Cover Design by alissamegan (Fiverr.com)

1

"It was a dark and stormy night."

"Oh, c'mon, really? You're starting your story like that?"

Giggles erupted.

Cody chided the young camper. Everyone had been taking turns telling ghost stories. Most were silly in Cody's mind, but the seventeen-year-old went with the flow. It was the last night of his last year as camp counselor. It had been a good run, but he was sad tonight because his younger brother, Jacob, had returned home two days earlier.

Jacob had come down with a bad cold and the powers-that-be determined he couldn't stay. They were concerned about the risk of spreading the illness. Cody thought the decision was overly cautious. Kids get sick. Colds are uncomfortable but not life-threatening. At least not usually. To deprive Jacob of the last two days of camp and all the festivities that went with that was cruel in Cody's mind. But he wasn't in charge.

He refocused his attention on the young camper who was now well into his story about green aliens invading the earth. Cody surreptitiously looked at his watch. They were fast approaching curfew. Time to wrap this up. He was about to interrupt when everyone groaned, signaling the story had concluded.

"OK, then," he murmured. "Everyone ready to turn in? Am I to anticipate nightmares tonight?"

Denials rang out as the dozen kids gathered their things and headed to their respective bunk houses. Cody gave them ten minutes, then did his bed-count rounds ensuring everyone was safely tucked in. He returned to his cabin which he shared with the head counselor, a gruff but kind man in his fifties.

"Everyone settled?"

"Yes. They should be set until morning, barring any late-night outhouse runs."

The man chuckled, then looked closely at Cody. "Your mom called about twenty minutes ago."

Cody looked up, slightly alarmed. His mother would not call him here unless it were something extremely urgent. "Is Jacob OK?"

"Can't answer that. But she said you need to come home tonight. I argued with her about that, but she was insistent."

"She didn't say why?"

"No. Just that you needed to come. You good to make the drive? It'll be late by the time you get there."

Cody had already been stuffing his things into his large backpack. "I'll be fine. Can you tell the kids goodbye for me? Tell them I'm sorry I had to go?"

"Yeah, yeah. I'll take care of that. Drive safely. No speeding. Cops love to break the balls of teenage boys exceeding the speed limit."

Cody laughed. "Yes, Dad."

"Don't be smart with me. Go on, now. Be careful. And you know you can call me if you need me, right?"

Cody was confused. *Why is he saying that?* But he nodded his head and held out his hand to shake goodbye. "I'll miss this place. I hope your next counselor is as awesome as me."

He ignored the man's exaggerated groan as he retrieved his keys off the hook where they hung. Without further comment, he opened the door and strode hastily to his car. It wasn't much to look at, and didn't have all the fancy electronics of the newer cars, but it got him from point A to point B. He was eternally grateful that his father had helped him purchase it. He tossed his backpack in the back seat and slid in behind the wheel. A few seconds later, he was pulling away from the cabin onto the dirt track that led away from the camp. Ten minutes later he pulled onto the main highway.

The drive home took three hours. It was just after one in the morning when he turned onto the small road that was essentially the family's driveway since they were the only house at the end of it. But Cody's heart took a turn for the worse when he saw flashing red and blue lights bouncing off the surrounding trees. He was motioned to stop some distance from the house by a uniformed officer who walked up to his door. Cody lowered the window.

"What's going on?"

"Who are you and why are you here?" the officer asked, ignoring Cody's question.

Cody identified himself and asked his question again, even though he could clearly see that the house he'd lived in since he was five was completely consumed in flames. It was obvious it couldn't be saved. His biggest concern was his family. He turned the car off and opened his door and stepped out. Before he could take a step forward, the officer put a hand on his arm.

"You can't go up there."

"But my family! Are they OK?"

"There's no one else around. But I'm sorry to say a man's body was removed from the house. He's badly burned, but if you're up to it, perhaps you can identify him? I'm sorry to ask this of you, but it will help in our investigation."

"Investigation?"

"The fire chief says the fire was intentionally set. We're approaching this as a murder investigation."

"Someone set fire to our house? Wait. Murder? What do you mean?" Cody was now almost in shock. Too much information was coming at him too quickly.

"The coroner says a gunshot wound was the likely cause of death for the victim. We're speculating the fire was set to cover it up."

Cody fell back against his car. He felt nausea rising and he wasn't sure if he could hold it back. The officer must have recognized the signs.

"Here, here. Let's get you sat down." He reached behind Cody and opened the car door and pushed Cody onto the seat. "You gonna lose it?"

Cody drew in some deep breaths. He almost smiled at the officer's concern. *Probably worried I'll upchuck all over his shoes.* "I'm good. At least as good as I can be."

"You able to take a look at the man we pulled out?"

Cody didn't think so, but knew he had to. If only to verify whether it was his father. He couldn't fathom it being anyone else. He nodded his head and pulled himself back up to a standing position.

"Let's do this."

He followed the officer towards the coroner's van. Glancing at the house, he noted the flames were almost out. There wasn't much left. He doubted he'd be allowed to go anywhere near it for a while. But he had to find a way. There was something he needed to retrieve, and he didn't want anyone else seeing him do it.

He waited while the coroner unzipped the black bag on the stretcher. The smell of burnt flesh reached him and he gagged, knowing that smell would be forever etched in his brain. The coroner studied him for a moment, taking in Cody's pallor.

"You ready?"

"I don't think I'll ever be ready." But he stepped towards the bag.

He only needed a quick glance. Turning away, he gagged again. The coroner put a comforting hand on his back while an assistant quickly zipped the bag back up.

"I'm sorry. I have to ask. Can you identify this person?" the coroner asked quietly.

"Yes. It's my father."

2

"Where's my mom and brother?"

"No one else here," the officer repeated what he'd earlier told Cody. "Do you know for a fact they were here? Maybe they were somewhere else when all this happened?"

Cody explained his mother had called the camp where he'd been working and told him to come home. Now. Tonight. He assumed she was at the house when she called, but he didn't know. The officer made notes of names and other information.

"Look. You obviously can't stay here. You have other family or friends close by where you can go? If not, I can take you somewhere for what's left of tonight and we can sort the rest later. OK? You're going to have to talk to a detective, but that can wait until tomorrow. Or later today," he corrected himself.

Cody looked again at the smoking embers of what was once his family home. When the officer quizzed him again, he turned and looked at the man.

"Yes. I have friends not too far away. I'll call them. I'm sure I can stay with them."

Without waiting for a response, he turned and walked quickly back to his car and got into it. He had already backed around and was facing out when the officer reached him. Ignoring the man's gestures, he accelerated down the road away from the scene and flashing lights.

What he'd told the officer wasn't a complete lie. He did have people he could go to. Not family. Not really even friends. But either way, it didn't matter. He wasn't going to them. His one goal now was to get as far away from this place as he could. He'd be back. But not immediately. Not until long after the officials were done with what they had to do. He knew there would be others after the local jurisdiction was done. Probably before that. And he knew those others would take over. There would be no funeral for his father. His body would be taken by the others. It would be like he never existed.

Cody understood all this while he drove through the remaining hours of darkness. Last year when he'd turned sixteen, his parents had spoken to him about things that, at the time, were incomprehensible to him. His confusion and feelings of betrayal had almost destroyed his relationship with his parents. But over the past year, Cody had begun to sort through all he'd been told and realized the life he'd been living was an illusion created for the outside world. The world of his parents, no, his family, was completely different. Things that had seemed not quite right in his younger mind, made more sense when framed in the new context. But Cody still struggled with the context. He hadn't totally reconciled everything he'd learned. And now he wasn't sure he ever would. A dead father and a missing mother and brother were not how he'd envisioned entering his adulthood.

In two days, Cody would turn eighteen and be legally responsible for himself. No celebration of that milestone, now. When he didn't show up for the detectives to question, he figured there would be a brief search for him. But he doubted they'd spend too many resources pursuing him. He wasn't a suspect. And he knew the others would assure the locals that they'd handle everything. Cody wasn't concerned about the locals. He was concerned about the others. And that's why he continued driving, stopping only to fill his car with gas. He had an ultimate destination. He only hoped it would be the safe haven his parents had assured him it would be.

A single tear rolled down his cheek.

"Goodbye, Dad," he whispered into the empty space. "I'm sorry I yelled at you before I left for camp."

3

"Where are we going?" Jacob asked his mom as he smothered a sneeze. "Where's Dad?"

Things had happened so quickly. Men storming into the house. Lots of yelling. A gunshot. His mom coming to his room and telling him to hurry. Literally dragging him out the back door and stuffing him into the old car they seldom used but kept in running condition.

Susan Winters was focused on the road, trying to suppress the memory of seeing her husband gunned down in front of her. She didn't know how to respond to her youngest son. Now was not the time to tell the boy his father was dead. And as for the other, where they were going, she couldn't answer that either. She didn't know. Not yet. She only knew she had to put distance between her and their home. No, scratch that. It had never really been their home. Only the place they'd lived for the past ten or twelve years. She'd lost track of the time. And the passing of time had dulled her survival instincts. But as she glanced at her son, she felt them returning with a vengeance.

"Mom?"

"Hush, honey. Try to get some sleep. We have a long drive ahead of us."

"What about Cody?"

"Don't worry about Cody. He's fine."

She hoped that was true. She'd had time to make a quick call to her friend George, the head counselor at the summer camp where Cody was working. The arrangement had worked well for the past three years. George had known the Winters before they were the Winters. While he didn't know the full circumstances of the name change, he knew enough to maintain his distance while still providing support. Encouraging Cody to be a camp counselor and caring for him had gone a long way towards fulfilling a debt he felt he owed to Susan and her family. A debt Susan didn't think existed but appreciated the outcome of the circumstances.

Cody had grown into a level-headed responsible young man under George's guidance. Even though the last year had been a bit touch and go, especially after Cody had learned the true situation of his family's life, the camp had provided a refuge. George had played a large role in helping Cody reconcile the initial feelings of betrayal. But Susan knew Cody still struggled. She feared things would get worse now.

Susan regretted telling George that Cody needed to come home. She'd called in a panic. Not thinking through to the fact she wouldn't be there when he arrived. That he'd be coming into a total mess. She could only hope that Cody would remember the things she and Tom had told him. That his survival would depend on his ability to stay undetected in a digital world designed to find anyone, anywhere.

4

Cody pulled into a motel just off the highway. He could barely stay awake to drive. He knew he needed to rest. But he also didn't have any money for a motel. He got out of his car and walked into the office, sighing a bit in relief to note the clerk was just slightly older than him.

"Help you?"

"I was wondering if I could pull around the back of the building and get some rest. I won't stay long, but I can't drive any further and I don't have money to get a room."

The young man looked Cody up and down, noting his youth and tiredness.

"How old are you?"

Cody was immediately on edge. "Why does that matter?"

"You running away from home?"

Cody laughed. "I'm on my way home if you really need to know. Look, can I sleep out back for a few hours or not?"

The man continued to study Cody for a few more seconds, then shrugged. "Sure, why not?" He glanced at the clock on the wall. "But you need to be gone by one. That's when the owner comes in. He won't be happy to see you there. He'll think you're a vagrant. Call the cops on you."

Cody also glanced at the clock, noting the time. He'd only get about four hours of sleep, but that was better than nothing. He noticed the snack bars on the counter. "Those for sale?"

"Yes. Two bucks each. But today's your lucky day, we're having a special. Two for a dollar."

Cody smiled tiredly and reached into his pocket pulling out some crumbled bills. He put two on the counter and picked up one of the bars. "Thanks." He turned to go.

"No, really. Take two. We're trying to get rid of them. No one wants them. They're kinda old, to be honest."

Cody turned back, fighting his inner honesty. He knew the clerk was lying. But he was hungry. He took another bar.

"Thanks," he said again. He walked back to his car and drove it around the back of the building, parking slightly away from the dumpster that sat at an angle. He glanced at his watch, still somewhat wishing it was the fancy electronic one he'd wanted to buy. Amongst all the other features offered, it had an alarm to wake up. He'd saved his money for it and was angry when his parents wouldn't let him get it, insisting he get the simple analog timepiece he was wearing. It wasn't until much later that he realized why they'd forbidden the electronics. While they'd never specifically said it, he'd figured out the gadget would make it too easy to track him. Once he knew that, he couldn't decide whether he was thankful for what he had, or more resentful of his overall situation. But right now, even though having an alarm would be helpful, he knew he was thankful for his parent's foresight.

He locked his doors and reclined the seat as far as it would go. He quickly ate the bars, then folding his arms across his chest, fell into a deep sleep.

The pounding on his window woke him. It took a few seconds for his heart to settle and his mind to sort where he was. The clerk was standing next to his car gesturing with urgency. Cody turned the key in the ignition enough to power down the window.

"It's almost one. You need to go. Now."

Cody nodded and started his car. "Thanks."

"You going to be OK?"

"Yes, I'll be fine. Thanks again for letting me do this."

"Yeah, yeah. Go on, now. You can drive around the dumpster and get out the other side. I gotta get back to the desk."

Cody nodded, put the vehicle in gear and carefully pulled forward around the dumpster. When he cleared it, he accelerated around the side of the building and pulled out of the parking lot. He glanced in his rearview mirror as he continued accelerating to the speed limit and noted a car turning into the motel. He wondered if it was the owner. Then he wondered if it might be someone more dangerous than the owner. Without being fully aware of it, his foot pushed the gas pedal a bit more.

Twenty minutes later he pulled over to the side of the road. He didn't know when the next gas station or other sign of civilization would appear, and his bladder was screaming at him. He quickly took care of his needs, then before getting back into the driver's seat, he opened the back door and pulled his backpack to him. It took only seconds to find the small atlas tucked into an inside pocket. As maps go, it wasn't the best, but it was better than the detailed topographical map of the summer camp area he also had stuffed in the pack. At least this gave him more information on a larger scale. He chuckled to himself as he remembered how annoyed he was when his parents told him to always have this resource available to him. Just extra weight to carry, was all he ever thought. Now he understood. He realized he might begin to understand a lot more of the things they'd always told him.

Thoughts of his parents reminded him that he still knew nothing of what happened to his mother or brother. The officer said no one else was at the house when they got there. Did that mean they'd left of their own accord? Or were they taken? If they weren't taken, why hadn't they waited for him? Or left some sort of message?

Message! His head snapped up. Unfortunately, he was still leaning into the back seat and the motion caused him to hit his head on the edge of the door opening.

"Ow!" he said and instinctively rubbed the bruised area. Straightening into a full stand, he looked up and down the deserted highway, thinking it weird no one was around this time of day. But the thought was more of a distraction than any particular worry. He found the page he needed in the atlas and studied it. He closed the back door, slid behind the wheel, and tossed the book on the seat next to him. He glanced at his gas gauge. He'd need to refuel soon. And he was running out of cash. He hoped he had enough money to get him to where he needed to go.

As he continued his journey, he thought about what, if any, message might be waiting for him. And whether it was at the house, or at his destination.

5

Susan drove through the night. Jacob had fallen asleep, the remaining stuffiness of his cold causing him to snore a bit. She smiled at the sound. Then sobered. The loss of her husband hit her hard and fast, causing her hands to clench the wheel. She took a few deep breaths. *Put it away, girl. Time enough later to mourn the dead. The living takes precedence.*

She worried about Cody. He didn't have access to the resources she did. She wondered if he was safe, if he'd eaten, if he had any money, if he remembered where to go. If he was even still free to go there. Had he been picked up? If not, would he remember to stay off-grid? Would he look for the box? The box that would give him things necessary to survive his new reality? Would he even comprehend how much he needed the box? What his new reality was?

She remembered how he'd laughed when Tom had explained the box as if it were a fairytale quest. She'd pulled him aside later and emphasized the importance of what he'd been told. Regardless of how silly he might think it was, he needed to remember the information he'd been given.

She sighed. All her worry was not going to solve anything. She also recognized her thoughts were a mixture of a mother's worry and a fugitive's mindset. Not that she was a fugitive in the sense of a legitimate meaning. But the world she came from, and the world her family had been forced into, gave words different meanings. That she'd been allowed to leave unharmed with Jacob surprised her. Until she remembered what the price was for that benevolence. She wasn't sure she'd be able to pay it.

The morning light was well established when she pulled into a gas station. She turned and looked in the backseat. Jacob was still asleep. She hated to wake him, but if he needed to use the facilities, this would be his last chance for a while.

"Jacob, honey. Wake up."

He stirred and rubbed his eyes. Looking around he asked, "Where are we?"

"Somewhere on the way to somewhere else," Susan smiled as she said it. "You need to use the men's room?"

He straightened in the seat and nodded his head.

"Go. Be quick. Go and come right back. No loitering. I'll fill the tank then see what might be available for munchies."

"Can't we stop and get breakfast?"

"Not right now. Maybe later we can stop and get something more proper. But I'm afraid it's snacks for now. You want orange juice or something else?"

"Orange juice is fine," Jacob said as he pushed the door open and got out. After a brief stretch, he headed for the restrooms around the corner.

She watched him, worried about what danger might be awaiting him. Then shook her head. Paranoia was helpful at times, but if regularly indulged in, will destroy a healthy mindset. She placed the nozzle in her car and reached for her credit card to start the process. Something flashed in her mind, and she quickly slid the card back into her small wallet. Chastising herself for almost being so careless, she walked into the store and up to the clerk. After prepaying for her gas, she hurried back out and started filling her tank.

She looked around and noted Jacob coming from the restrooms. When he came closer, she told him to make sure there was no overflow and walked quickly back into the store. It didn't take long to gather a few things. The items were not overly healthy, she knew, but it would suffice for now. She paid for her purchases and returned to the car. Jacob was just pulling the nozzle out and placing it back in the pump.

"Any problems?" she asked.

"No. It stopped by itself."

Susan glanced at the numbers displayed, surprised the vehicle had taken the full amount she'd given the clerk.

"Good enough. Hop in. Let's blow this popsicle stand."

Jacob giggled. The sound warmed her heart. The saying was one her father had always used. Growing up she'd thought it silly, but somewhere in life, she'd started using it with her kids. She knew they thought it just as goofy. But they never chided her for it. If anything, they'd enthusiastically claimed it as a family ritual.

Back on the road she remained on high alert for a while. Slowly that dulled from the monotony of the miles until she found herself humming the melody of a popular tune.

"Can we turn the radio on?" Jacob asked.

"Sure, why not? What's the flavor?"

"Old-time rock and roll."

Susan smiled. The kids had been raised on a wide variety of musical genres. The definition of old-time rock and roll was something the entire family good-naturedly argued about, never fully agreeing on the subject. She fiddled with the dials. Something from The Doors was playing.

"Good enough?"

"Yeah." Jacob shifted in his seat. "Mom, where are we really going, and will Cody be there? What about Dad?"

When Susan didn't immediately answer, Jacob continued, "Dad's dead, isn't he? That was the gunshot I heard just before you came into my room, wasn't it?"

Her son's words caused Susan to jerk the wheel slightly, they'd been that unexpected.

"Jacob," her voice was soft. He interrupted her.

"It's OK, Mom. I know. I heard the yelling. I don't know what it all meant, but I understand that you and Dad didn't want to do what those men wanted. Why'd they shoot him? Are you and Dad spies?"

Susan sighed and looked for a place to pull over. This was not a conversation to be had while driving. She'd underestimated Jacob's ability to put the pieces together, even if he was not drawing completely correct conclusions. *He may only be twelve,* she thought, *but it looks like I'm going to have to tell him everything Cody didn't learn until he was sixteen.*

She wondered if Jacob would react as Cody had.

6

Cody pulled into the quiet residential street going just under the posted speed limit. He was trying to read the numbers on the houses while still maintaining an awareness of the general environment. He vaguely noted some kids playing ball in a front yard and a young woman walking a dog.

"There!" he voiced his triumph even though he was the only one to hear it.

The house he'd been searching for looked structurally like all the other houses. Nothing made it stand out from the rest, except perhaps, its color. Most of the houses on the street were white, gray, or some other muted color. This one was a darker blue. Cody thought the color nice and that some of the others should be painted with darker hues to add variety.

He passed the house, looking intently at it. He couldn't tell if it was empty. It didn't look deserted. In fact, it looked well-cared for. The lawn was trimmed, flowers were blooming, and there was a small floral flag hanging off the porch.

He tried to remember what his parents had told him about this place, but his thoughts were still jumbled from everything he'd experienced in the last twenty-four hours. One thing rang loud and clear, though. *Can't stop. Can't be seen here.*

He continued to the end of the block and took a left. Midway to the next intersection, he noted what appeared to be an alley. He turned into it. As he slowly rolled along, he realized that this offered access to the backs of the properties. Most were fenced, and all that were had gates. A few had obvious driveway access although no garages, simply providing additional off-street parking for the residence. The house that interested him had such a setup.

A fence on either side of the driveway enclosed the rest of the yard, but there was no gate. Cody could see the full backside of the house and he noted two windows and a door. He also saw that the door was accessed by ascending two steps onto a small deck attached to the house. He absorbed nothing else before he was past the property and realized he was almost at the end of the block. He took a right onto the main street and drove away from the neighborhood. He had much to think about.

He pulled into the parking lot of a large Catholic church. The size of the building surprised him, considering its location. But he appreciated that it offered an over-sized lot and that there was enough pedestrian and vehicle traffic to allow him to park without drawing much attention to himself. As he sat there observing the comings and goings, he soon realized that the building contained a school. He wasn't sure if that helped or hurt him. If he stayed too long, someone might think he was a pervert or something just sitting there in his car. He decided to pretend he was studying his map. He figured that would allow him to remain unnoticed while he thought things through.

He was wrong. About ten minutes later, a tall man who looked to be in his late twenties, early thirties, rapped on his window. Cody looked up to see that the man was wearing a priest's collar. While that fact relieved some fears, it created others.

"Yes?" Cody asked after lowering his window.

"Are you lost, son? Do you need assistance?"

Cody smiled, realizing the question could mean more than one thing. He chose the less spiritual interpretation.

"Not really. I just needed to study the map and thought it safer to be parked than trying to do it while I was driving."

"A wise decision, to be sure. Perhaps I can offer you some direction?"

Again with the double meaning, Cody thought.

"I seem to be in a large residential area. Is there somewhere more commercial nearby? Somewhere I can get a bite to eat?"

"Ah. 'Tis food you need. As it happens, tonight is our weekly community dinner. You probably noticed the increased foot traffic? Our volunteers are busy preparing the meal. You are welcome to join us. The offering is simple, but nutritious."

Cody thought about that. Doubtful he'd have to pay anything, which was good. He only had a few dollars left. On the other hand, there was probably some expectation that he donate to the church. But that would be less than purchasing a meal. And he was hungry. He'd had nothing but the snack bars at the motel. And that seemed like three days ago.

The young priest correctly interpreted Cody's silence as an internal struggle of some sort. He gently suggested that he would be more than welcome to eat his fill with no financial expectations of any kind.

"Maybe I could help with the preparation in exchange for my meal?"

"That is kind of you to offer. I'm sure you could be put to work with some task. Come. I'll show you the way. Then perhaps we can discuss what other assistance you might need."

Cody kept his face averted, hoping to hide his expression from the priest as he climbed out of his car. He was uncertain how to interpret this sudden good fortune. He'd had lots of time to think during his drive. Too much time if he were honest. Everything his parents had told him a year ago was bouncing around in his head. He was tired and anxious. He was also worried about his mom and brother. He'd pushed the loss of his father aside for the time being, recognizing that dwelling on that subject would dull him to potential threats he needed to anticipate. The problem was, he didn't know what threats were out there, if any. Was he really caught up in a major storm as his parents suggested he might be should something happen to either of them? Or had he blown everything out of proportion when he'd fled from the scene of his burning home? Were people really after him? Was there really a box with a message waiting for him?

He realized the priest was walking towards the church, obviously expecting Cody to follow. He stumbled in his efforts to catch up. *Food first. After that, maybe I can sort through things. It's a church. What could happen?*

7

"So you're not spies?" Jacob asked, obviously disappointed. His active mind had built a world filled with action figures and adventure. One where he got to play a hero figure. The reality was almost boring.

Susan had found a pullout area that included picnic tables and several parking spots. She'd backed into a space and kept one eye on the road while giving her son a general summary of the family's true circumstances. She smiled. "No, dear. We're not spies. But we still have a few challenges to overcome."

"Does Cody know all this?"

"Yes. Most of it. But you know a bit more than him."

That distracted Jacob. He knew more than Cody! Being younger, he always felt excluded from important conversations. He wasn't a child. He was twelve! Almost a teenager. That his mother had told him more than she'd told Cody made him swell with pride.

"I can help, you know. I'm not a baby."

"Of course you're not a baby. But you also don't have many of the skills that might be needed on our journey."

"You can teach me, though, can't you?"

Susan looked at her child with a mixture of pride and sorrow. Pride in how the boy was developing into a solid young man. Sorrow that he was going to have to grow up much faster than she would have liked under normal circumstances. But these weren't normal circumstances. Far from it.

"I can teach you some things. Others you'll have to figure out on your own. What works best for me, or anyone else, might not work for you. Only you can decide that. But the first thing we need to discuss is situational awareness. And, while we're at it, let's get out and I'll show you a couple of moves you can use if someone grabs you unexpectedly. You up for that?"

"Yes!"

They spent the next half-hour practicing some simple but effective moves to get out of three of the most common grabs an adult might use on a child or someone smaller than them. Susan realized Jacob had an innate talent for the physicality of the responses, but she noted his general lack of attention to the other matters she was trying to teach him. She wasn't sure whether it was his age or an overall childhood sense of invincibility. After he answered the same question incorrectly for the fourth time, she threw up her hands in exasperation.

"Jacob! This is extremely important! You need to listen and absorb the information. Truly, your life could depend on it."

Deftly deflecting her wrath, he asked, "How do you know all this stuff, anyway?"

She was about to chastise him again when she noticed a large white SUV slowing to turn into the small lot. Alarm signals burst in her head.

"Jacob, get in the car. Quickly."

"But, Mom—"

"Now!"

The vehicle had not pulled into a parking space. Instead, the driver positioned it broadside in front of her car. It had barely come to a complete stop when three doors opened, and men stepped out. Jacob took one look at the size of them and ran for his open car door, closing it behind him as he got into the backseat. Susan walked to the front of her vehicle and stood. Waiting.

No one spoke for a few moments. Then one of the men, obviously the leader of the group, addressed her.

"Mrs. Winters. You seem a bit far from home."

"Who are you, and what business do you have here? I don't appreciate your parking skills I might add." The tone of her voice was aggressive.

"Come now. No need to be so hostile. We're here to offer our assistance."

"What do you mean? And you didn't answer my question. Who are you?"

While she stood tall and projected as much strength as she could, Susan was concerned. She had no immediate means to protect herself or Jacob other than her bare hands. She had a weapon, but it was locked in the trunk. She hadn't wanted it too accessible to Jacob. She regretted that decision now.

The man stepped closer. Susan instinctively backed up but found herself up against the front bumper with no room to maneuver. *Not a good situation,* she thought.

"Don't be difficult."

"I'll be as difficult as I want. I'll ask one more time. Who are you? And while I'm at it, how did you find me?"

"You should turn your phone off. You've become stale. Doubtful you'll survive long. You or your son. That is your son in the car, right? Would be unfortunate for something to happen to him, wouldn't it?"

"Nothing will happen to him. He's under my protection."

"Like you protected Tom?"

The man's words hurt more than an actual punch. Both about Tom and that she'd left her phone on. *Stupid! Stupid! Stupid!* She sent him a look that left little doubt she was angry and dangerous.

"Look. We know that those who shot your husband didn't get want they came for. Give it to us and we'll see that you don't have to worry about the others again."

"I don't know what you're talking about."

"Yes, you do. You can make everything go away with a simple act. Or we can do this the hard way."

Susan centered her body weight and stood as tall as she could. "Move your vehicle. I'll only ask nicely once."

"Or what? What are you going to do against the three of us? You may have been hot stuff in your day, but that day is long past. Not only are you older, but you've had it way too easy this past decade."

She half-smiled. He wasn't completely wrong. She was older. But she'd made a point of staying in shape and working her skills. Tom had laughed at her, saying she couldn't let go. But she'd always known this day, or a day like it, would come. She'd warned Tom constantly not to let his guard down. But he'd waved her off. Now he was dead, and while she hadn't yet sorted out her feelings of guilt over that fact, she knew without a doubt that had he been better prepared, events might have gone differently that night. Might have.

"I'm losing patience. What's it going to be?" The man took another step closer. The other two moved into better positions.

"I'm not giving you anything."

"I was afraid you were going to say that."

The words were barely out of the man's mouth when he lunged forward, arms outstretched to grab Susan. She waited until the last possible moment then moved sideways and, using his forward momentum, deflected his arms and pulled him so he fell onto the hood of the car. Not giving him a chance to recover, she stomped down on the back of his knee causing his body to jerk backwards as his leg collapsed. Grabbing his chin, she punched his exposed throat with all her strength. He fell to the ground coughing and gasping for air. She was about to stomp on his head when she was grabbed from behind.

Without consciously thinking about the movement, she slammed her fist downward, catching her attacker in the groin. Before his brain could process that her blow had not been debilitating, she spun inwards and drove her elbow upward under his chin. She finished her movement by delivering an open-hand strike to his nose. The man fell backwards a step, his hands instinctively going to his face to stem the flow of blood coming from his nose.

"Stop." The deep voice got her attention and she paused. But what caused her to freeze where she stood was the pistol she saw in the man's hand. He waved it, clearly motioning for her to step away from the two men.

As she cautiously slid to her left, widening the distance between her and the two injured men, a large rock, coming seemingly from nowhere, hit the man squarely on the side of his head. The unexpectedness of it caused him to drop the hand holding the gun and stagger slightly in Susan's direction. She didn't need any further invitation. She threw her body at the man in the best imitation of an open-field tackle any football coach would have been proud to see.

Both fell to the ground in a tangle of arms and legs, the gun flying out of the man's hand. As they rolled around, each trying to gain a superior position, Susan managed to free a hand and before the man could secure it, she struck out at his eyes, one finger hitting her target square on. With a cry of pain, the man pulled back. It was all Susan needed. The shift of the man's weight gave her the leverage she needed to flip him onto his back. Sitting atop him, she delivered punch after punch, focusing mostly on his throat, but managing to hit his nose a couple of times in the process. He went limp beneath her.

She climbed off him and looked around. What she saw stunned her. Jacob had picked up the handgun from the ground and had it pointed at the other two men. While his hands shook slightly, his finger was on the trigger and she could see he was extremely focused. Apparently the men could see it also. They didn't want to risk the boy shooting them whether by intent or inadvertently. They stayed where they were.

She walked over to Jacob and placed a hand gently on his shoulder. Reaching out with the other hand she said quietly, "Give me the gun, honey."

Jacob let his mom take the gun from his hands, but he didn't move, staring fiercely at the two men.

Susan reached into her front pocket and pulled out her key. Without thinking about whether he even knew how to do it, she told Jacob to start their car. It took a couple of seconds for Jacob to process her instructions. Then he reached for the key and slid into the driver's seat and started the engine. Without being told to, he climbed over the middle console into the passenger seat.

Susan looked at the three men in various stages of recovery. She pointed the gun at the man who seemed most able and instructed him to help his buddies into their vehicle. Being on the wrong end of the gun and with little option to do anything else, the man did as she said. Moments later the SUV pulled out of the lot, tires squealing. Susan watched it go.

She looked at the handgun, absently noting that it didn't have an external safety. She did a quick press check, seeing the bullet in the chamber. If Jacob had squeezed the trigger, the gun would have gone off. He might possibly have hit one of the men. She shivered at the thought of her twelve-year-old wounding or killing someone. Later, when they both calmed down a bit, she would give him some instruction on safely handling a gun. She didn't want to; it was something she hoped never to have to do. But it was clear that their new reality required it.

8

Cody finished off a second helping of the meat and potatoes on his plate. Surprised at the sheer volume of people who'd filed into the church's community center to get a meal, he'd asked one of the servers if this was a normal night.

"Yes. There is a lot of need in this community."

"But I drove through the neighborhood. All the houses look well-cared for. Surely the people living in them make reasonable incomes."

"You must have driven through the nice side. Go a half-mile further down this street and you'll see a different vision."

Cody thought about that. He'd seen things like that on television but had never experienced it in real life.

"Is it safe to go into that area?"

The server laughed. "Yes. The people are struggling economically. They're not thugs. This church serves all who come to its doors."

Cody didn't know much about that. His family had never really been church-goers. Now that he thought about it, his family hadn't participated in many organized activities. He and his brother were home schooled. Their parents had encouraged many interests, but organized sports or other social activities had never been high on their list. When they'd proposed he serve as a camp counselor, he'd been surprised but pleased. Meeting and working with George had been a hoot. And educational in its own way. He'd always figured Jacob would follow in his footsteps in another year or so.

The thought of Jacob sobered Cody. He wondered if his brother was OK. And his mother. Were they together? Were they safe? He glanced at the watch on his wrist. It was well past eight.

"Do you want me to help with the clean up?"

"Thank you for offering. You've been more than helpful today. I think we can give you a pass on that. But Father Timothy would like to see you if you have a few moments?"

Cody immediately felt on edge. Why would the priest want to talk to him? He swallowed his anxiety and asked where he could find the man. The server pointed towards a door.

"Go through there and down the hallway. His office is on the left. I think he's there now."

Cody stood and picked up his plate to carry it to the kitchen.

"Leave that. I'll take care of it. Go on, now. The Father is waiting."

Cody put his plate down and turned towards the door the server had pointed to. He said his thanks and walked to the door, opening it, and stepping through. On the other side he stood and drew a few deep breaths. He walked down the hall and tapped lightly on the office door.

"Come in, please."

Cody opened the door and poked his head in. "I was told you wanted to see me?"

"Yes. Please come in and have a seat. Did you get enough to eat? The volunteers said you were very helpful this afternoon."

Cody stepped into the office, closing the door behind him. He stood still for a few seconds glancing around and taking in the setting. More ornate and cluttered than his father's office, it still had the normal work tools such as a computer, printer, desk phone, etc. A small file cabinet was pushed into a corner. What caught Cody's eye the most were all the pictures and statutes depicting religious scenes. While his family had never attended church, his education included a deep study of the Bible and various philosophical scholars. He recognized most of what he saw. When his eyes settled back on the priest, he realized the man had been studying him. Father Timothy gestured to the chair in front of the desk.

"Please. Or if you prefer, we can sit over there." He gestured to a corner furnished with a small love seat with an armchair placed at a ninety-degree angle to it.

Cody was undecided. He figured the straight-back chair in front of the desk would keep him more focused and aware, but the small couch looked inviting. It also had the advantage of not putting his back to the door. He chose the couch and began walking towards it.

Saying nothing, the priest stood and walked over to the area and sat in the chair once Cody had settled himself on the couch.

"I don't think I ever got your name in all the hustle-bustle today."

"Cody."

"Just Cody?" At Cody's hesitant nod, he continued, "Well, thank you again for your assistance today. I get the distinct feeling you're not from this area. What brings you to our humble doors?"

Cody almost laughed at the priest's description of the huge ornate church. Humble was the last way he would categorize the building.

"Just passing through."

"Any particular destination?"

"Not really." Cody had no intentions of telling the priest his business.

"You seem rather young to be on your own. May I ask how old you are?"

Cody felt his anxiety rise. "Eighteen."

The priest looked at him until unnerved, Cody admitted he'd be eighteen the next day. The priest nodded. In his experience, young people always inflated their age. Ask the very young and they'd add in the months. Ask the in-betweens and they'd often stretch to the next birthday. Or at least clarify when they turned the next number. As in, "I'll be thirteen in two months." Adults, however, tended to do the opposite. They could be a day away from their next birthday and proudly state their age as a year younger than what the next day would bring.

"Still pretty young to be on your own."

Cody shifted on the couch. "Is there something in particular you wanted to talk about, Father?"

"Not really. I just sense that you're troubled and was wondering if you needed an ear or another's opinion?"

As Cody sat silent, the priest said softly that whatever was discussed would remain private and between the two of them. In the same soft voice, he went on to relate a story from his past and how he'd resisted assistance from anyone. The resulting consequences had taught him to appreciate sincere offers of help.

Cody looked at him. The man's voice and the warm food in his stomach was lulling him into a state of intense relaxation. The past hours of stress and limited sleep helped move him closer to a desire to share his worries.

Almost.

He was just about to give the priest an abbreviated version of the past thirty hours or so when there was a sharp knock on the door, and it opened to reveal an older woman clearly in distress.

"Father Timothy! There's a fire!"

The priest stood. "Where? Is anyone hurt?"

"Come quick! It's that blue house down the street. Someone set it on fire!"

Cody felt his body react as if hit by a bolt of electricity. The blue house! It could only be the one he'd been looking for! Who would set it on fire? And why now? Just hours after he'd located it? Had he been followed? And what about the box that was supposedly waiting for him? Had it been destroyed? Or had whoever set the fire found it and taken it?

He stood and started toward the door.

"Wait," Father Timothy said.

"No! I know that house. I need to get to it. Now."

Father Timothy put a hand on Cody's arm to stop his forward movement. "How do you know that house? What meaning does it have for you? No one lives there. Hasn't for years. The church maintains it, using a small fund granted for that purpose."

Cody pulled his arm away and continued forward. "I need to get there."

Realizing he'd get no answers from Cody in his agitated state, he hurried to catch up. "We'll go together. Can you drive us there?"

Cody didn't answer but slowed enough to allow the priest to catch up with him. Together they hurried down the hall towards the main door. In the parking lot, Cody nearly ran to his car. He'd already slid behind the wheel and started it by the time Father Timothy caught up. Pulling on the passenger door, he knocked on the window indicating Cody needed to unlock the door. Cody reached across and did so.

"You know how to get there?"

"Yes," Cody responded as he put his car in gear and stepped on the accelerator.

"There will be several first responders around. Doubtful you'll be able to park very close. We'll probably have to walk a bit."

Cody just nodded and navigated the neighborhood streets he'd driven through a few hours prior.

"Here," the priest pointed to an open spot a block from their destination. The flames and smoke could be seen from their location.

Cody pulled into the spot and shut off the engine. The priest's next words stopped his hand from completing the act of opening his door.

"Cody. Who are you? It seems an odd coincidence that you suddenly appear, then there's a fire in a house that's been unoccupied for years. What is your connection to that house?"

Cody looked at the priest who stared back at him intently. Cody wilted under the intensity of that look.

"I was told by my parents that if something should happen to either of them and I was unable to contact the other, I must come to this house and find a box that contained a message."

Father Timothy absorbed that statement, which raised several questions. He asked the one he thought most pressing.

"And did something happen to one or both of your parents?"

"My father was killed. Our house was set on fire. I don't know where my mom or brother are."

As he said that, a tear slid down his cheek. He quickly brushed it away, taking a deep breath as he did so. He stared resolutely out the windshield, refusing to look at the priest.

"I'm sorry, son. You must be feeling the loss deeply. But you won't find any box at the house."

Cody looked at him. "What do you mean? How do you know that?"

"As I said earlier, the church has been maintaining the house for several years. A fund was set up to allow for it. Every year, an additional small deposit is made to the fund. We don't know where it comes from or who is providing it. It just appears. I am personally in charge of this project now as Father Geoff transferred it to me when he was reassigned last year. I'm afraid I don't know any more history than that."

"Then how do you know there isn't a box within the house? Have you been inside? Have you looked?" Cody's tone was accusatory.

"I have been inside, but only to be sure that all is well. I haven't searched anything. There is only minimal furniture, anyway. Or was. I'm sure it's all burned now. But I didn't need to look through anything because I was told all the cupboards and closets were empty. I took that statement at face value, seeing no need to verify the accuracy of it."

"Then how do you know there isn't a box hidden away somewhere? I'll need to look myself."

"You won't be able to come close to the place for a while. The police will have it cordoned off. And afterwards, I'm sure the neighbors would report it if they saw a stranger poking through the remains."

"But—"

"Cody. You won't find a box there. Even if one existed, based on the flames we're seeing, I'm sure it's been destroyed with everything else."

Cody slumped in his seat. He worried the priest was correct, but he still felt the need to look himself. He was so focused on figuring out how he was going to do that, he almost missed Father Timothy's next words.

"However, what you're looking for may, in fact, be at the church."

"What do you mean?"

"When Father Geoff transferred the responsibility of the place to me, he gave me a small chest. I must admit, it looks like something out of a fairytale quest. Has a rather ornate and mystical appearance."

"And did you look inside?" Cody was sure this was what he was looking for. He remembered how his parents had presented the information, almost like a knight's quest from tales of old. He'd laughed at his father's embellishments.

"No. Of course not." Father Timothy smiled. "Besides, it has a big padlock on it. Father Geoff said he didn't have a key and thought it likely one was never included when the chest was deposited at the church."

"But he didn't know for sure?"

"I can't answer that. I can only tell you what he told me."

Father Timothy could see that the glow from the flames in the distance were diminishing. He assumed that the fire was being contained.

"Do you still want to walk over and see what's going on? Or do you want to return to the church and look at the chest?"

Cody was torn. He wanted to see with his own eyes the extent of the damage to the house. But he also knew there would be many officials on the scene and the one thing his parents had emphasized was that he needed to stay out of the limelight. Off grid, they'd said. He hadn't fully understood what they meant then. He had a better idea of it now. Feeling slightly defeated, he agreed to return to the church.

9

Susan put the car in gear and pulled out of the parking area. Jacob was quiet and she wondered what he was thinking. He looked a little pale but not too agitated.

"What's on your mind?" she asked him as she reached into her inner pocket and pulled out her phone.

She still couldn't believe she'd been so careless. To her knowledge, the only two people who had this number were Tom and George. It was why she hadn't thought to turn it off. But it was now obvious someone had known how to track her number, even though it was registered to another name.

Before shutting it down, she checked for any messages, text or otherwise, even though she knew it was unlikely she'd have any. She knew that after her call, George would know to not try and contact her. And Cody didn't have a phone. She sighed. *Where are you, son?*

"Those were bad men, weren't they? Are they the ones who shot Dad?" Jacob interrupted her thoughts, bringing her back to the present.

"No, they didn't shoot your father. As to whether they're bad men or not, I suppose that depends on who you ask."

Jacob was about to ask what she meant by that, but she cut him off.

"Were you scared holding the gun?"

"Yes."

"You were very brave to have picked it up and point it at the men. And by the way, great aim with the rock. You might have ultimately saved both our lives."

"Really?" Jacob puffed his chest out a bit.

"Yes. Really. But we need to talk about gun safety. You had your finger on the trigger. The gun could have gone off with even the slightest jerk of your hand. It's very dangerous to hold a gun like that. I must emphasize to you that you should never point a gun at someone unless you mean to use it. And even then, you only put your finger on the trigger when you fully intend to squeeze it."

"I would have shot them, if I'd had to!"

"That's a very serious thing to say. You're too young to truly understand the consequences of such an action. Real life isn't a video game. People you shoot don't just reappear as living when you reboot the game. Do you understand? You can't reboot the game in real life."

Jacob slumped down in his seat. He didn't want to continue this particular conversation. He knew what his mother meant. He knew what death was. In all honesty, he wasn't sure he could have shot those men. But he didn't want to admit it.

"Where are we going now? Are those men going to come back? Are we ever going to get something to eat? I'm really hungry."

Jacob spewed out everything pressing on his twelve-year-old mind. Susan suppressed a smile at the incongruity of the thoughts.

"Can you hold on for a little longer? We should be at our destination in about an hour. When I get what's there, we can stop and eat. As for the men, I don't think they'll bother us again."

Susan hoped that was true, but she knew it was wishful thinking. Not only was it a near certainty that they would encounter those men or their colleagues at a later date, others would also be looking for them. She needed to acquire the articles she'd stashed in a safe house location, then she needed to make sure that she and Jacob disappeared. Her heart ached at the knowledge Cody was out there somewhere on his own. She had no current way to contact him. All she could do is hope he'd listened to all he'd been told and that he could figure out the rest on his own. Her hopes didn't comfort her much.

She realized Cody's eighteenth birthday was tomorrow. While that made him an adult in the eyes of the legal system, she knew he was unprepared for all that would confront him. Not being able to guide him through the rest of his teens both angered and saddened her. But worrying about that took her mind off her immediate situation. And she couldn't afford that.

She slowed to take a familiar turn off the road. The bump from the pavement to a gravel road roused Jacob who had dozed off. He looked around.

"Where are we?"

"No place in particular. Can you stay alert for the next few moments?"

"Yes. Why? Are those men here?"

"No, honey. The men aren't here. But I want you to practice your situational awareness and tell me everything you observe in the next ten minutes."

She knew that would keep him occupied and stop the questions coming from him. She needed to focus on the upcoming stretch of road. While she didn't anticipate any trouble, she also knew that if anyone was aware of her destination, the next half-mile would be a perfect place for an ambush. Fortunately all was calm, and she reached her destination without incident. Jacob stared at the rundown cabin.

"What is this place? We're not staying here are we?"

Susan chuckled at both his tone and expression. It was obvious he wasn't impressed. She maneuvered the car so it faced back the way they'd come.

"No, we're not staying here. I just need to get something that's inside. I'm going to leave the car running. I want you to stay alert while I'm in there. No daydreaming. If you see anything that makes you nervous, yell 'cream cake' three times as loud as you can."

"Cream cake? Seriously, Mom? Can't you come up with something better than that?"

"OK. What's your suggestion?"

Jacob thought for a moment. "Purple pants!"

Susan gave Jacob the same look he'd given her a moment before but went along with his suggestion. "Purple pants it is!"

She got out of the car, reminding him to stay alert, and hurried to the door of the cabin. Expecting it to be locked, she was surprised and alarmed to find it wasn't. *Maybe just kids breaking in and causing mischief.* But she proceeded cautiously, just in case.

Taking a moment to allow her eyes to adjust to the gloomy interior, she glanced around and noted that nothing seemed out of place. Not that there was a lot to move around. The cabin was almost empty. Two wooden kitchen chairs and a small table were in the center of what should have been furnished as a living room. As she moved further into the room she remained on high alert. She decided to clear the other rooms before retrieving what she'd come for.

Keeping as quiet as she could, she moved down the hallway and verified that the one bedroom and the small bathroom were empty. Some graffiti defaced the wall in the bedroom confirming her first thought of kids breaking in. She retraced her steps and went into the kitchen. Some old food wrappers were on the counter and a few crumbs littered the sink. But otherwise, there was no obvious damage or indication that someone was squatting in the cabin.

She went to the area where there would normally be a refrigerator. Running her hand along the wall until she felt what she was looking for, she slid her hand downward to the floor. She was happy to see the lack of disturbance in the dust that covered the wooden planks. She knelt and counted over three planks from the one directly below where she'd slid her hand.

She pulled out a small pocketknife and inserted it between a seam. It took a bit of wiggling, but she'd soon pried up the board. She reached into the revealed cubby and pulled out a small duffle bag, breathing a sigh of relief it was there. She quickly replaced the board and stood. She turned and took a step to leave, then stopped. It wouldn't do to leave the marks in the dust. Glancing around she saw no sign of brooms or other cleaning materials. She swiped her feet around to disturb the rest of the area where she'd been, as well as several feet in both directions. It wasn't ideal, but it would have to suffice.

Jacob eyed the duffle in her hand when she returned to the car.

"What's that?"

"Something we need. You see anything that seemed out of place?"

"No. Are we going to eat now?"

"Soon. We've got one more place to stop first."

Jacob gave a loud dramatic sigh and settled back into his seat. Susan asked him to tell her his observations from before they'd reached the cabin, knowing it would keep him distracted while she drove to her next destination. He sighed again, but dutifully began cataloging everything he'd seen.

By the time he'd finished, she was almost at her next destination. She pulled up to a small storefront. The sign read mechanic and handyman.

"What's here?" Jacob asked.

"Our new car."

"We're getting a new car?" He sat up straighter.

"Well, not new as in brand new. Just new to us."

"What about this car?"

"We're leaving it here."

Jacob was about to respond when a young man stepped out of the door. Susan thought he looked familiar, but he wasn't the person she was expecting.

"Help you?" he asked.

"I was looking for Charlie. He around?"

"My father passed two months ago. Cancer. I took over the shop. My name's Daniel."

That explains the familiarity. Susan expressed her condolences and considered her next move. Did Daniel know about her? Did he still have the vehicle that Charlie kept in good running order?

"I knew your father for years. Good man. He was storing a car for me. Is it still here?"

"That old beat-up Chevy?"

"Yes. That's the one. You still got it?"

"You Jane? Dad left a note for you. C'mon into the shop. Yes. The car is here and it runs fine. He changed out the motor. He tell you that?

Put some super hyped-up thing in there. I thought he was crazy, but he said you'd appreciate his efforts."

Susan was surprised. She'd never suggested to Charlie that he do such a thing. But knowing the man and how meticulous he was, she had no concerns that whatever he'd done, he'd done well and she'd have no complaints. She followed Daniel into the store. He went behind the counter and rummaged around for a few moments before pulling out a letter-sized sealed manilla envelope. It had a bulge in it, which Susan assumed was the key to the car.

It was. She pulled out the note and saw that the date was approximately three months earlier.

Jane. I'm sorry I'm not here to greet you. I'm also sorry you're reading this. It means your life has taken a turn for the worse. It's been a long time. When we made the arrangement, I was certain this day would never come. But I should have known better. People like us can never fully hope to just live out our days peacefully. I came close, but this cancer got me in the end. Maybe it's better than the alternative. I don't know. I hope you get through whatever is causing you to seek my assistance, even though I am now unable to personally give it to you.

My son will make sure you get everything you need. He doesn't know the back story. He only knows we're old friends who saved each other's lives once. Please don't tell him anything more. He doesn't need to carry that burden. The car has been maintained beautifully. The new engine gives it power no one would expect from such a rust bucket. While I hope you won't need it, my gut says that if you're here, you will.

Take care of yourself. And may God protect those you love. I know you'll do everything to protect Daniel and keep him off the radar of any threats you might represent to him. Forever in your debt, Charlie.

Susan stifled the tears that were building and swallowed a few times to clear the lump forming in her throat. She and Charlie went back a long time. Before she was Susan. Before she met and married Tom. And long before Cody and Jacob. She would miss him dearly. But she knew he was now at peace. And he'd never have to worry about the past catching up with him. She wasn't sure how, yet, but she'd make sure their past wouldn't catch up with Daniel.

"You OK?"

Daniel's words brought her back to the present and made her realize she needed to finish her business here and move on before she inadvertently involved Daniel in her current troubles.

"Yes. Sorry. Can you show me the car? It has a full tank? Everything is working?"

Daniel looked intently at her for a few moments, then nodded his head. "Follow me. It's in the barn out back. No room to keep it in the garage. But I promise you. It runs like new. Better, actually." He smiled.

"Dad said you'd be leaving whatever car you came in here. He told me I could part it out. Is that true?"

"Yes. It's true. You can even keep it or sell it. But you need to paint it before doing that. You understand? You can't keep it the same color. And I'll be removing the plates from it."

She knew the car was old enough that he wouldn't need a title to get new plates. All states differed on that matter, but this state allowed it. She repeated her caution about changing the color.

Daniel looked at her but didn't comment. She had an idea Charlie had told his son not to ask any questions. Just to make sure she got the car and anything else she might need. He swung open the large barn door revealing the Chevy inside.

"You want me to pull it out for you?"

"Thanks. But I'll do it. It'll give me a chance to get familiar with it."

She hurried to the car and slipped in behind the wheel. Seconds later she was inching it forward out of the barn into the daylight. She manually rolled down the window, smiling at both the need to do so and at Daniel.

"It literally purrs!"

Daniel grinned back at her. "Just be sure you're strapped in if you stomp the gas. Thing'll take off like a rocket. It may look like a rusty old car, but it's both structurally sound and can rival some of the best muscle cars out there."

Susan laughed. "Do they even say muscle car anymore?"

Daniel smiled sheepishly. "It was one of Dad's favorites."

Susan could appreciate that fact like no one else. It sobered her to again realize she'd never see Charlie again.

"Your dad was a good soul. I'm sure he's proud of the man you've become."

Daniel's smile faded a little and he nodded his gratitude for those words.

"You need anything else? Dad told me if you ever came, I was to provide whatever assistance I could."

While she would have asked far more of Charlie than the car, had he been here, she didn't want to involve Daniel in her intrigue any more than with the exchange of the vehicles.

"I've got everything I need. Thanks. I should get going. You need to put my car in your barn. I'd suggest not letting anyone see it until you change the color. If you decide to part it out, you'd do well to dismantle it as quickly as you can. And Daniel, this is important. I was never here. OK? You never saw or talked to me. I can't explain more than that. But I don't exist. You got that?"

Daniel nodded. "Dad told me you'd say something like that. He said not to question you and just do whatever I'm told. He said if push came to shove, and someone questioned what happened to the

Chevy, I was to say it was stolen and I didn't report it because it was just an old junker. But I don't think anyone even knows about it."

"Good. I need to transfer a few things from my car to this one. Then you need to get that one in the barn immediately."

She drove the car around front and parked it next to hers. She got out and made the transfers as quickly as she could, telling Jacob to get into the new car and buckle up. She gave him a silencing look when he opened his mouth to protest. By the time she was finished, Daniel had come to the front of the building. She tossed him her key and thanked him. Then without further comment she slid behind the wheel and was soon pulling away from the place.

Jacob waited all of three minutes before he started pelting her with questions. The only one she answered was how long it would take them to find a place to eat.

10

Cody fidgeted on the couch he'd vacated less than an hour ago, wishing Father Timothy would hurry up and bring the chest he'd referenced. Cody still wanted to go to the house and look for anything else, but he admitted that the priest was probably right. The chest was what Cody was likely looking for. *Bring it, already!*

The door of the office opened, and Father Timothy entered carrying an object that was approximately two feet long by about a foot wide and maybe ten inches or so tall. Cody smiled. Father Timothy had told the truth. The thing did look like something out of a fantasy quest book or movie. He wondered how heavy it was. He couldn't tell from the way the priest was carrying it.

Father Timothy placed the chest on a small table in front of the couch. Cody could see the large padlock thread through the latch loop. *How am I going to get past that if nobody has a key?* He reached out and touched it, feeling the rough wood. Leaning more forward, he used both hands to lift it. It was heavier than he thought. He looked at the priest.

"You're sure no one here has a key?"

"I'm sure."

"Any note or anything? A clue to where a key might be found?"

"Nothing. Just the chest. Father Geoff said he'd gotten it from the priest before him who'd gotten it from the priest before him. None of them had anything to offer other than instructions that the chest was to be kept safe. And that at some point, someone may come asking for it. But then again, no one might ask for it."

"Didn't you find that just a bit weird?"

Father Timothy laughed. "Have to admit I did. I even asked several questions. None were answered. I don't think anyone knew how to answer them."

"Then how do you even know it's connected to the blue house?"

"An excellent question, young man. One that shows you have a fine mind for critical thinking."

Cody was not to be put off. "Well? How do you?"

"The chest appeared at the same time as the fund was set up for maintaining the house. There was a note then, now that I think about it. It—"

Cody interrupted. "Can I see it?"

"I'm afraid it was lost through the years. I never saw it myself. But I was told it gave the instructions I've already given you. Keep it safe. Someone may come for it. Or not."

"Nothing else?"

"Not that I was told."

Cody leaned back on the couch sighing his frustration. "And you think I'm the person that might someday come for it? How do you know I'm not just trying to rob you of the chest?"

Father Timothy looked at Cody. "Are you?"

Cody blushed. "Of course not! I don't steal!"

"I thought not. As to why I think you might be the right person, the events of today lead me there. You appear. You know the house. The house catches fire. You're distressed, needing to find a box with a message. I have a box, so to speak." He gestured towards the chest. "Came to us at the same time we were given the task to maintain the house. Does this chest have a message for you? I don't know. Does it have anything in it? The weight appears to so indicate. We've had it for years. You're the only one to come. I think it's meant for you."

"What if you're wrong?"

"Then may God forgive my error. How do you plan to open it?"

"I don't know."

"Perhaps you should sleep on it. We have a few empty beds in our school dormitory. You're welcome to make use of one."

"But—"

"The chest will be safe. You need your rest. It's obvious you haven't slept in a while. Tomorrow morning you can decide what to do."

Cody realized how exhausted he was and also that he wasn't going to solve the riddle of the padlock tonight, nor be able to explore what was left of the house. The priest had offered him a place to sleep. A place more comfortable than his car.

"All right. But you'll lock this back up?" Cody pointed to the chest.

"Yes. I'll do that now. Then return and take you to the dormitory."

Father Timothy stood and reached for the chest. Cradling it close to his body, he left the room. He was back within five minutes.

"Come," he said. "Let's get you set up for the night. Your car will be fine where it's at. Do you need to get anything from it?"

"I have a backpack with some essentials."

"I'll walk with you to go get it, then show you where you'll sleep."

11

THREE YEARS LATER

Cody sat staring out the window of his small efficiency apartment. Even calling it an apartment was questionable. The large room contained a double bed, a small table with two chairs, a bookcase, and a clothes rack on wheels. In one corner, a counter and a sink comprised the kitchen. Cody had added a hot plate and a small refrigerator to the mix. A door separated this room from the bathroom. He almost tripped over the toilet every time he entered the room, it was so small. All in all, it wasn't much. But it was all he needed.

Today was his twenty-first birthday. His celebration was a store-bought cupcake and a single-serving bottle of milk. As he stared at the treat, he let his mind wander back over the last three years. So much had happened. And yet so little.

The biggest thing that hadn't happened was his mother and brother reentering his life. He'd followed up on a few thoughts, but nothing had panned out. He didn't even know if they were alive. He was convinced no closure was harder than accepting their deaths. And until he knew for certain, he would continue looking for them.

A couple of times, in the early months, he'd contemplated contacting George, his senior camp counselor. *Maybe if I had, he might have had information for me.* But it was too late now. He'd tried calling a few weeks ago and learned George had passed from a heart attack almost a year back.

He remembered Father Timothy with fondness. He'd ended up spending almost a year at the church, helping in any capacity that he could, from minding the younger children to tutoring, to yard work. Whatever needed doing. The church paid him a small stipend, fed him, and allowed him to sleep in the dormitory. He'd debated Biblical passages with the priest, often coming away with a different perspective from what his parents had taught him. But sometimes, he'd given the priest something to ponder. He knew this because the thoughts came out in Sunday messages during mass. And once Father Timothy learned Cody had been home-schooled, he wasted no time in building on the knowledge base the boy had acquired. Cody knew that in those few months, he'd received the equivalent of several college courses. He was grateful, since he knew college was something he would not have access to in the foreseeable future. Maybe someday, but only time would tell. And if he were totally honest with himself, he wasn't sure he even wanted to go to college. He wouldn't know where to begin when it came to picking a major to study.

He glanced in the corner where his bed was. The mysterious chest had been tucked away, nearly forgotten but not quite. He'd never tried to open it while at the church. With food, a safe place to sleep, and a small amount of money in his pocket, he hadn't seen the need to disrupt his life more by whatever might be in the thing.

One night he'd snuck over to the ruins of the burned house. He'd sifted through the debris for about an hour, receiving nothing for his efforts but dirty hands and clothes and a need to sneeze continuously. He never mentioned his midnight adventure to Father Timothy, although he had an inkling that the priest knew of his escapades but been kind enough to not mention anything.

Since he'd left the church, Cody often came close to breaking the lock off, then decided not to. He was never sure what held him back. But something deep inside told him he'd know when the time was right.

Now, here he was, about to eat his birthday cupcake. Alone. No drinking celebrations with friends or family. He knew a few people, but no one amongst them were deemed worthy of sharing this moment with him. He pulled the wrapper off and ate half the small cake in one bite. He chased that with several swallows of milk, then ate the other half, followed by the remaining milk.

"Happy birthday, Cody," he said to the empty room. "May this coming year bring all you could hope for." He let out a small bitter laugh.

Without stopping to contemplate his actions, he stood and walked the three steps to his bed and reached under it. He pulled out the chest and carried it back to the table.

"It's time, you miserable box."

Earlier that day, he'd purchased a hacksaw and a few other tools. One way or the other, he was getting into the chest today. He sat down in front of it and grabbed the padlock, giving it a strong yank. As expected, nothing happened. He looked at the keyhole, wondering if he could force the screwdriver into the opening and manipulate the mechanism. He gave the idea a half-hearted attempt with no success. Sawing through the thing was going to be a lot of work. He spun the thing around and studied the hinges thinking he could simply remove them. But whoever had built it had been clever. They'd somehow concealed the mechanics inside, leaving nothing to tamper with.

"Maybe I should just smash the thing with a sledge hammer," he murmured into the room. But he knew he didn't want to destroy the last thing that connected him to his family. Whether it be empty or full of treasures, the container itself had taken on a larger-than-life significance to him. And he knew it wasn't empty. It was too heavy for that.

Sighing, he picked up the saw and began working at the top of the shackle, figuring he could pry it apart enough to pull it from the chest if he cut through it. An hour later he was still working at it. He was tired, frustrated, and annoyed with the mess he was making. He stopped just short of throwing the saw on the table when he stood to stretch his legs and back. He paced back and forth in his room, stopping only to get a drink of water from the faucet.

He stood by the table and looked down at the chest sitting there. *Why leave the thing for me and provide no way to open it? Doesn't make sense.* He reached out and rubbed his hand over the top and sides. He'd done that several times over the past three years, almost as if he expected it to magically open for him. It never did.

He sat down in front of it and repositioned it so he could continue with his sawing. However, as he lifted it, his little finger felt a slight indentation on the bottom. He stopped, trying to remember if he'd ever felt that before. He didn't think so.

Carefully tipping the chest on its side, he ran his fingers lightly over the entire bottom. *There! I felt it again!*

Feeling excitement bloom, he looked closely at the spot. It didn't look any different from the rest of the bottom. Just a slight indentation, barely noticeable. He fought disappointment as he used his thumb to push in the middle of the dent.

The sound was so soft he almost missed it. A quiet click. Had there been any background noise, he would never had heard it. Quickly placing the chest upright, he ran his hands all along the top seam, while at the same time trying to lift it up. He felt a slight give.

He slid the box around examining every side carefully. One side's seam was slightly wider than the others. He jumped up and grabbed a butter knife out of his kitchen drawer. He carefully pushed the tip of the knife into the opening. Wiggling it up and down did nothing, so he tried sliding it along the opening. About half-way along, the knife hit an obstruction. Cody wiggled the tip, then tried to force its path. For a second, the knife didn't move, then suddenly whatever was obstructing his movement gave way and the knife slid to the corner.

Slowly, hopefully Cody pulled on the lid again. It came apart from the chest, the only thing keeping it connected was the clasp and padlock.

"Noooo! Seriously??" Cody murmured the words aloud. He studied where the hinges had protruded on the back. He immediately saw that they were simply an interlocking clasp designed to deceive the eye. Whoever had come up with the idea was a genius. He took a deep breath and shifted his focus to the inside of the chest.

At first, it looked empty. Then he realized he was staring at a black velvet bag. Barely breathing, he removed it and set it on the table. Part of his brain registered there was minimal weight to the bag. Slowly, he opened the drawstring closure. He grabbed the end and gently tipped it upward spilling the contents out in front of him.

The first thing that caught his attention was a photo. He picked it up and studied it, feeling his eyes moisten with emotion. The picture had been taken when he was fifteen. He remembered the day as if it were yesterday. The whole family had enjoyed a hike and picnic. At the end of the day, his dad had insisted everyone crunch together while he took the picture of them, barely getting everyone in the frame. An inexpensive digital model, the camera had been a birthday gift to his father, who'd used it at every opportunity. The family, tired of having to always pose for pictures, made funny faces at the camera. At first slightly angry, then joining in the fun, his dad took another picture making his own funny face. The picture Cody now stared at was the second, goofy-faced photo of his family. Not realizing he'd been holding his breath until it came out in a whoosh, the sound was a mixture of a chuckle and sob. He put the photo down, knowing it had instantly become his most prized possession.

The next item to catch his eye was an envelope. He picked it up and saw it was sealed and addressed to him. His hands shaking slightly, he opened it and pulled out a folded piece of paper. Unsure what to expect, he unfolded the paper slowly. It was a hand-written note.

Dearest Cody,

If you're reading this, it means you've had to flee from our home. It also means you're probably alone, and one or both of us are no longer alive. Not knowing which situation is true, your mom and I hope Jacob is with you. We know you'll do everything you can to keep him safe. If your brother is not with you, please find him and guide him into his adult years. We can't emphasize enough how much we wish you weren't reading this note.

Remember everything we've told and taught you. You didn't know it at the time, but all our outings and activities were designed to give you and Jacob survival skills. The games all had purpose. You may not even recognize that you've used some of the skills imparted, but it's important that you never forget. Take every opportunity you can to build on those skills. I'm sad to say, you'll need them.

There are people who will want to use you for their own distorted, likely criminal, benefit. Others will say you must help them for reasons of national security. All will want something from you that you cannot give them, for the simple reason that you know nothing of what they ask. They won't believe you.

The best way to stay safe is to stay invisible. Avoid as many of the modern conveniences as you can. They are all designed to monitor your existence and activities. And there are those who would do just that to find you. Stay safe son. Use the contents of this chest to do so. We love you. –Dad

P.S. Cody, if you are uncertain whether both of us are gone, or you know for certain that one of us is out there, possibly with your brother, find us. You can do it. Remember our family story times. The clues for where to look are all within those tales. To keep you safe, we can't come for you. You must figure out how to find us. Whoever is left, is waiting for you. And it gives me deep pain to acknowledge this, but if you truly are alone in this world, know that your dad and I are sorry we're the cause. Live your life, son. Be happy. Love, Mom.

Cody reread the letter three times. He didn't fully understand the message. What skills did he have? What doesn't he know that is putting him at risk? He placed the paper on the table and stood, knowing if he held it any longer, he might just rip it to shreds. He had enough composure to know that would not be a good thing. But his frustration was quickly overtaking any semblance of common sense. He paced his small apartment, using the movement to help vent his emotions. So many thoughts were going through his head. What if he'd opened the chest sooner? It's been three years since he found it. A lot could happen in three years. A lot had happened. Were his mom and Jacob even still alive? How long before he must acknowledge he'd never see them again?

He sat on his bed, then swung his feet around and stretched out on the mattress. He needed time to think. To process. To understand.

12

Susan watched Jacob fiddle with the Rubik's Cube. At fifteen, he was taller than her and she could tell by his physical development that he had the makings of a very muscular young man. It made sense. He had little to do to occupy himself other than the lessons she insisted he keep up and to work out in the makeshift gym they'd created. It wasn't much of an existence for a young man who should be involved in so many outside activities.

She reflected on the last three years with a mixture of sadness and joy. The sadness came from not knowing about Cody. She continually prayed that he was safe and thriving. But the not knowing was difficult. The joy came from seeing Jacob safe regardless of the other challenges he faced and would continue to face.

Other than the incident at the park, she'd been left alone. She wasn't sure whether that made her feel safer or more at risk. She was convinced unseen forces were still at work looking for her. But she'd managed to gather the things she'd stashed and kept herself and Jacob off the radar of others for three years. It was a minor victory, compared to the fifteen years she'd had with her husband and family in their previous home. But it was a victory, nonetheless.

She glanced out the window at the cold Colorado landscape. Not her first choice for a place to stay off-grid, yet it was the most suitable. The cabin they were in was far enough from town to keep any busybodies at bay, but they were close enough to access the services they needed. That the cabin had no hardwired telephone or internet access was more of a plus than a minus in her mind. She knew Jacob would disagree with that assessment. And in some ways, he was right. Even though it denied him the various distractions he would seek out if he had access, it made his ongoing education more difficult. But she compensated in other ways. Lately she'd been taking him out and showing him the rudiments of hunting and scavenging off the land. He'd been an eager and enthusiastic student of bushcraft, quickly learning the skills she imparted and coming up with innovative approaches she'd never considered.

Her latest burner phone was on the table in front of her. It was the fourth one she'd acquired since going off grid. Like the others, this one tied into a central number via a service that routed all calls through several layers of security. Since fleeing the scene of her husband's murder she'd received no calls or messages. The lack of any outside communication offered several scenarios. All were concerning.

Had Cody found the chest? Had he figured out how to open it? If so, had he deciphered the coded number? Did he not want to reconnect? Was he afraid to try? Or the worst possibility, was Cody even still alive?

She sighed. Sitting here and letting her mind wander into places best left alone was not going to help. She looked at Jacob.

"Want to go out and see if we can find something to shoot or catch for tonight's dinner?"

He looked up from his cube. "Sure. Can we go to the other side of the mountain today? You said we'd explore that some time. The weather is clear. Why not today?"

Susan smiled. "Yes. Why not? Go get your things together and we'll head out in about fifteen minutes. OK?"

Jacob grinned at her, stood and quickly headed for his room. It took Susan less than ten minutes to gather all that she needed. And to her, that time frame was still too long. *Need to tighten things up. Never know when it might be necessary to escape into the wilderness. Preparedness will keep us alive. When we get back today, I'll sort things out.*

Jacob came out of his room, his backpack secured to his frame and his rifle held loosely in his right hand, barrel pointed down.

"Ready."

"You're sure? You have everything to survive a night outside?"

"Mom. We've gone through this a hundred or more times. I'm ready."

She gave him a 'mom' look but relented. "I know. Old habits die hard."

She let him lead the way out, closing and locking the door behind them. "You know which way you want to go?"

"Yes."

"Then take us there."

They hiked in silence for over twenty minutes, navigating the deeper spots carefully. Those areas that looked less treacherous, they hurried through with little thought for any hazards that might be lurking.

"Mom, do you think Cody is still alive?"

The question came out of nowhere as far as Susan was concerned. But then again, if Cody was on her thoughts, why wouldn't he be on Jacob's?

"Yes." She said definitively. Then continued more hesitantly, "At least I pray he is."

"Then why hasn't he contacted us? He knows how, right?"

"I can't answer either of those questions, hon."

"I miss him."

"I know. I do, too."

Jacob abruptly stopped and turned to his mother. "It's been three years! Doesn't he want to be with us? Do you think he's just forgotten us and moved on with his life?"

"I don't think he's forgotten us."

"Then why—"

Jacob stopped at his mother's gesture. He noted her tense posture and looked wildly around him.

"What?" he whispered.

"I thought I heard something. Something not part of the environment," she whispered back. "Quick, get over to those trees."

They both hustled to the tree cover and dropped to a half-squat position, on high alert. Susan pulled a small pair of binoculars from her chest pocket and surveyed the landscape. Jacob focused on regulating his breathing after the unexpected shot of adrenalin had disrupted it. He waited for his mother to indicate whether all was clear, or if they were in danger. He studied the area around them, automatically looking for and evaluating escape routes. In one sense he wasn't aware how naturally he did this. In another, he recognized the training his mother had been imparting to him over the past three years. In a matter of moments, he'd discarded two directions based on terrain alone.

He was calculating the odds of success with his third choice when he heard it. A buzzing sound. Electronic or mechanical. Maybe a combination of both. He closed his eyes and listened with his entire body, trying to pinpoint the direction. When he opened his eyes, he scanned the sky. He realized his mother had already been doing so with her binoculars. *How had she even heard that while they'd been talking?*

"Drone?" he whispered.

Susan nodded.

"Who?"

She shook her head and shrugged, indicating she couldn't answer that question. Jacob understood that her lack of words conveyed her intention to not talk, even if in whispers. He respected that. He tapped her shoulder to get her attention then pointed in the direction of his choice for retreat. She looked in that direction, then glanced at the two other routes he'd already discarded. Her decision was almost instantaneous and when she nodded her head at her son, he was amazed at how quickly she'd evaluated the options. *I'll have to ask her how she does that. It took me much longer to choose.*

She tucked the binoculars back in place and rose into a crouched ready position. She gestured for Jacob to take the lead. She hoped he'd stay vigilant for threats ahead of them while she covered their backs. As he moved out, she gently eased her handgun from the place she'd secured it under her outerwear, careful to not distract her son with the movement.

As they moved further into the woods, Susan was glad to see Jacob move from tree to tree, obviously thinking of maintaining a barrier between him and whatever might be ahead. She knew that most might take a direct path in favor of speed over caution. She wondered if Jacob even realized what he was doing. She continually glanced behind her. She couldn't hear the drone anymore. She didn't know if that was due to their going deeper into cover, or if whoever had been flying it had moved on to other parts of the mountain.

After approximately a half-mile of trekking, she reached out and touched Jacob's shoulder. He stopped instantly, becoming as still as one of the trees. She saw the slight movement of his head, indicating he was surveying his surroundings. She nodded to herself. *He's learned.*

"I think we're clear," she said softly. Not quite a whisper, but also not her full voice.

"What do you make of all that?" he asked in the same volume.

"Not sure. Could have just been folks out playing with a new toy. Could have been something else."

"How will we know?"

"We won't."

He looked closely at his mother. Her face had a bland expression, as if she hadn't a care in the world. He knew better.

"Do we continue with our day's plans, or head back?"

"What do you think? Consider all your options. Tell me your decision and why you made it."

Jacob was surprised at his mother's response, but he tried not to show it. Instead, he took her at her word and considered his choices. She waited patiently.

After several minutes he spoke. "I think we head back. But take a different route. Come in from another direction rather than straight in the way we left."

"Why do you say that?"

"If we continue with our day's plans, we'll only be distracted by what happened. Doubtful we'll have a successful hunt. And even if we do, we'll be faced with the prospect of packing the kill out and wondering if we're walking into something unprepared due to our preoccupation with our loads. If we go back, we should be careful. We don't know what, if anything, that might be waiting for us."

He paused and drew a deep breath. "And I think it's time to leave Colorado."

She stared deeply into his eyes. She could see several emotions. She knew now was not the time to explore them.

"I agree with everything you said. Lead the way, son. Stay alert."

He nodded and maneuvered himself around her to start back. She didn't say anything when he followed the track they'd been on. But she smiled to herself when within a few hundred yards he veered off trail and to the left.

Jacob led his mother through a maze of twists and turns. At one point, she began to wonder if he was lost but didn't want to admit it. Even though they'd both explored their surroundings considerably over the past three years, when one was in the woods off-trail, it was easy enough to lose direction. But she soon understood that he knew exactly where he was when she recognized the outer boundary of their cabin area. She felt a swell of pride at his abilities. *He'll be OK. Regardless of the circumstances, he'll be OK.*

She wasn't sure if she was trying to convince herself or was already convinced. Either way, she called out softly to him.

"Jacob, hold up."

He stopped immediately and half-turned towards her, a question in his eyes.

"Let me go first."

He looked as if he were going to object, then silently moved aside so she could pass him. His eyes widened when he noticed she was holding her handgun in a ready position but pointed downward. Without conscious thought, he removed his rifle from his shoulder and held it in a manner that he could easily deploy it if needed. Susan looked at him closely, then slightly nodded and took the lead.

They moved silently to the edge of the clearing. Jacob saw them first and put his hand on his mother's shoulder. Both knelt to better conceal themselves in the brush as they watched the two men move in, out, and around their cabin. It was obvious the men were speaking to each other, but neither Susan nor Jacob could make out their words. After approximately ten minutes, the men climbed into their Jeep and drove away. Susan waited another five minutes before gesturing to Jacob that they could approach. They did so cautiously.

When they entered the cabin, Susan took in the devastation with a calmness that was almost eerie. Jacob, however, was stunned. And angry.

"Who were those guys? Why would they do this? What were they looking for? We have almost nothing!"

"Calm down, Jacob. What's done is done. Go to your room and pack the rest of your belongings. We're leaving in fifteen minutes or less."

"But Mom. What—"

Susan shook her head. "Not now. We need to leave."

Jacob grunted and strode to his room. His rifle still over his shoulder. Susan heard him mumbling to himself and the sounds of drawers opening and closing. She quickly gathered her own things, as well as retrieving what she considered the most important items. The sack with those things she'd gathered from her safe-stash three years ago. She was relieved the men hadn't found her hiding place. She stuffed it in her duffle, not wanting Jacob to see it and be reminded of that time. She also didn't want the questions she was sure he would ask.

Jacob stepped through his door just under ten minutes later. His backpack still securely attached, he now had a small duffle in his left hand and held his rifle, barrel down, in his right.

"Ready. Other than some tossed-around clothes, it seems they left my room alone. Nothing like what it looks like in here. I assume I can bring my rifle? If so, I have a couple boxes of shells for it."

Susan smiled at his commentary. "Yes. Bring the rifle. We'll put it in the back. You've unloaded it I presume?"

"Of course."

"Then go stash your stuff in the trunk. I'll be out in a couple of minutes."

He looked at her. "Anything I can help you with?"

"No. I just need to finish up."

She watched him exit, then returned to gathering the rest of what she needed. She was ready within two minutes. She hated leaving the mess behind that she was leaving. The landlord would certainly not appreciate it. But at least nothing was broken; just things strewn about.

She took one last glance around the cabin before closing the door and locking it. Although Colorado hadn't been her first choice, she was now sorry to be leaving. The last three years had been peaceful. She wasn't exactly sure who the men were or which side of her life they represented. But she did know that staying here was no longer an option.

She quickly walked to their car and tossed her stuff into the backseat. Jacob was already in the passenger seat, waiting for her. She did a walk around the vehicle, checking for tracking units. Then raised the hood and looked for any obvious signs of mischief. Seeing none, she closed the hood and slid into the driver's seat. She looked at her son, reminded again of how much he'd grown and matured.

"Ready?"

"Yes. Where to?"

She smiled. "How do you feel about Montana?"

13

Cody awoke with a start. He glanced at the clock, amazed to see he'd slept almost three hours. He sat up and rubbed his face. The chest on the table caught his eye. He didn't want to deal with it, yet knew he had to finish what he started.

He stood, walked to the table, and stared down at the letter and photo. Sitting, he pushed them aside and sorted through the other items that had fallen from the bag. There wasn't much. A silly plastic decoder ring from a Cracker Jack box. A rodeo belt buckle. And a wooden stick. No, it wasn't just a stick. When Cody picked it up and looked at it more closely, he realized it was a Lincoln Log from an old set he and Jacob used to play with. They'd seen it at a yard sale and his parents had purchased it for them.

"What an odd assortment of things," he murmured to the empty room. "Why would they put this stuff in a chest and make such a big deal out of the whole thing?"

He looked into the box. There was nothing more inside. Picking it up, he shook it slightly, noting the weight. *Has to be more to this. The chest itself can't be this heavy.* He shook it again and thought he heard something shift within. *Gotta be a false bottom!*

He put it down on the table and spun it around several times, looking for a crack or some other indication there was another opening. Seeing nothing, he tapped the interior sides and bottom. Nothing seemed out of place, yet he knew there was more to the puzzle. He dropped his chin into his hand and stared at the chest as if by looks alone he could force it to tell its secrets.

Finally, he picked it up, flipped it over and soundly smacked the bottom. He thought he felt the weight distribution change. He smacked it again and again. Without warning the hidden contents of the chest disbursed, hitting the floor in a loud plop.

Flipping the chest upright, he looked inside and saw that what had first appeared to be the bottom was simply a thin board wedged in to hold in place what was beneath it. His shaking and smacking had dislodged the piece and it now hung crookedly, half in and half out of the chest. Quickly checking to see that there really wasn't anything left in the box, he placed it on the table and fell to his knees to scoop up the materials on the floor.

Two square manilla envelopes, a key, and an Allen Wrench were the bounty. Cody dropped the items on the table and sat again. He picked up the key. He thought it looked like it would fit a suitcase or briefcase or something along those lines. He put it down and picked up the Allen Wrench. He twirled it in his fingers for a moment then put it down next to the key. *Odd.*

He picked up both envelopes and explored their weight and contents by running his fingers over them. He put the thin one down and hefted the thicker one in his left hand. *Here goes nothing.* He ripped it open and tipped the contents out. A passport, driver's license, birth certificate, social security card, and several one-hundred-dollar bills fell out. There was a note. Before looking at the other items, he picked up the note and read it. It didn't say much. Only that he would need the enclosed items and should put them to use immediately. He tossed the note on the table. Frustrated, he picked up the driver's license. It had a picture of him at seventeen, the last one he remembered his father taking of him. But the name said Cody Walters, not Cody Winters. Confused, he looked at the passport. Same photo, same name. Then he looked at the birth certificate. The date was his birthday, but again, the name was Cody Walters. And it said his state of birth was Montana. As far as he knew, he'd never been to Montana. He was told he'd been born in some small town in Colorado.

He ran his hand through his hair. *I'm so confused! I don't understand any of this!* He counted the money. It totaled two thousand dollars. More than he'd ever had at any one time.

He pushed everything aside and sat staring at it for several minutes. Almost afraid, he reached for the second envelope. This one was thin, indicating there wasn't much in it.

Inside was a single sheet of paper containing a typed nursery rhyme. He recognized it immediately. As kids, he and Jacob had learned and recited the rhyme often. If either forgot the words, one of his parents would prompt them until they could recite the whole thing without mistakes. Just seeing the words on the paper brought back many memories. He remembered once asking why they had to learn the sing-song rhyme only to be told it was a family secret, that he should never forget it, and someday he may need the message contained in it. When he'd asked about the message, his mother had simply said one day he'd understand.

Well, one day was today. And he didn't understand. Cody tossed the paper on the table and stood. Without consciously aware of it, he began pacing again. Back and forth across the small apartment, his mind a tangled mess.

At some point, he started mumbling the nursery rhyme in time to his steps. He realized he'd learned it by repeating the words given him. He'd never seen it in written form. He stopped. Something clicked in his brain. He hurried to the table and picked up the sheet of paper and studied it.

All the words are right. Just as I memorized them. But something is off.

Then it hit him. Whenever a number was mentioned, it wasn't spelled out. The numerical representation was used.

"Why do that?" he asked the empty room. "It's not something you would usually do. Is it?"

His only answer was silence. He chuckled when he realized he'd actually expected to hear a response.

He counted the numbers. Ten. He wrote them on a separate piece of paper in the order they appeared. At first, he thought them random numbers. But as he stared at them, an idea began to form. Not sure why, he spoke them aloud as he rewrote them. Something about the rhythm triggered the thought these might represent a telephone number. Separating them into the proper groupings, he was now convinced that's exactly what they were.

He stood and went to the landline telephone that hung on his wall. He'd never acquired a cell phone. Partly because, since being on his own, he never had the money to buy one, and partly because he remembered his parents' aversion to modern technology. His hand absently rubbed the simple watch on his wrist.

Punching the numbers in, he waited in anticipation. But any fledgling excitement he felt was quickly crushed when a recorded voice announced that what he'd entered was not a working number. He gently hung up the receiver, returned to the table, and sat. Chin in hands, he stared at all the items in front of him.

What are you trying to tell me? Please! Just reveal your message!

He decided a walk might help clear his mind. He didn't have to work today. Sal, his boss, had told him to take the day off for himself. Sal ran the local deli a block from his apartment. He gave Cody counter hours from time to time and the small amount he received kept Cody up to date with his rent. But that's about all it did. Eating at the deli kept him alive. And luckily, Sal was always telling him to eat up. That he was too skinny.

Cody grabbed his jacket from a hook and slipped into it. Almost as an after-thought, he scooped up all the identification documents and zipped them into an inner pocket, along with the cash. He put the key and Allen Wrench into his front pants pocket, leaving the other items on the table.

Just as he was reaching for the door handle, he turned. Not sure why, he went back to the table and picked up the paper with the nursery rhyme. Carefully folding it into a small square, he pushed it into his back pocket. He also picked up the photo and tucked it next to the paper. A quick glance around the apartment satisfied him it was as neat and tidy as it would ever be. He opened his door and stepped through without another thought.

He wandered the streets for almost thirty minutes, having no clear destination in mind. The cool air felt good on his face. Feeling slightly hungry, he decided to go visit Sal and see if he could wrangle a sandwich from him.

As he turned the corner, he saw a young woman slip and fall on the sidewalk. He hurried to her, asking if she were OK. Before she could answer him, he felt two strong arms grab him from behind. Reacting immediately, he kicked out behind him and felt his boot strike a target. He didn't know if it was a knee or shin, he just knew it was enough to make the person who grabbed him flinch. He turned into the man and pushed him hard on the chest. The move dislodged the man's arms. He was about to execute another move when he felt something stab his arm. He turned and saw the woman who'd fallen holding a syringe. Confused, he struck out, hitting her on the chin. This time when she fell, she didn't immediately get up.

Luckily for Cody, the man who'd grabbed him went to the woman. Cody used the opportunity to run. He'd taken about six steps when he felt himself getting dizzy and disoriented. *What was in the syringe?*

He forced his legs to keep moving and just as he felt himself starting to fall, he reached for the door in front of him, opening it and falling onto the floor of Sal's deli.

"Cody! What the hell?"

Sal's voice came from far away, but Cody had nothing left in him to answer. He closed his eyes and relaxed into unconsciousness.

14

Susan yawned. She'd been driving almost non-stop for twelve hours, stopping only for gas and potty breaks. Jacob had slept a large part of the trip. She envied his ability to do so. They were only a few miles from the Montana border.

"Jacob, hon. Wake up."

Jacob's eyes opened immediately. "What's wrong?" She heard the alarm in his voice.

"Nothing. I'm sorry. I didn't mean to scare you."

"Wasn't scared. Just asking."

She chose to ignore his comment, understanding how the mind of a fifteen-year-old boy worked. "We're almost in Montana. Just wanted you to see the area."

He looked around at the empty plains surrounding them. "What's to see?"

She chuckled. "I'll give you that. This part of Montana is pretty flat. But we're headed towards the mountains."

Jacob noted a road sign and grabbed the atlas to study it. "Why are we taking this route? Wouldn't it have been faster to stay towards the west?"

"Yes, but there's a small town I need to stop at."

Jacob had learned over the past three years not to ask additional questions when his mother made statements like that. She never answered them. And he knew her reasons would be revealed to him either through her actions or the consequences of her actions. He hoped there weren't going to be any bad consequences.

"How much further?"

"About another hour. Can you handle that?"

"Maybe."

She glanced at him. "Need me to pull over?"

He hesitated, then nodded, slightly embarrassed.

She schooled her face to a neutral expression and glanced in the rearview mirror to make sure they were alone on the highway. She slowed and pulled to a stop.

Jacob climbed out of the car and moved to the only cover presented, a couple of scraggly shrubs next to a fence post. Making sure his back was to the car, he quickly took care of his needs then returned to the vehicle. He noted is mother was looking out the opposite window, away from him. He slid into his seat and closed the door.

"Thanks," he mumbled.

"No problem. There's some water and a couple of snacks in the back-seat. Help yourself."

She pulled onto the highway without further comment, accelerating to ten miles above the posted speed limit. They rode in companionable silence for the next fifteen minutes or so.

"Can we talk about Colorado?"

Susan inwardly winced. She'd been dreading this moment, even though she knew it would come at some time. She swallowed her sigh. Keeping her voice light, she asked if there was anything in particular he wanted to talk about.

"Do you know who those men at the cabin were?"

"No."

Jacob looked at his mother closely. He knew from experience he had to form his questions carefully to get any real answers.

"Do you have any suspicions?"

Her answer was so slow in coming that Jacob had nearly given up that she would answer at all. When she did finally answer, he wasn't sure she'd really said anything.

"I don't know which side of my life they might be connected to. But either side is not something I want contact with right now."

Jacob decided to switch tactics. "They appeared to be looking for something. Do you know what? And did they find it?"

Again, her answer was long in coming. Finally, "Yes. I know what they were looking for. And no, they didn't find it."

Jacob was quiet for several minutes. The next question was asked in a quiet, hesitant voice.

"Will they kill to get it? I mean, are we really living a life-and-death existence?"

Susan smiled. "Not to sound flippant, but everyone is in a life-and-death existence. We're not special that way. But to specifically answer your question, yes, I do believe they would kill to obtain what they're looking for."

"You've never said what it is, or why it's so important."

"And I won't. You're safer not knowing."

"But what if they have me and don't believe that I don't know anything?"

She slowed a bit as she looked at her son. She could see real concern on his face. "Jacob. Please know that I will do everything in my power to make sure they never have you, as you phrase it. But I will be honest. Even if you knew the information and could give it to them, it's likely they would still kill you. I don't want to scare you or give you more to worry about, but you are old enough and mature enough to understand the real world is not always a happy place. There are bad people in it. I've kept you safe for fifteen years. Granted, these last three have not been the idyllic childhood I wanted for you, but we've been safe. I will continue to keep you safe and give you the skills you need to stay safe. Do you trust me to do that?"

Jacob nodded as he surreptitiously wiped a tear from his eye. The silence stretched as Susan accelerated back to her earlier speed.

"Mom? Do you think Cody is still alive?"

"I hope so, hon. No. I know so. I would feel it if he weren't."

She said the last with so much conviction that Jacob didn't question her further on that topic. But he returned to his earlier one.

"How did those men know where to find us? It's been three years. Do you think they've been looking for us all that time?"

"I must admit I've been wondering the same thing. I would probably have put the drone incident down to a random incident if it hadn't been for the trashed cabin. In some ways, we're lucky they were so careless. It allowed us to escape. But, and I'm thinking out loud now, how they found us is a bit of a mystery. And yet it's not."

"What do you mean?"

"The town we were by. It's where Cody was born. That information wouldn't necessarily be hard to find out. It would be a natural process of elimination to check it out. Even if they thought it a complete longshot. They know it's the two of us. Wouldn't take much to ask around and find out a woman and her son were staying in a cabin up the mountain. Easy enough to check out the terrain with the drone. They may or may not have even seen us. I'm thinking they didn't, or they wouldn't have left after searching the cabin. They would have waited for us, knowing we'd return at some point."

"If their questions revealed we were still there, why didn't they wait anyway?"

"I don't know. Either total inexperience, or something else is going on. But the people who would be looking for us? They wouldn't be so incompetent. At least not in my day."

"Then maybe it wasn't anyone associated with your past. Maybe it was just hoodlums."

Susan chuckled at Jacob's use of such an old-fashioned description for mischief-makers. In that moment he reminded her of her husband Tom, prompting a deep stab of sorrow.

"Be that as it may, we're better off not being there."

"Will they find us here in Montana?"

"Maybe. But not for a while. And if so, we'll be prepared. Don't worry yourself. Focus on how you plan to provide meat for the table."

As she'd hoped, her comment distracted Jacob. "Oh, don't you worry. I'll provide the meat. I'm the best hunter I know."

She laughed at that. He was the only hunter he knew. But she let him have his moment. She slowed to take a turn. To Jacob, the terrain looked more of the same. Flat and uninteresting. To Susan, she knew she was only five miles from her destination.

When she pulled in front of a small post office, Jacob moved to get out. Susan placed her hand on his arm.

"Wait in the car. I'll only be a few minutes. Then we can get something to eat at that diner over there. After that, we'll get back on the road."

"But you've been driving forever! Shouldn't we stay here so you can get some sleep?"

"I'll be fine. We'll find something further down the road. I want to get a little closer to our destination before we stop."

"What is our destination?"

"You'll see." She smiled. "You'll like it. I promise."

15

Cody awoke in a dark room. Panic immediately enveloped him. He sat up, some part of his brain registering that he could sit up and that he wasn't tied up. He saw movement in the corner and tensed.

"You're awake. Good."

Sal's voice calmed Cody. A small lamp clicked on, illuminating the room, which appeared to be a bedroom. He wondered if Sal slept here. *Doesn't he have a home? Does he live in his shop?* He looked at Sal.

"What happened?"

"I was about to ask you that same question. You literally fell into my shop. I dragged you into the back. And none too soon, I might add. Just after I closed the back door, this man and woman came in asking about you. I played dumb. Said I didn't know what they were talking about. No one had been in my shop for over an hour. Asked them if they wanted a sandwich."

Sal's laugh at his own cleverness made Cody smile. But he sobered at Sal's question.

"Who were those people?"

"I don't know."

Cody described what had happened. When he finished and Sal asked why they would target him he could only answer with another denial of knowledge.

"You must have some inkling."

Cody debated whether to tell Sal about the last three years. While he worked for the man, he really didn't know much about him. And since his father's death, he'd developed an approach in life of not trusting people. It had taken several weeks to trust Father Timothy, but in the end, Cody recognized how much he'd leaned on the priest for support and advice. He missed that closeness.

Sal had been watching him. "C'mon. Let's make a couple of sand-wiches. You must be starving. Then you can decide what you want to tell me."

Cody looked around the room. Sal laughed. "Not here, you goof. Come into the kitchen. Can't see the lights from the front and the store is closed anyway."

Sal led the way into the shop's back kitchen and began pulling meats and cheeses out of the large walk-in refrigerator.

"How long was I out?"

"A little over two hours. Whatever they stuck you with was powerful. How are you feeling?"

"Weird."

Sal laughed. "Can you be a little more specific than 'weird'? Are you nauseous? You have a headache? Anything like that?"

"Yeah, a little sick to my stomach. But I'm good to eat."

"Figured as much."

Sal had put together two large sandwiches while they'd been talking. He took their plates to a small table in the corner, then went back into the fridge to grab a couple of single-serve milks.

"C'mon. Making these has made me hungry."

Sal sat in one of the chairs and picked up his sandwich. Not waiting for Cody to sit, he took a huge bite, his cheeks puffing out from the effort.

Cody sat at the table and stared at the sandwich. He made no effort to pick it up.

"You sure you're good to eat?" Sal asked around another mouthful.

Cody jerked as if just waking up. He smiled as he reached for the sandwich. Taking a smaller bite than Sal's initial one, he murmured, "Yes. I'm good."

They ate in companionable silence. Sal waited for Cody to decide if and when he would talk. He'd just convinced himself Cody wasn't going to say anything when the young man began his story. He summarized his last three years and how he came to be at his current location. He also described the chest and its contents.

"You have everything on you?"

"No. There's still a couple of things at my apartment. I should probably go get them. Put them somewhere safe. I may not know what their purpose is, but I'm sure they wouldn't be in the box if they weren't important."

"I agree. But I'm not sure it's safe for you to return to your apartment."

Cody's eyes widened in alarm, and Sal hastened to reassure him. "We'll go together. Get your things. You can stay with me while you figure out what you plan to do."

"That's very kind of you, but I can't take advantage of your hospitality like that."

"Nonsense! It's clear you're meant to complete some kind of quest. But you'll need all those box contents to be prepared for whatever is waiting for you. If I weren't so old, I'd be begging to come along."

Cody smiled. Sal wasn't old, but he was settled in his life. And Cody knew that whatever was waiting for him, he had to face it alone.

"I'm thinking I should leave town as soon as possible."

"Where will you go?"

Cody tried not to show his disappointment that Sal hadn't urged him to stay. "Colorado?" he asked hesitantly.

Sal nodded his head. "As good of place as any. Especially since you were told you were born there. Maybe you'll find something that will help you figure out what's what."

"And if I don't?"

"Then, Mr. Cody Walters," Sal used the name on the papers Cody had shown him, "I suggest Montana might be on your list of destinations."

Cody sat quietly for several minutes. Sal wondered what was going through the boy's head. When Cody looked up, Sal was surprised at the question.

"Will you come with me to the apartment now? It won't take me long to pack what I have."

"Absolutely. Grab your coat. I'll get mine."

Both stood to retrieve their outer garments. Sal added an additional item to his. Cody's eyes widened when he saw the small handgun Sal tucked into his jacket pocket.

"No need to worry. Only want to be prepared. I'm sure it's just extra weight in my coat," Sal said in a calm voice. As Cody stood there, uncertain, Sal gestured to the door.

"Let's get this done, boy. I'm a busy man, you know."

Cody chuckled as the two left the deli shop and walked the short distance to Cody's apartment. Once there, Sal suggested he go first. He tucked both hands in his pockets to avoid alarming Cody. But his intent was to make sure his gun was in his hand and ready.

The door to Cody's apartment was slightly ajar.

"You leave it like that?" Sal whispered. Cody shook his head.

"Then stay here. I'll check it out." This time Sal made no effort to hide the fact that his gun was in his hand. He crept cautiously towards the door and pushed it further open with his foot and waited. When nothing happened, he moved so he could see into the room. The place being small and the only other door being to the bathroom, and it was open, Sal was able to easily see that the place was empty. But it was a mess. Someone had obviously been there.

"Not much on housekeeping, are you?" He spoke in a normal volume.

"What do you mean?" Cody's tone was defensive until he looked into the room. "What the—"

"C'mon, get inside and close the door."

Cody did so, making sure he locked it. Then he turned back to the mess that met his eyes. He didn't know what to say, so he said nothing as he looked around the space, taking a mental inventory of his possessions.

"Anything missing?"

"Nothing obvious. Wait, the stuff on the table is gone."

Both moved to the table. Sal glanced around and saw the chest on the floor against the wall.

"Maybe not," he moved to pick it up. "Check around and see if the items are on the floor like this chest."

The floorplan being what it was, there weren't many places to look. Cody spotted the decoder ring under the toe kick of his kitchen cabinet. He bent and retrieved it. He figured that whatever the people were looking for, a cheap plastic decoder ring wasn't it. He saw the Lincoln log not far away and snatched it off the floor. He looked around.

"I don't see the belt buckle."

"It's over here, under the chest." Sal had already grabbed both items and set them on the table. "Anything else?"

"Just the letter. I don't see it anywhere. Do you think they took it?"

"Maybe. Do you remember what it said? Did it have any information in it that could put you in danger?"

Cody sat and dropped his head into his hands. "I don't know! It was personal. Talked about one or both being gone. Apologizing for putting me in this situation. Some other stuff. I can't remember!"

"Calm down. Let's look once more to see if it's here. If not, then you'll need to try and remember more completely what was in it. If they took it, they must have thought it important in some way."

They did another sweep of the small apartment but didn't find the letter. Cody was getting more agitated by the minute. Sal sought to distract him.

"Why don't you pack up your clothes and stuff. Maybe while you do that, something will come back to you. If not, we'll get out of here and think about it somewhere else. I don't think whoever was here will be back, but no sense in tempting fate."

When Cody just sat there unmoving, Sal gave him a nudge. "C'mon, Cody. Get your stuff together. What can I do to help?"

Cody sighed and stood. "Nothing. It'll only take me a minute or two. I don't have much."

Sal could see that by the few clothes that hung on hooks. He thought the kid only had two, maybe three sets of clothes. He shook his head slightly as he watched Cody gather the things and stuff them into a backpack. He found a plastic grocery bag in the cupboard and put the chest and belt buckle in it. He'd seen Cody put the decoder ring in his pocket and the Lincoln log in his pack. There was nothing else to gather up.

"Ready?"

At Cody's nod he went to the door and unlocked it. He opened it slowly and glanced both ways down the hall before stepping out. He looked back over his shoulder.

"Let's get out of here. We'll talk about anything else that needs talking about back at my place."

Sal led the way and they were soon back at the deli.

"You really live here?"

"Yes. Well, not here," Sal indicated the room Cody had been in earlier. "I'll show you."

Sal opened a door that Cody had never noticed as it was partially hidden behind a large storage unit. A bright light came on from somewhere inside.

"Motion detector light. Greatest invention ever!" Sal stepped through the open door and onto a stair landing. "Come on. Close the door after you." He proceeded down the stairs.

Cody followed, careful to close the door behind him. At the bottom of the stairs there was another door. This one had a combination lock. Sal had already entered the code and opened it by the time Cody caught up to him.

"Welcome to my home, or rather, my cave. No windows, but it won't seem like it. When I bought this place, the previous owner said this area was used for storage. But I saw its potential immediately. Why spend extra on rent somewhere else when everything I need is right here. Of course, I had to do some work to bring plumbing in. Made a few other upgrades, too. It's all I need. And the commute to work is quite convenient, I might add." Sal laughed.

Cody stepped into what at first appeared to be a bunker. But as his eyes adjusted to the ambient light, he saw a living area that looked quite comfortable. He could understand Sal's pride in what he'd accomplished. Framed and curtained areas gave the appearance of windows, and Sal had rigged up some kind of lighting that made it look like there was sunlight on the other side.

Sal saw him looking at those and explained how the lighting dimmed to give the effect of city street lights. As long as he didn't pull the curtains back to expose the cement wall behind, he could convince himself and others the windows were real.

"I've got a small kitchen area, but honestly, who needs it since the deli is upstairs. It's convenient for making coffee and such, though." Sal pointed to a closed door. "Full bathroom. Spared no expense there." He pointed to what looked to be a large cabinet. "See that? Murphy bed. And over there, my favorite chair. It's all I need."

As Cody looked around, his first thought was that Sal was right. The place wasn't much bigger than his apartment but comfortably provided everything a person really needed. His second thought centered on the lack of space for him. He couldn't stay here. There was simply no room for a second person. Rather than point out the obvious, he focused on another thought that had occurred to him.

"How do you breathe down here? What's your air source?"

"That's the most ingenious thing of all. See that piping over there?" Sal pointed to a series of pipes that varied in diameter. "Not sure exactly how it works, but between all that wizardry you see on the wall, fresh air comes in and stale air goes out. It's never failed in the five years I've lived here."

Cody took his word for it. He was too tired to dwell on the intricacies. He looked around once more. Then finally forced himself to ask the question.

"Doesn't seem like there's room for a guest. You sure you want me to stay here?"

"It isn't much, but there's a bed hanging on the wall. Those pictures over there? They're secured to the bottom of the bunk that drops down. Pretty good camouflage, right? Go on. There's a latch on top. You'll see it. Release it and the bed will fold out. Be careful. You'll need to hang on to it as it comes down."

Cody walked to where Sal had pointed. He quickly saw the latch and released it, easing the bed down into a lateral position. Sal was right. It wasn't much. But for a night, maybe two, Cody could endure it. He put his backpack on it and turned back to Sal.

"I really appreciate this. You didn't have to do any of what you've done."

"Nonsense, boy. Anyone would do the same."

Cody knew that wasn't true but didn't say so. He sat on the edge of the bed. "Would it be OK if I tried to sleep? I'm feeling exhausted."

"Go ahead. You've had an eventful day. I'm going to read a little, then turn in myself. Use the bathroom, make yourself at home."

Sal pressed some hidden button on the cabinet and his bed came down on hydraulics. Cody thought it pretty slick. Sal reached over and turned on a small reading lamp.

"Will this bother you?"

"Not at all."

Cody grabbed his pack and went into the bathroom. Not wanting to take a full shower, he washed up as best he could then donned a clean t-shirt. Exiting the bathroom, he quickly climbed into bed, turning away from Sal. Within minutes Sal heard his light snoring.

Poor kid. He's got a lot on his plate. Don't envy him at all.

Sal used the bathroom to take care of his own needs, then crawled into bed, and reached for his favorite book. He'd read it several times, but it never got old. He was half-way through it and figured he'd read for an hour or so. He found his reading glasses and settled in.

CODY OPENED his eyes and listened. He wasn't sure what woke him, but his senses were on full alert. He glanced at his watch. Three in the morning. *There! I heard it again!*

"Sal!" Cody whispered the name aggressively. "Sal! Wake up!"

Sal rolled over and moaned. "What is it boy?"

"I hear something."

Sal sat up and listened. They looked at each other when both heard a crash.

"Someone is upstairs in the deli."

"That ever happen before?"

"Never. And I don't think it's random now."

"You think it's connected to me, don't you. I've brought this down on you."

"Let's not worry about that. We're safe for now. But let's get prepared, anyway."

"What do you mean?"

Sal was up and rummaging in a drawer. He ignored Cody while he found what he was searching for. He turned to Cody.

"You ever use a gun before?"

"Target practice on the farm. That's all. I don't think I could use it on a person."

"I'm good with that. Can you hold it steady? No shaking hands? It's only for show anyway."

Sal knew better, but he didn't want to make Cody any more anxious than he already was. He placed the 9mm handgun on the bed and went to his jacket, removing the small pistol he'd had with him on their trip to Cody's apartment. He checked that the safety was on then went to Cody.

"Here. Hang on to this. The safety is on. Won't fire that way. But if you need to, this is how you release it."

Sal showed him the lever and explained how to know when the safety was engaged or not. Cody held it in both hands, barrel pointed down.

"Good job. Keep it pointed that way."

They heard another crash, knowing it was pans being knocked to the floor.

"Might just be vandals. They haven't found the door yet, so we're still good."

Sal had barely finished those words when they heard the door at the top of the stairs open. Sal went to a small screen on the wall and flicked it on. Cody hadn't noticed it before. It cleverly blended in with the items around it. He stood by Sal and watched as two men came down the stairs, clearly visible due to the motion-sensor light.

"Not kids being vandals," Cody muttered.

"Nope. You ever see them before?"

"No."

"You sure? Never in the shop? Not around town. Hanging out by your apartment?"

"No. None of those places."

"OK. Since I've had no trouble in five years, and suddenly these men appear on the night you're here, we must assume they're interested in you. Not me or my measly shop."

"How do they know I'm here?"

"Must have followed us."

"What do we do?"

"Wait. In the meantime, I'll call the police."

Sal grabbed his cell phone off a counter and made the call. Cody was somewhat amazed he had service but was glad he did. He felt better knowing law enforcement was on the way. They watched as the men stood in front of the door observing the electronic locking system. Sal quietly slid a bolt into place further securing the door. Cody wasn't sure how effective it would be, but figured it was better than nothing.

Suddenly, one of the men pulled a gun from inside his jacket. Cody tensed, wondering if they were going to shoot the lock. The man didn't, but used the butt of the gun to pound on the electronic panel. Sal chuckled.

"What?" Cody asked.

"Watch and see."

A red flashing light engaged, making the stairwell look like something out of a science fiction movie. At the same time, a foggy mist descended on the two men. Although it obscured details, Sal and Cody could still see their body movements. Both had turned and were working their way back up the stairs, having abandoned their attempts to disengage the lock by destroying it. They soon lost the men to the mist.

"Let's wait."

"How long?" Cody's hands were sweating. He was having a hard time maintaining his grip on the handgun.

"Either the cops will get them topside, or the sirens will scare them off."

"How will we know?"

Sal looked at Cody, noting his general anxiousness. He suggested Cody put the gun on the table and sit. He continued to watch the monitor.

It was several minutes later when two more men descended the staircase. Sal watched closely. When he was certain it was law enforcement, he pushed a small button and spoke into a speaker system, explaining he was the owner of the shop and the one who'd called. He told them he was opening the door, but that it would be a minute.

He turned and hurried to the table. He grabbed the small handgun there and put it, with the one he was holding, in a drawer out of sight. He told Cody to stay seated and avoid talking any more than necessary.

He opened the door, warning the officers just before pulling it back. They stepped in and looked around.

"You live here?" one of them asked.

"Nah, just a fancy saferoom. Apartment is being renovated. Since it's small, perhaps we can return to the kitchen upstairs?"

After a brief hesitation, the one who spoke nodded and gestured for Sal to lead the way. The gesture included Cody, who stood and followed Sal.

"What's your name, son? Why are you here?" the officer asked.

Sal spoke before Cody could. "This is Cody Winters. He works for me."

"What's he doing here?"

Sal didn't answer, as he climbed the stairs. Since Sal didn't speak, Cody also remained quiet. A few seconds later, Sal stepped into the kitchen and gazed at the few pans that had been knocked to the floor. He was relieved to see no real damage to the kitchen, and hoped the customer side of the deli shop was also intact.

"How'd you get in?" Sal asked the officers before either one could follow up on their question about Cody.

"The door was open."

"Busted?"

"Not the door itself, but you'll probably need a new lock mechanism."

Sal was about to say something else, but the officer returned his attention to Cody. "Why are you here?"

"His place was infested with roaches. Nasty creatures. Landlord can't do anything for another couple of days. I invited him to stay with me."

If Sal thought that would satisfy the cop, he was sadly mistaken.

"Thought you said your place was being renovated. Why would you invite someone to stay with you if that's the case?" He turned to Cody. "How old are you?"

When Cody gave his age, the officer seemed to relax a bit. Cody wasn't sure what that was all about, but when asked to show his identification, he realized he was still in his t-shirt and underwear. He blushed.

"I have to go back downstairs to get it. It's in my jeans." Cody hesitated. "I'd like to get dressed, anyway, if that's OK?"

The officer looked intently at Cody for a moment, then gestured with his head towards the stairs. His partner, without being asked, followed Cody. They were both back within a couple of minutes, Cody wearing his jeans and holding out his license.

It took a little over thirty minutes for the officers to gather the information they needed. Sal did most of the talking, offering to download the recording of the men in the stairwell and send it to them.

"You have some way to secure the door?"

"I'll figure it out. I'll call a locksmith later this morning when places start opening."

"All right, then. Doubtful the intruders will return, but we'll increase patrols for the next few hours. Stay alert." A short hesitation, then, "You're sure you didn't recognize them?"

Both Sal and Cody shook their heads.

The lead officer nodded, and both filed out of the shop. Sal pushed the door shut and asked Cody to grab a chair from one of the tables. When Cody brought it over, he wedged it under the door handle and tested the result.

"Good enough for now."

He looked at Cody. "I think it's time you left this city."

"Me, too. But I need to get my car. It's in a garage on the other side of town."

"What's it doing there?"

"Couldn't leave it on the street. Would have had to continually move it or risk it being towed. That garage was the cheapest."

"Grab your stuff. I'll drive you to your car. I don't think you should wait any longer. I don't know who those guys were, but I have a feeling they're going to be more persistent than we'd like."

"Will you be safe?"

"Don't worry about me. I have resources to call on. Let's get you going. C'mon. The clock's ticking."

Cody practically ran to the room to retrieve his things. While he was gone, Sal made a couple of calls. He hadn't lied. He did have resources available to him, and he'd use them. In the meantime, he'd make sure Cody got out of town safely. After that, he hoped the kid could take care of himself.

16

I t took Susan only five minutes to accomplish what she needed to do inside the post office. It had taken longer to prepare. Even in such a small town, she had to assume the premises were monitored with some type of video surveillance. She preferred not to be visually identified if so. The box she accessed could be readily determined. But that didn't mean much. The name registered to the box was an alias.

"Ready?" she asked as she slid behind the wheel.

"Can I get a big breakfast? I'm really hungry."

"You can get whatever you like. Small town diners usually don't skimp on the food. I'm sure you'll be more than satisfied."

She drove to the end of the street and parked facing outwards. There were only two other cars in the lot. Susan assumed at least one, maybe both, belonged to the staff.

She glanced quickly around the room when they entered the establishment, noting one man at the counter, and an older couple in a booth at the end of the aisle. She indicated the booth at the opposite end of the diner when the woman at the counter acknowledged them. After getting a nod, she ushered Jacob to the booth, careful to make sure she sat on the side facing the door and the room.

A few seconds later the woman came to them, two mugs and a coffee pot in her hand. She looked at them.

"Coffee? You're out early. Where you headed?"

Susan smiled. "Yes, coffee for both. With cream please."

Susan avoided the last question. The woman didn't seem to notice, or if she did, took no offense. Instead, she filled the mugs and pushed them to the center of the table.

"Cream and menus right there." She gestured with the pot. "I'll be back to get your order."

Susan watched as Jacob put enough cream in his coffee to turn it almost white. She hid her smile. He'd formed the coffee habit a year ago. She hadn't been happy but wasn't about to nag on such a small thing. She added a tiny amount to her own and reached for the multi-page menus, handing one to her son.

They'd barely got through the first page when the woman came back.

"Ready?"

Luckily the specials were the first thing listed. They ordered and relaxed against the padded backrests.

"Won't take long for you to go into a food coma. Sure you'll be able to drive? Maybe I should take over."

"Nice try. I'll be fine."

Jacob grinned. He knew she wouldn't let him drive, but it never stopped him from asking. It wouldn't be much longer before he'd be old enough for formal lessons. He wondered how that would work, given the way they lived their lives.

"How much further do we have to go?"

"Montana is a big state. Takes longer to drive across it than most realize. And we're going almost to the Idaho border."

"What's there?"

"Safety. Hopefully."

Before Jacob could ask another question, the woman brought their food.

"Here you go, folks. Enjoy."

She placed their plates in front of them and hurried back to from where she'd come. In the time it'd taken to get their food, four more customers had entered. Susan had evaluated each of them as they'd taken their places at either the counter or a booth. None had triggered an alarm within her. She rotated her plate and picked up her utensils. Jacob was already stuffing his food into his mouth. She chuckled.

"Slow down. You'll choke. Or give yourself indigestion."

Jacob's only response was to swallow and prepare another forkful of pancake. She focused on her own food. She hadn't realized how hungry she was until she'd seen and smelled the food in front of her.

They ate in silence. Susan kept track of the comings and goings of the customers, as well as the activity in the lot. She didn't know if Jacob was aware of her doing it or not. She decided to test him.

"How many people are in the restaurant right now?"

He looked up from his plate. Without turning his head, he answered, giving both the location and genders of the people. She was stunned at his accuracy.

"You've been stuffing food in your face like a starving homeless person. How'd you do that?"

"I've a good teacher. And if you think about it, I am a starving home-less person."

"I supposed that's somewhat technically correct, but really, how'd you do that?"

"Window reflections. But they're fast going away."

"You're quite an amazing person, you know that, right?"

Jacob colored slightly. "Ah, c'mon, Mom."

"You are. Anyway, we need to get moving soon. Things are starting to get busy." She looked at his plate. "You good here by yourself for a few minutes? I can go get the car filled while you finish."

Jacob looked at her plate. "Aren't you going to finish that?"

She smiled. "You can have it if you have room for it."

Jacob grinned as he reached across with his fork and stabbed the remains of her pancake. "Go on. I'll be fine."

"Stay aware."

Susan got up and caught the eye of the woman at the counter and mouthed that she'd be back. She hurried out to the parking lot and slid into the driver's seat. Just as she was pulling the door shut, a hand reached out and grabbed it, stopping its momentum. Susan looked up alarmed.

"You!"

The man stepped in between the door and her opening, effectively blocking her in.

"Hi, Susan."

"So they sent you?"

"No, I wasn't sent. I came on my own."

"Why? And how did you find me?"

"I came because I was concerned. And finding you was a guess, based on your past. I got lucky. That's all."

Susan looked at the man. He hadn't aged in looks even though she knew him to be ten years older than herself.

"So, what now, Ray? My son is inside."

"I know he is. I'm not here to cause trouble. I'm here to warn you."

"Warn me?"

"Yes. They know about your place in western Montana. You can't go there. They're watching it. Waiting for you."

"How'd they find out?"

"I don't know. But I do know this. You can't trust any of them. They'll say they're only trying to bring you in to protect you. It's not true. They want what you have. And if they get it, your future health is highly questionable. You and your sons. Both of them."

"Both of them? Cody? You know where he is? Is he safe? I've had no contact. It's been three years. I'd almost given up hope."

"He's safe. For now."

"What's that mean? Where is he?"

"He's safe. And I'll do my best to see that he stays safe. I know this is late coming, but I am sorry about Tom. I didn't find out what they'd planned until it was too late to stop it."

"Why'd they kill him? He knew nothing."

"A message to you. They want what you have. They'll go to any lengths to get it."

"Ray, it's been over twenty years. Why now? What's changed?"

"The world has changed, Susan. The players we knew? Most of them are gone. This new generation has a different agenda. It's not about saving the world from itself. It's about grabbing all the power. It's why I retired a few years back. Couldn't support their vision."

"You retired?"

"Hard to believe, I know. Been trying to stay off-grid. But when I heard what happened, I had to make an effort to find you."

"Have you brought them with you?"

Ray looked at her. "You know better."

She did. Ray had been one of the best in the business. Probably still was, despite his self-declared retirement. She didn't believe for a minute that he wasn't still working quietly behind the scenes. He was too valuable an asset for those in power to completely let him go. Unlike her. She'd served her purpose. Almost been killed for it. Likely the only reason she was even still alive and had had almost twenty years of peace was because of what she possessed and knew. But that had changed three years ago. And the death of her husband marked the severity of the change.

"What do you suggest?"

"Go back to where you came from."

"I can't. They've already been there. Not safe to return."

"Then go to a different town. It's unlikely they'll think you've gone back if they've already made a play in the first location."

"Maybe. But how long before they reconsider?"

"Long enough. Things change fast in this business. You know that."

She looked at him. She wasn't sure if he'd just sent her a message or not. Was he actively working to remove the threat from her life, or simply making an observation?

"I need to go. Jacob is going to wonder what's taking me so long."

"Does he know?"

"He knows about the witness protection."

"Not the other?"

"No. And I hope to keep it that way."

Ray stepped back away from her car. "Stay safe, Susan. The world will be a lot less bright if you're not in it. My number is the same. If you call it, I'll answer."

She looked deep into his eyes one more time. Memories of their past flashing through her mind at rapid speed.

"Thank you, Ray. For everything. Past and present. And hopefully the future. You stay safe, also. If they find out you've connected with me, you'll be in as much danger as I am."

"Don't worry about that. Won't be an issue. Go on now, you've been here longer than advisable."

Before she could respond, he turned and walked quickly away, not looking back. She watched his retreat, wondering where he'd come from and where he was going. Rather than get the car filled, she went back into the diner and hurried to Jacob. Both plates were gone, and the check was on the table. Glancing at it, she pulled enough cash from her pocket to cover the amount and leave a decent, but not extravagant, tip. She didn't want to be remembered for that.

"C'mon, let's go. We still need to get gas."

"I thought you were taking care of that?"

"Got distracted. You need to use the facilities?"

"No. I'm fine. What was the distraction?"

"Never mind, now. Let's get out of here."

Jacob opened his mouth to protest but quickly shut it at her look. He stood and followed her out of the diner, giving the woman at the counter a slight wave and smile just before exiting.

Once in the vehicle, Susan drove out of town without a backward glance.

"I thought we needed gas?"

"We've enough. We'll get it at the next town."

"Mom, what's going on?" He noticed they were retracing the route they'd come in on. "Are we still going to where you said we were going?"

"No. We're going back to Colorado."

"But—"

"Jacob, please. Just for now can you let it go? I need to think."

Jacob settled into a sulky silence as the miles flew past his window. Whatever had happened while he was finishing his breakfast had obviously spooked his mother. He felt a deep unease beginning to form.

17

Cody checked his watch. Three hours. He'd been driving non-stop for three hours. He glanced at his gas gauge. *Gonna have to stop soon.* He read the upcoming road sign, noting the distance to the next exit.

The traffic had been minimal, and he'd seen nothing to indicate anyone was following him. While he admitted to himself that he probably wouldn't recognize a tail, he'd looked for consistency in the headlights behind him and watched for any long-term patterns. Seeing nothing to concern him, he assumed he'd made a safe getaway.

He thought about the last twenty-four hours, trying to put some order to them. He wasn't sure he'd have managed if Sal hadn't provided support. He hoped the man was in no real danger. *Who were those men? What did they want? It's been three years since anyone strange or anything weird has occurred. Why now? How'd they find me? I wish I could remember more what was in that letter. Did it give them more information, or only confirm what they already know? And just what do they know?*

Cody's thoughts kept swirling in his head. Almost in rhythm to the noise the car tires made on the pavement. It was a song he didn't want in his head. He took the next exit and pulled into a gas station. After filling the tank, he walked into the store hoping to buy some snacks to keep him going.

"Howdy. How can I help you?"

Cody glanced at the store clerk. He gave a slight wave to acknowledge the person but didn't speak. He wandered up and down the aisles picking what he thought was most healthy of the junk food displayed. He carried his selections to the counter.

"That's a lot for a snack. You traveling a long distance?"

Cody barely kept his face from showing his annoyance. He didn't want to engage with the person, but then realized the guy was probably sick of being alone in the store for hours overnight.

"A fair bit."

"Where you headed?"

"Out west. Family."

Cody thought it best to not be too specific. Then realized what he'd said could be too much. He suppressed a sigh. *Too many things to think about.*

The clerk eyed his hundred-dollar bill with alarm and suspicion. "Not sure I can break that."

"I'm sorry. It's all I have. Don't forget to add the gas to it. Not sure why it let me pump without first paying, but it did."

Cody waited patiently for the clerk to decide what he was going to do. After several seconds of inaction, the young man rang up the items and counted out change, murmuring something about that pump needing service. Cody gathered up his purchases, wished the clerk a good day and made haste to his car. Tossing the things on the passenger seat, he glanced around the area. He wasn't sure why, but his nerves were suddenly on edge. Not seeing anything that alarmed him, he pulled out onto the road, turning the direction the highway onramp signs indicated.

Once on the highway, he relaxed slightly. But his thoughts kept swirling. Suddenly he had a thought. *Remember our family story times. The clues for where to look are all within those tales.* That thought triggered others. As more and more of the contents came back to him, he wondered if whoever had taken the letter would understand the clues. Depending on their existing knowledge, it revealed more of his situation than he'd initially realized. Much more. He felt his body flush with warmth. He mentally berated himself for leaving the letter on the table.

After a few moments, he consciously stopped his thoughts from going further into a dark zone. He instinctively understood it wouldn't help his situation. Might even make it worse. But one thought came through with clarity. *Gotta write down what I remember before the details slip away.*

He pulled onto the shoulder of the highway, checking his rearview mirror for any traffic. He wasn't sure if the lack of it made him feel better or more isolated. But not wasting any further time, he rummaged for a paper and pen. It took him twenty minutes to record everything he remembered of the letter. Once he'd started, more came back until he was fairly certain he'd recalled most of it. But he couldn't shake the feeling he was missing something extremely important. He reread what he'd written twice, but nothing more came to him. *This'll have to do.* He stuffed the paper in his jacket and, checking his mirror, pulled onto the highway to continue his journey.

Two hours later he was barely able to keep his eyes open. Opening his windows and cranking up the radio station didn't help. He knew if he didn't pull over and rest soon, he risked falling asleep at the wheel.

He checked his watch. Mid-day. Not really a good time to check into a motel, and he didn't want to spend money on one anyway. He read the approaching road sign. Two miles to some form of civilization. He decided to explore what the location had to offer.

He rolled into the small town slowly, looking down the main street with interest. *The place looks like something out of an old western movie.* He pulled into an angled parking spot and sat for a moment trying to decide what to do. The knock on his window set his heart thumping. He looked at the person standing on the other side of his door. The man was wearing a uniform. Cody lowered his window.

"Yes sir?"

"You realized you pulled into a reserved parking space?"

Cody looked towards the front of his car and saw the sign indicating the space was reserved for the town's mayor.

"I'm sorry. I didn't see the sign. I'll move."

"See that you do." The officer looked at Cody closely. "You visiting? I don't remember seeing you around."

Cody felt a spark of concern. "Just got here. Passing through. But need to find a place to rest for a while. Any recommendations?" Cody hoped the last question would distract the officer from pursuing any further queries of his own.

"You looking for a motel or a campground? We have both. The campground is a bit further out. Cheaper, though."

"Campground."

The officer nodded as if his assessment of Cody's situation had just been confirmed. He gave directions to the campground. Then as an after-thought, recommended the local diner for a good meal at a reasonable price. Cody thanked him and carefully backed out of the space. He put the car in gear and pulled away, glancing in his review mirror and noting the officer was watching him drive off. He felt another jolt of concern. His car was registered in the name of Cody Winters, but he was using the new identification. If he got pulled over, he'd be hard-pressed to explain the differences.

He was still pondering that thought when he saw the sign for the campground and followed the road to the entrance. It wasn't much to write home about, but he figured he could get a good snooze in. He pulled up to the office and entered. When asked how long he was staying, he decided to press his luck.

"Do you think I could just pull over at the end of the row and grab a bit of sleep? I don't really have plans to stay in the area. I just need to rest a bit."

The girl at the desk looked him over carefully. She was young but Cody didn't doubt she'd sized him up well.

"I'm not really allowed to let you do that, but if you leave before six, when the manager checks in, you should be okay."

Cody glanced at his watch. That would give him almost five hours of sleep. More than enough to continue his journey. He smiled.

"I really appreciate it. I'll be gone before six. I promise."

She waved him off and turned to attend to something on the far side of the office. Cody took that as his cue to escape before she changed her mind. He quickly climbed back into his car and maneuvered it to a spot well out of the way of regular traffic. He made sure he was pointing outward so he could simply drive out when he needed to. He looked around the area and spotted a rest room a bit further in. He got out and walked to it, glancing at the multiple tents spotting the grounds with their various colors. A small part of him wished he could be part of that group. Camping and enjoying a short vacation with few to no worries. He wondered if he'd ever have that opportunity.

He washed up as best as the facilities allowed and returned to his car. Adjusting the seat to as far as it would recline, he made sure the doors were locked. Before falling into a deep sleep, he reflected upon his luck that twice, now, he'd been able to secure a place to rest that hadn't cost him anything but the minor discomfort of his car seat.

18

Jacob held his silence for almost two hours before he returned to his earlier question.

"Why are we going back to Colorado?"

"Because the people I'm trying to stay away from are aware of the place in Montana. I'm sorry for that. I know you would have liked it there."

"Won't they come to Colorado when we don't show at the Montana place?"

"Maybe, but they'll have to find us. We're not going back to where we were."

"Then where?"

Susan refused to admit she didn't know. Instead, she tried making a game out of it, suggesting Jacob study the map and pick a place that he fancied. She snuck glances at him while he studied the atlas. She wondered how much he'd figured out. He was an observant kid. He didn't ask as many questions as she would expect. She knew he had an analytical mind. Somehow, she had to figure out how to determine what his conclusions were surrounding their situation. And she had to do that without revealing more than was prudent. His question interrupted her thoughts.

"How about someplace big, like Denver? Hide in plain sight. Plus, there will be more to do. I'll have access to libraries and can more easily continue my studies."

Susan smiled at the last bit. While Jacob never seriously complained about how he was schooled, she wasn't convinced he was thinking about access to libraries as the reason for picking Denver. It was true that sometimes larger cities provided better cover than small rural places, but they also increased the need for constant surveillance.

She made her decision. "Tell you what. If we can find a small cheap apartment, we'll give Denver a go. But you'll need to be situationally aware at all times. And be prepared to leave in a hurry."

"Nothing new about that," Jacob murmured.

Susan let his comment go. She felt guilty about how unsettled his life had been the past three years. If it had been just her, she would have long ago taken the fight to those who pursued her. But with Jacob to consider, she was forced into this game of hide and seek. It wasn't sustainable. She knew that. But she needed to maintain the status quo until Jacob was old enough to truly fend for himself. She thought back to her encounter with Ray. If what he'd said was true, Cody was still out there somewhere. Alive. But she knew that could change in a heartbeat. And he wouldn't see it coming. At least, she didn't think he would. But she didn't know. He'd had three years on his own. Who knew how he'd grown and developed?

They pulled into the outskirts of Denver in the late afternoon. It was one of those clear spectacular days where the sun was glistening off the mountain snow. Looking at the breathtaking views, one could almost feel all was right with the world. But Susan knew better.

"We'll get a motel, then start seriously apartment hunting in the morning. Sound good?"

"Sure." Jacob cleared his throat. "What about dinner?"

Susan laughed, relieving some of the tension she'd been holding. "Always thinking of your stomach. Have no fear, we'll stop and get something."

Susan recognized very little of the Denver and its neighborhoods she was driving through. She'd last been in the city years before they'd settled on their farm. Much had changed. Too much. It made her uncomfortable not knowing what was now considered safe and what wasn't, but she was careful not to let Jacob see her concerns. She saw a gas station and decided to pull in and ask for recommendations on where to stay. She also needed gas. Pulling up next to a pump, she asked Jacob to handle the fill up while she went inside to speak to the clerk and pay for the gas.

A small bell jingled as she stepped into the store, and a young woman looked up from the book she was reading. She slid off the stool she was perched on, pushing her book to one side. Susan guessed her age to be around twenty, give or take a year. She greeted the girl and took care of the gas transaction before quizzing her on places to stay.

"You'll want to be somewhere other than here," the clerk stated.

"Why's that?"

"This isn't the best part of town. Lots of crime in the neighborhood."

"Yet you seem to be okay working here alone?"

The young woman smiled. "I'm off limits."

Susan raised an eyebrow in query.

"My dad owns this station. Been part of the neighborhood since his teens. No one messes with him. Hence, no one messes with me."

Susan wasn't quite sure how to respond to that, so she held her comments. She figured the girl's dad must be gang affiliated or something. Nothing she wanted to explore. Instead, she repeated her original question on where might be a good place to stay that wasn't too expensive.

After giving it some thought, the clerk named three different areas. Susan saw a Denver city map stuck haphazardly in a rack and grabbed it, asking the young woman to circle the areas she'd mentioned. The look she tossed at Susan made it clear she couldn't believe Susan didn't just pull out her phone and use the GPS app. Shrugging and with no further comment, she did as requested, handing the map to Susan.

"Anything else?"

Susan smiled. "No. But I appreciate your assistance."

"Yeah, no problem." The woman had already reached for her open book, pulling it back in front of her, dismissing Susan from her focus.

Susan went back to her car. "All set?" she asked Jacob as she slid into the driver's seat.

"Yes. But I don't think what you paid for completely filled the tank."

Susan started the engine and checked the gauge. He was right, but it was close enough. She tossed the map at Jacob.

"Here, figure out how to get to one of these areas circled."

She gave him a few minutes before pulling away from the pump. "Which way?" she asked as she approached the exit.

"Take a left. Go about three blocks or so. There should be a sign to get on the main route through town. I'll tell you when to get off."

Susan followed the instructions, proud of Jacob's command of the situation. She'd briefly glanced at the map on her way to the car and based on his directions, she figured he had chosen the area she'd picked herself.

A little over a half-hour later, she pulled into the lot of a medium upscale motel. The design of the building signaled that entrance to the rooms were all internal. Not Susan's first choice, but she didn't expect any trouble. No one knew they were in town. Jacob looked at it with misgivings.

"Looks expensive."

"Probably a little more than I wanted to spend, but at least it should be clean. C'mon. Grab your pack. Let's get checked in. There's a restaurant attached. We'll have dinner there."

Twenty minutes later they were seated in a booth at the restaurant.

"Mom, when we get settled, could I go to the local high school?"

The question came out of nowhere. Susan paused her fork's journey to her mouth.

"Before you say anything, I know it's risky. I'll be careful. But please? It would be nice to experience a real high school environment."

Jacob rushed to make his case. He was certain she would refuse, but he thought it worth a try. He was surprised and hopeful at her comment.

"A real high school environment may not live up to your expectations."

"Maybe. Won't know until I try it." He hesitated. "Does that mean you'll consider it?"

She wasn't ready to commit and said as much. But she left the door open for further consideration. Jacob knew he had to be content with that. To push it any further would garner a hard no. He changed the subject.

"Do you have a plan for our apartment hunting?"

"I will by tomorrow." She smiled. "Finish up. Let's go get some rest. It's been a long couple of days."

Susan let Jacob commandeer the bathroom. She checked her burner phone for messages. Nothing. Grabbing the map to study it, she turned the TV to a local news station hoping to get a sense of the city from that. Jacob came out of the bathroom and with a murmured goodnight, crawled into the second bed.

"Will the TV bother you?"

"Nah."

She watched him roll over on his side. It wasn't long before she heard his deep even breaths. *He must have been more exhausted than he was willing to admit.* She was, too. But she had things to do. She wanted to call Ray and ask for advice, but it was too soon after they'd met. He was a resource she didn't want to waste. She thought through her short list of trusted contacts, and decided none would be of help. Sighing, Susan flipped the covers open and crawled into her bed fully clothed. She'd watch TV for a while and hope something resembling a plan of action came to her.

"Mom! Wake up!" Jacob's urgent whisper next to her face caused her eyes to fly open and her body to tense.

"What is it?" she whispered back.

"Someone's outside the door. I heard them try and turn the knob."

Susan was on her feet and half-way to her pack for her handgun as she instructed Jacob to go into the bathroom and close the door.

"But—"

"Now, Jacob!" she whispered fiercely.

He responded by making an exasperated noise but complied. Once the door was closed, Susan positioned herself next to the door and listened intently. There was no further activity outside her door, but she heard noise further down the hallway. Carefully, she removed the chain and turned the bolt. As quietly as she could, she turned the knob and opened the door enough to look down one side of the hallway. She hoped the threat wasn't on the side she couldn't see without opening the door wider.

She saw movement midway down the hallway. A man was staggering from door to door, his cardkey in hand. She watched as he methodically, if sloppily, inserted the card in each door and tried the handle. She studied his body movements. She saw nothing more than what he appeared to be. A drunk looking for his room. But she continued watching. She knew from experience that things weren't always as they first seemed. Finally, the man's card allowed a door to open, and he stumbled into the opening. Susan waited and watched a few minutes longer, then opened her door enough to scan the other side of the hall. Seeing no threats, she closed the door and re-engaged the lock and chain.

"It's OK, Jacob." Her voice was a normal tone and loudness.

He opened the door and poked his head out. His eyes widened at the sight of the gun in her hand.

"You sure?"

"Yes. Just a drunk looking for his room."

At his skeptical look, she reassured him all was well. She checked her gun to be sure the safety was on, then replaced it in her pack.

"Thank you for waking me. I'm surprised you heard him."

Jacob walked out into the room. "I was just rolling over and I heard the noise."

"Well, I'm glad you did because I certainly didn't. Some protector I am."

Jacob chuckled. "You were, as they say, dead to the world asleep."

Susan suppressed a shiver, glad she wasn't just plain dead. And Jacob, too. She mentally scolded herself for her lapse. She glanced at the clock on the nightstand. Three in the morning.

"You going to be able to go back to sleep?"

"I don't know. I'm pretty awake right now."

"Me, too. Maybe there's a movie we can watch."

Susan grabbed the remote and started flicking through the channels. They settled on one that had been released over five years ago. They'd both seen it and had enjoyed it the first time so figured it would do for a second viewing.

"Too bad there's no popcorn," Jacob said with a grin.

"Always thinking of your stomach."

His response evoked a chuckle from her. They settled into their respective beds; pillows fluffed to accommodate their viewing angle.

Twenty minutes into the film, Jacob asked again about high school.

"We'll see."

After the scare she'd just had, Susan wasn't sure she could handle Jacob being out of her sight for a large part of the day. She fell asleep still contemplating the issue.

19

Cody awoke to the sound of giggling. Slowly turning his head, he saw two very blue eyes staring at him from outside his driver's window. They were attached to a small face framed in curly blond hair.

He sat up and lowered the window.

"Hi," she said with another giggle. "What are you doing there?"

Cody smiled. "I was sleeping until some small person woke me up."

The little girl jumped up and down. "That was me!"

"Indeed."

He looked around, not seeing any adult in the area. "Where are your parents? You're too young to be wandering around on your own."

"I'm six!" she declared with all the confidence someone that age could muster.

"Are you, now. And what's your name, Miss Six-Year-Old?"

"Beth. But Mom calls me Bumper."

"And why is that?"

"Because I'm always bumping into things."

Cody adjusted his seat to a sitting position and glanced around the area again. "You didn't say where your parents are."

"It's just me and my mom. She's in the store. We're camping." She turned and pointed towards a small tent. "That's us. Where's your tent?"

"I don't have one. It's why I'm in my car."

"But you have to have a tent! You can't camp without one!"

Cody rubbed the remainder of the sleep from his eyes and glanced at his watch. Five o'clock. It was fortunate the little girl had woken him. He needed to be on his way. He was just about to respond when an older version of the girl stepped out of the store.

"Bumper! Where are you? Come here! I told you to wait by the door."

Seeing her daughter next to the car spurred the young woman into a near run as she dropped the bag she was holding and came to her daughter. She looked at Cody accusingly.

"Who are you? What are you doing with my daughter?"

Cody felt her mixed fear and aggression come at him in waves. He quickly reassured her, explaining the situation.

"Mom, he doesn't even have a tent. How can he camp without one?"

"Hush, dear." She studied Cody's face, taking in the light stubble on his cheeks and chin. She must have seen something else because she asked when he'd last eaten.

Picking up on that, Beth demanded that Cody share their dinner. Cody observed the mom's reaction to that and hastened to assure her that he needed to be going and he couldn't possibly take the time for a meal.

When it looked like both would insist, he more firmly emphasized his need to leave. He thought they both looked half-starved. He didn't know what their situation was, but he knew he couldn't be drawn into it. It wouldn't be safe for any of them.

"I really need to leave. I should have been gone some time ago. If you'll step back away from the car," he left the sentence hanging.

The woman grabbed Beth and backed away as Cody started the engine. He put the car in gear, then looked back at them.

"You take care of your mom, Bumper. And do as she tells you. No wandering off. All right?"

Beth nodded and sidled up next to her mom. Cody noted that the mom looked both relieved and distressed. Cody let the car roll forward slowly, careful to give them room. Not sure why, he met the woman's eyes and said quietly as he rolled past her.

"Stay safe."

He glanced in his rearview mirror as he left them behind. Both were watching him. The girl's hand in her mother's.

He thought about them for several miles, wondering at their situation. He hoped they were just on a girl's camping trip, but a part of him understood there was more to it than that. Knowing he was powerless to help them, he silently wished them nothing but the best. He had his own life to manage, and right now, it didn't seem like he was doing such a great job of it.

Two hours later he entered the outskirts of a sizeable town. He pulled into the lot of a shopping complex and found an empty place to park. He sat in his car for several minutes watching foot traffic come and go out of the large grocery store that appeared to anchor the other stores. His stomach growled. He studied the other businesses, noting a small coffee shop at the end of the row.

He knew he had to eat, as well as take care of other bodily needs. He just didn't know which avenue was best to pursue. He decided on the grocery store, figuring it offered more options. He counted the money in his jean's pocket, realizing he would need more than the few small bills in his hand. He pulled another hundred-dollar bill from his inside coat pocket and pushed it, with the rest of his money, back into his pants pocket.

He grabbed a cart as he entered the store, his eyes scanning for a restroom sign. Thirty minutes later, with a cart full of both hot deli food and other items he could snack on, he checked out and headed towards his car. As he approached, he saw three men, slightly older than himself, hanging out by his car. He slowed and watched them. They appeared to be looking in the windows and generally checking out the vehicle. He called out as he pushed his cart forward.

"Hi, guys. Something I can help you with?"

"This your car?"

"Yes. Why?"

"We just think it's well kept for such an old thing. How long you had it? Does it run well?"

"Quite a few years. Runs fine." Cody looked at the three of them, shifting his position slightly. "What's with all the questions?"

As if the speaker suddenly realized Cody's tenseness and how the situation might appear, he spoke quickly.

"Relax dude. We're not here to cause you any trouble. We really were just admiring your car. Don't see too many like this around anymore."

Cody relaxed slightly but still maintained awareness. "My dad helped me buy it when I was seventeen."

"Cool, man. He still around? Your dad?"

"No. He died a few years back."

"Sorry. You're obviously not from around here. Where you headed?"

"Out West. Looking to hook up with family."

Cody was hesitant to unlock the car and start loading groceries into it with the three of them still surrounding it. While he was less concerned than earlier, there was still something pulling at his instincts, telling him to be careful.

As if reading his mind, the speaker asked if Cody wanted help loading his purchases. When Cody refused and looked directly at the man wishing him a good day, the two shared an extended stare-off. Finally, the man looked to his buddies and signaled for them to back off.

"Have a safe trip," he threw over his shoulder as he and his buddies walked away.

Cody released a sigh of relief, watching them increase the distance. When he was sure they were far enough away not to be able to take him by surprise, he quickly unlocked his car, tossed his stuff into the front passenger seat, and literally ran the cart to one of the nearby corrals. Deciding he might be better off finding another place to pull over and eat his hot food, he drove out of the lot, scanning it for the three as he turned right onto the main street through town.

He waited until he was about twenty miles out of town before finding a place to pull over and eat his food, which was no longer hot. While disappointed at the barely lukewarm offering, he was hungry enough to enjoy the casserole he'd purchased and downed almost a full quart of milk before he began to feel full. He stuffed a brownie into his mouth, almost choking on its gooey richness, then finished off the rest of his milk. His thoughts turned to whether he should drive through the night or find a place to sleep. He decided to drive. He studied his map to get his bearings, then pulled out onto the road.

It was near midnight when he pulled into the parking lot of a road-side motel. He entered the office and was surprised to learn the nightly rate was quite affordable. He decided a night on a real bed would do him wonders so paid the amount. He backed his car in front of the door to his room and grabbed his pack. Not bothering to undress or even crawl under the covers, he threw the spread off and literally fell onto the bed. He was asleep within seconds.

He awoke the next morning refreshed, with a sense of renewed hope. Sometime during his sleep, his brain had worked on the nursery rhyme puzzle. He had a new theory about the numbers. Quickly getting himself put together, he pulled the paper from his back pocket and reread the document. Searching the motel room, he found a pen and some paper and wrote the numbers down in the order they appeared. Tucking the nursery rhyme paper in his back pocket, he walked to the office hoping he could use their phone.

The woman who looked up when he came in was about the age of his mother. He hoped she'd be understanding. He approached her and asked if he could use the phone.

"Can't call long distance," she said without hesitation.

He showed her the paper and briefly explained the numbers in the nursery rhyme. He thought the digits represented a telephone number but that he'd tried it and it hadn't worked. She glanced at the series of numbers, then back at him with a raised eyebrow. He felt compelled to continue, explaining that last night he'd thought it might be written backwards.

She looked at the number more carefully.

"If it is, that area code isn't local."

"Could I try it? If it didn't work the other way, it may not work this way and then there'd be no charge. And even if there were, I can pay you."

She took so long in answering he was convinced she was going to refuse. Surprisingly, she consented and pulled the desk phone into the center of the counter. Cody's hands shook slightly as he lifted the receiver and punched in the numbers. When he glanced up, he realized the woman's full attention was on him. He quelled his momentary feeling of unease. A few seconds later a recorded voice indicated the number he'd dialed was not a working number. He sighed as he replaced the receiver.

"Didn't work?"

"No. But thanks for letting me try."

He started to turn away when she spoke again.

"You know, I have a sister who lives in Colorado. Those first five digits are the same as her postal zip code. Have you thought about it that way?"

When he asked her where the sister lived, he was astonished to learn it was the town where he'd been told he was born. He felt a spike of excitement. But it died almost as quickly.

"But that's only five numbers. It doesn't explain the other five."

"True, but you know they have that four-digit extension. No, that wouldn't work. It would leave one number hanging out there. Why do that?"

"Yeah, doesn't make sense. Can you think of anything else? An address? A house or street?"

The woman tapped her fingers on the counter as she stared at the numbers. Almost as if speaking her thoughts aloud, she rambled through various scenarios, rejecting each one immediately after speaking it. Finally, she admitted defeat.

"I'm afraid I can't help you. Run out of all my possibilities. Maybe if I read the rhyme I might see something else?"

Cody hesitated. He didn't want to share it with anyone else. He was protective of his family. But then he wondered if fresh eyes might see something he didn't. With great hesitation, he pulled the paper from his back pocket and smoothed it out on the counter. The woman picked it up, causing Cody's hands to jerk uncontrollably. But he stuffed them in his pockets and waited.

She stared at the paper for a very long time. Cody was near twitching with impatience and the need to snatch it back from her when she finally spoke.

"It's kind of silly." When he stiffened, she added, "No, don't be offended. I didn't mean the rhyme. I meant my thought."

Cody expelled a breath he didn't realize he'd been holding. "What do you mean?"

"Well, this line about looking as far as the eye can see. It's kind of silly, but Lookout Mountain is in Colorado. And the first five digits being the same as my sister's in Colorado. Seems too much of a coincidence. But maybe I just have Colorado on my mind. Haven't seen my sister in a few years and I was thinking of taking a vacation and going to visit."

Cody just looked at her. His own thoughts were racing. He hadn't made that connection. But then again, why would he? Other than being told he was born in Colorado his parents had never really talked about the state. His birth added a third dimension to the coincidences the woman identified. It was if an invisible hand was pushing him in that direction.

"Do you see anything else in the rhyme that makes you think of Colorado? Just curious."

She studied the paper again.

"No. Can't say as I do. But I've only been to the state a couple of times. And to be honest, this whole rhyme seems rather jumbled in its message. Your folks never explained it? Put some context to it?"

"No. It was a game to my brother and me. We had contests as to who could memorize it the quickest. And we used to exaggerate certain words with funny accents. Mom and Dad would get a little mad at us when we did that, but then they'd just laugh it off. Only correcting our mistakes if we didn't recite the words exactly as written."

"Seems an odd family tradition. But every family has their own way of doing things. I could curl your hair with stories from my childhood." She smiled as she said the words and Cody returned her smile. Then she got serious.

"But tell me why you're trying to puzzle this all out. Has something happened to your family? Is this a secret message or something?"

Cody instinctively took a step back. "I really need to get going."

She read the alarm on his face and in his body language.

"I'm sorry. I don't mean to pry. Nothing sinister in my question. Whatever your reason for working through the rhyme, I wish you success." She switched the topic, "You're checking out? Not staying another night?"

"No. I really need to be going. I only planned the one night. Needed to rest. Thank you for letting me use your phone, and for sharing your thoughts. Gives me something to think about."

As he was speaking, Cody had been slowly backing towards the door. She half turned away from him, pretending to busy herself with straightening paperwork.

"If you still need to clear your stuff, then just leave your key on the desk in the room. No need to come back to the office."

"OK," he replied as he opened the door and stepped through it.

She stared at the closed door for several seconds, thinking about their exchange. Then shrugging, she said into the now empty room, "Good luck, Cody. Stay safe."

Cody hurried back to his room and grabbed the few things he'd brought in with him the previous night. Ten minutes after leaving the office, he was in his car and driving away from the motel. His stomach growled. He wished he'd asked the woman about a place to eat. No matter. He'd find something somewhere. He had a lot to think about, the most important being how long it would take him to get to Colorado. While only a vague idea before, he now knew with certainty he was destined to go there.

20

"C'mon, sleepy head. Get up."

Susan gave Jacob a soft nudge on his shoulder. Somewhere in the middle of the movie they both fell asleep. Jacob groaned.

"What time is it?"

"A little after eight. I'm surprised we both slept in that long."

Jacob stretched and commented that he could easily sleep another hour or so, but Susan was having none of it. She wanted to get busy looking for a more permanent residence. Still protesting, Jacob rolled out of bed and stumbled into the bathroom. Susan heard the shower a few minutes later.

Smiling, she dug through his pack for some clean underwear and a pair of pants. She picked up his t-shirt from the bed and gave it a sniff, her nose crinkling. *It'll have to do for now. I don't see an alternative in his pack. We need to find a laundromat.*

She snuck into the bathroom and left the clothes on the closed toilet seat, then waited for him in the main room. She flicked through the TV channels as she waited, skipping the usual local traffic and weather reports, as well as the most recent developing international crisis. She wasn't sure if she was just restless or if something else was pushing her to channel surf.

She got her answer a few seconds later. The closeup face of an overly animated reporter was commenting on a private jet crash somewhere near Chicago. Initial reports indicated all on board had perished. Speculations were that a bomb had caused the crash. Names were not being released, but the reporter left no doubt that important people had been on board. Susan felt a deep unease forming. She continued to flip between the various news stations, finally landing on one that provided additional information on the passengers.

The list of names confirmed what Susan suspected. One name on the manifest was Ray's alias. One he seldom used, but she knew it from the old days. Her body went limp. *Did they know he'd met with me? Was that why he was killed? Or was it something else? Someone cleaning up historical messiness?* She didn't know, but she did know the action confirmed the danger she was in. *I'm sorry Ray. I believed you when you said meeting with me wouldn't be an issue.*

Jacob came out of the bathroom and looked at his mom. "What is it? What's happened?" The alarm in his voice was apparent. Susan hastened to reassure him that nothing was wrong.

"I don't believe you. What aren't you telling me? Mom, I'm old enough. You have to stop treating me as if I'm still twelve."

Susan looked at her son. He was right. She knew it. But she still had trouble accepting it. She took a deep breath.

"There was a plane crash near Chicago. Someone I knew was on it."

"Who? A good friend? Have I ever met them?"

"No. You've not met him. He was a mentor of mine from the past." She gave him a sad smile. "I just wasn't expecting to hear about his death on the news, that's all. It shook me. I'll be fine."

"You don't look fine. Maybe some breakfast will help."

Susan chuckled. "That stomach of yours! But yes, let's go get something to eat. If nothing else, I could use a strong cup of coffee."

After they'd finished eating, Jacob picked up the topic of searching for an apartment.

"How are we going to look for one?"

"I'll get a newspaper and we'll check out the classified."

"Why don't we just get a modern phone and search the internet?"

Susan looked at Jacob without saying anything.

"What? Everyone has a phone. People look at us weird for not having one. Everyone my age has one, too. If I don't have one in high school, the kids are going to give me a hard time."

Jacob's words came out in a rush. He slumped a bit in his seat when he finished. Afraid he'd blown any chance for both high school and a phone, he waited. The length of time his mom took to respond confirmed to him that he was doomed to a life of unnatural solitude. When she did answer him, he was shocked.

"If I get you a basic phone, do you promise to be responsible in its use? I'm not promising you anything fancy. And you simply mustn't do anything that reveals your identity to the larger world. I mean it Jacob. Your life and mine, possibly Cody's, depends on that requirement."

The mention of Cody momentarily distracted Jacob. "You've heard from Cody? Is he okay? Where is he? What's he doing?"

"No, I haven't heard from him. But I've heard of him. He's alive and well. At least he was a couple of days ago."

"How do you know?"

"That friend I mentioned? The one who died in the plane crash? He told me."

"How did he know?"

"I can't answer that. But if he told me Cody was alive and well? I believe him."

"Then why hasn't Cody contacted us?"

Her answer confused him. "You remember the nursery rhyme you two were taught when you were young?"

"Yes. It's burned into my memory. Sometimes it pops into my mind unexpectedly. But what does that have to do with anything?"

When she didn't answer him, but switched back to the topic of the phone, he swallowed his frustration. Not wanting to miss the presented opportunity, he let the other subject drop. After again eliciting his promise regarding the phone use, she suggested they go shopping and apartment hunting, effectively stalling any further questions from him.

Three hours later both had new phones. Not as basic as she would have liked, but she recognized that if Jacob was going to interact with other kids his age, he couldn't run around with what they would consider a prehistoric phone fit for dinosaurs. Susan had paid a year in advance offering no explanation other than it was more cost effective.

"Why'd you tell them our name was Walters?" Jacob had kept his silence during his mom's transaction, but now in the car, he demanded answers. "Our name is Winters."

"No longer. If you want a phone and to attend high school, you better get used to your new name."

"Wait. High school?"

"Yes. When we get settled in an apartment, I'll register you for high school. On a temporary basis, mind you. You better not mess up the name or be an idiot with the phone."

"I won't. I promise!" A moment of silence then, "I'm going to high school!"

"One more thing. You need to answer to Jake, not Jacob. That's how I'm going to register you. No questions. Just accept it."

Jacob stared at his mom. There was so much he wanted to ask but he knew better. *Jake Walters.* He tested the name in his mind. He'd have to focus. He'd never been called Jake. Not even as a nickname. His family and those few friends who'd visited had always called him Jacob. And Cody always called him Jacob, never shortening the name even when they were alone. He felt a growing excitement. And a growing fear. He couldn't screw this up. A new phone. A new name. An opportunity to attend a real high school. Maybe even have new friends. His whole world had changed in what seemed a fraction of a second. The completeness of it forced a question.

"Mom?"

"Yes?"

"Will everything be OK? I mean, I don't have to go to high school. We can continue as we've been if it's safer."

"It'll be fine. You deserve this opportunity to have a more normal life. But we need to talk further about your name and your background. It's important, Jake." She emphasized his new name.

He grinned and nodded his head; then pulled out his new phone and began tapping buttons. She watched him out of the corner of her eye as she focused on the traffic around her. She refused to acknowledge her misgivings.

"Look. Here's the first place we circled in the paper." She turned into the lot of a four-story building.

Jacob studied the property. "Looks like an office building."

"It does, rather. Maybe that's a good thing."

It wasn't. The person who'd met them to show the apartment began instantly quizzing them. So much so, Susan felt her alarm growing by the second. They'd barely looked at the place before she quickly made some excuses and dragged Jacob with her back to the car.

"Let's go look at the next place," she said in a no-nonsense voice. Jacob had the sense to remain silent.

They saw three more places before she settled on one that fulfilled an internal checklist. Jacob offered a small protest.

"Mom, it's kind of run-down looking."

"We'll clean it up. It'll be fine."

"But—"

"It'll be fine Jacob." She corrected herself. "Jake."

She knew this neighborhood, although she could tell by the condition of the residences that it had fallen into a different status from her earlier memories. She didn't share with Jacob her familiarity of the area. Better he not know. But she knew it would be easier to stay under the radar here, than at any of the other places they'd looked at. Her biggest concern was the school system. How far from grace had it fallen? Would her son be able to resist its possible pull into a lifestyle she didn't want for him? *Only time will tell,* she thought with a suppressed sigh.

They were able to move into the apartment two days later. Susan furnished it with mostly second-hand things found in a local shop. The only splurge was the beds. The day after, Susan registered Jacob for school. Walking the hallways, she reflected on the rather rough-looking crowd of kids. She hoped she was doing the right thing. Seeing the excitement on Jacob's face as he peeked into each class-room they passed, she again felt guilt at the life he'd lived these past three years. She hoped the next three would be better. She wondered if they'd still be in Denver three years from now.

"Will I start tomorrow? What if I'm way behind everyone else?"

"Can't see why you won't start tomorrow. And don't worry about being behind. If anything, I bet you're much further along in all your subjects than your soon-to-be fellow students. If, for some reason, you're behind in a topic or two, you'll easily catch up. I know you will. Remember all we talked about."

"I will. I promise. Thanks, Mom, for letting me do this."

The paperwork was easily accomplished. Because he'd been home-schooled for his entire school career, the administrators insisted on testing him in various subjects. They said it was to make sure he was placed in the correct classes. Susan wasn't convinced that was the real reason, but she knew Jacob would pass all their tests with minimal effort.

She was right. They ended up placing him in several honors classes. Susan hoped that meant he'd not only be challenged, but that the students he would spend most of his time with would be of a more stable group than some of the others she'd seen wandering the hall-ways. In any event, she would keep a close eye on him and his associates.

"Susan? It is, isn't it?"

Susan stopped at the voice. A chill ran down her spine. She turned slowly.

"I was right! It is you! What are you doing here? How long has it been. Years! You haven't changed! Who's this? Your son?"

The questions came fast and furious. Jacob looked back and forth between his mother and this unknown man.

"Hi, Turner. How have you been?"

"How have I been? That's all you can say? How have I been?"

Turner rushed to her and enveloped her in a big bearhug. "It's great to see you! You really haven't changed a bit. I'm not kidding."

Susan pulled away and introduced her son.

"Jake. This is Turner. Turner, Jake Walters my son." She looked at Jacob, "We knew each other years ago." She turned to Turner. "I assume you're teaching here?"

"Yes. Honors math."

"Then you'll probably have Jake in your class. Make sure he doesn't slack off."

"What's your last name?" Jacob asked.

"Johnson. That's how you'll address me. Mr. Johnson." Turner offered his hand and Jacob shook it. Turner turned back to Susan.

"Walters? That's not the name I remember. I thought—"

"Married name," Susan hastily interrupted. My husband passed three years ago. We've just recently moved to the Denver area.

"Oh, I'm sorry to hear that. But welcome to Denver. We should get together."

A bell rang and classroom doors opened. Students spilled into the hallway interrupting any further conversation. Susan took the opportunity to make her escape, ushering Jacob ahead of her. She was worried. Having Turner in the mix changed things slightly. He knew more of her past than she was comfortable with. And there was no way she could keep Jacob away from him. Especially if he was, in fact, Jacob's math teacher. She worked on the puzzle of how to minimize interaction with the man. Based on his comments, she thought that might be difficult to accomplish. She didn't want to raise undue curiosity in Jacob by too obviously avoiding the man. She'd have to navigate those waters carefully.

"Did you and Mr. Johnson date?" Jacob's question caused Susan to burst out laughing. They were in the car almost at the new apartment when he asked.

"No. But we had a friendship of sorts. He never met your father. Be careful of any questions he may ask about Dad. Try to avoid answering them without seeming like you're doing that."

"Why?"

"It's better. Believe me on this, hon. We don't want Turner inserting himself too deeply into our lives."

"But why?"

"He can't be trusted. That's all I'll say. You must accept my direction on this. Tread carefully around him. If he truly is your math teacher, you can't avoid him. But you can control how much you share with him. And I'll repeat what I've often said. You must always be aware that even what appears to be inconsequential information might be the very thing that brings destruction upon us."

"I don't understand, but I'll do as you ask."

"Thank you. Turner's presence makes me want to immediately pull you from the school." At Jacob's widened eyes, she quickly added, "I won't. But you must be cautious."

"I will. I promise."

"Well, here we are. Home sweet home. Let's get inside and I'll fix us some dinner. You've got a big day tomorrow. We should have a relaxing evening."

She ignored Jacob's snort as they entered the apartment and she locked the door behind them.

21

Cody drove for several hours before pulling over to fill his car. He hadn't bothered stopping at any of the roadside places to eat. He still had plenty of snacks from his shopping trip and, if not exactly healthy eating, they kept him feeling full.

As he was paying for his gas, he asked the clerk for an estimated time to his destination. The response was close to what Cody had guessed it to be. He felt relieved. Perhaps once there he could settle for a bit and figure out his next steps. He quickly filled his car and continued his journey.

He rolled into the small Colorado town shortly after four in the afternoon. The sun was low in the sky, and while he knew there were several hours of daylight remaining, he wondered if the towering mountains would make twilight seem earlier than it should. As towns go, it wasn't much to write home about. Similar to the other town he'd recently been in, he thought this one also looked like a set from an old western movie. As he slowly drove the length of the main street, he noted a small bed and breakfast with a vacancy sign in the window. Although he figured the odds he might lose the room if he explored the town further were slim, he decided better safe than sorry and pulled over into an open parking space.

He felt instantly at home when he walked through the door. He could smell something baking and the scent caused his mouth to water and stomach to growl. He looked around the small sitting room, noting the comfortably overstuffed chairs arranged around a small wood-burning fireplace which crackled merrily behind its screen.

"Help you?"

He turned in the direction of the voice. He saw a man that he thought had to be at least ninety. As he came closer to the makeshift counter, he revised his estimate. *Maybe seventy? Perhaps younger?* He smiled.

"You still have a room available?"

"How long do you need it?"

"I'm not sure. A week? Maybe longer?"

The man pushed a registration book towards Cody. "The longer you stay, the better rate I can give you."

Cody thought that rather odd but didn't comment. As the silence stretched, the man fiddled with a pen he'd picked up.

"You take cash?" Cody asked. "I don't have a credit card."

The man chuckled. "Gotta say, that's a new one. Most kids your age, they don't know what cash is. Everything is electronic this, electronic that. But yes, I take cash. Will give you an even better deal since I won't have to pay processing fees."

"Seems fair," Cody said. "What would you charge me if I stayed a month?"

"A month, is it? Well, let's see," the man looked off into space. Cody figured he was doing math in his head and gave him the space to do so. The number the man quoted when he next spoke surprised Cody.

"Really?"

"Too much?"

"No, no. It's very reasonable. Almost too reasonable." Cody hesitated, "you don't have anyone else staying here, do you?"

"Can't say as we do. That make a difference to you?"

Cody shook his head. He quickly filled out the book and pushed it back towards the man, who looked at what Cody had written.

"Walters? You from around here? I remember a Walters family from way back. Well, not a family at first. Moved away shortly after the woman gave birth to a boy."

Cody stared at the man wide-eyed.

"What? You look like you've seen a ghost."

"It's just that my parents told me I was born in this town."

"You don't say. You think you might be that boy?"

"Do you remember the first names of the people?"

"Can't say as I do. Been a long time. How old are you, boy? You look to be, oh I don't know, late teens? Everyone looks twelve to me nowadays."

Cody smiled. "I'm twenty one."

"Ma!" the man called, startling Cody. "Come out here, will you?"

A woman wearing an apron liberally sprinkled with flour came through the door asking what all the ruckus was about. The man quickly explained the situation. Cody felt himself being studied and he shifted his weight.

"Could be. He has a familiar look to him."

"Please, tell me what you remember," Cody pleaded.

The man spoke quickly, "Look, why don't you take your things upstairs and get settled. Dinner is in about a half-hour. You hungry? You look like you haven't eaten since the wagon train got stuck on the mountain." He laughed and laughed at his own private joke.

"Oh, Donner, you really need to quit with that line," the woman scolded him. Then she turned back to Cody. "I agree with my husband, get yourself settled. I'm Anna, by the way. My husband, Donner, named after the famous mountain pass, can be a bit much at times. We can have a civilized conversation over a meal. You like fried chicken with mashed potatoes? And there's chocolate chip cookies for dessert."

"Yes, ma'am. And I can smell the cookies. My mouth's been watering since I stepped through the door."

"Go on, then. Come down as soon as you're settled."

It took Cody about forty-five minutes to present himself at the kitchen door. He'd decided to shower, shave, and change into clean clothes. Anna looked at him and smiled, then ushered him to a large table in a separate dining room located between the kitchen and the front sitting room. As she dished up a plate and set it before him, he had all he could do to not attack the food like some kind of madman. *Wouldn't do to freak out my new hosts,* he thought as he downed several mouthfuls within the first minute or so before forcefully ordering himself to slow down.

"This is delicious," he said as he reached for a basket containing buttermilk biscuits.

"It's good to see someone enjoy their food," Anna commented. "Not like Donner, here, who is always complaining about something."

"I don't complain, woman!"

"Don't shout. And yes, you do."

Anna smiled at Cody and winked. Cody smiled back. He was fast settling into the first home environment he'd experienced for some time.

"So you were born here?" she asked.

"Yes, ma'am."

"Oh, please. Don't be so formal. Call me Anna. And him," she gestured with her head towards her husband, "Donner."

Cody nodded his acquiescence. "My parents told me I was born in this town. I came to check it out."

"Where are your parents now? What are their names?"

"My dad passed a little over three years ago."

"I'm sorry to hear that. And your mom?"

Cody shifted. He didn't want to share his family situation with these people. Nice as they were, he had learned over the years to be on guard about such things.

As if Anna had somehow read his mind, she shifted the topic slightly.

"I remember the young couple Donner mentioned. Her name was Susan, I think. Can't really remember the man's name. And as he told you, they moved shortly after she gave birth to a boy. You really think you might be that boy?"

"My mom's name is Susan," Cody blurted before he could stop himself.

"Is it now," Donner inserted himself into the conversation as he looked at his wife. "Woman, your memory ain't what it used to be. While you were talking, I remembered the man's name. Tom, or Thomas, or Tomato, or something like that."

"You old fool," Anna shot back. "No one is named Tomato!"

Cody watched the interplay between the two. Despite the way they spoke to each other, he could tell there was a deep love between them. He'd seen that kind of love between his parents. Their memories of the couple convinced him they were speaking of his parents. A wave of sadness hit him, overwhelming in its suddenness.

"How long have you lived in this town?" he asked.

"Forever. All our lives." Both answered at the same time, then smiled at each other.

"Then you would have known my parents. Dad's name was Thomas. Tom for short. Unlikely there were two couples named Susan and Thomas who lived here and had a baby boy. What can you tell me about them? Anything, even the slightest memory would be a treasure to me."

"Really can't say much, I'm afraid," Anna answered. "They came into town one day, rented a place up the mountain somewhere. Didn't engage with the locals much. She had her child," She smiled. "You, I guess. At the birthing center. We don't have a real hospital here. They left a couple of weeks after you were born."

Cody nodded, but inside his hope for more information deflated and popped like an old balloon. He pushed his mashed potatoes around on his plate, forcing himself to take another bite.

"Now you know all that, you still gonna stay a month?" Donner asked. He winced, indicating Anna must have kicked him under the table. She took over.

"You look tired, dear. Why don't you go on up to your room. Take a couple of cookies and your glass of milk with you. You want a refill?"

"No thanks." Cody stood and took two cookies off the plate they were stacked on. He looked at Donner. "Yes, I'll stay the month. I still need to pay you."

"We'll take care of that in the morning. Go on, now," Anna said before Donner could respond.

Eager to be alone and think about what he'd just learned, Cody made his escape. In his room, he quickly stripped to his underwear and crawled under the covers, placing his hands behind his head. He contemplated the coincidence of landing at this place, with these people, and getting such information so quickly. What really intrigued him was that they knew the name Walters. Did that mean it was his real name? That Winters was the fake one? He wondered how hard it would be to get a copy of his birth certificate. He wondered if there was any other information he could find in the public records. He doubted it. If his parents had stayed somewhere outside of town and didn't engage with the locals, unlikely he'd find much of anything. He wasn't sure it was worth staying the month, but then again, he was tired of constantly driving and wondering where he'd end up each night. *Yes. I'll stay and rest. Maybe I'll find more information, maybe I won't. But it's surely safe enough for me to remain here for a bit.* With that thought, he drifted off to sleep.

"You gonna tell him?" Donner asked his wife as they washed the dishes together.

"Not sure. Probably not. Susan told us never to reveal our true identities. Remember? She said it could mean our death."

"But the boy. He should know."

"Let's see what other questions he asks. Or what else he figures out. He's staying the month. Let's just enjoy the unexpected gift of getting to know our grandson. Even if we can't tell him. And I'm warning you, you old fool, you better not let anything slip. It could put him in danger as well as us."

"See you mind your own advice, woman," Donner murmured as he dropped the dish towel on the counter and wandered into the other room, muttering to himself.

Anna heard the television and knew he was settled for the night. She stayed in the kitchen indulging in busy tasks, as she called them. She thought about the sudden turn of events and sent a silent thankful prayer upwards that she had met her grandson. She thought about her daughter, whom she hadn't seen for nearly twenty years. She wondered what other surprises the next few days would offer.

22

Jacob burst through the door of the apartment. He dropped his backpack of books on the floor, and kicked off his shoes as he continued a non-stop flow of talk on his way to the refrigerator. His head disappeared while he looked inside for something to snack on.

Susan watched him, both amused and slightly alarmed by how animated he was. Obviously his first day of school had been memorable. She quizzed him lightly about his fellow students and classes.

"Mom, can I join the basketball team? I think I'd be good at it. Cody and I always played against each other, but I think I have enough skills to add to the team. I played with a couple of guys during lunch. Goober said I was pretty good."

"Isn't it too late to join sports teams? And who is Goober?"

"Basketball season is just starting. It runs through the end of the school year. Goober is really Gerald, but everyone calls him Goober. I'm not sure why."

Susan swallowed her misgivings. She feared Jacob getting too deeply involved in extra-curricular activities. However, it seemed churlish to deny him all opportunities attached to his first-ever high school experience.

Jacob interpreted his mother's hesitation as a refusal and rushed to justify his participation. The objective part of Susan admired Jacob's skills at presenting his case. But the part that worried about excessive exposure won out.

"How good is the team?"

"They've been city champions for two years running."

His answer confirmed Susan's fears. There would be media coverage. The games might possibly be televised, even if only on local stations. She looked at his face. He was so eager. She couldn't bring herself to immediately crush that eagerness.

"Let me think on it. There are aspects to this that I need to sort through."

"But—"

"I'll give you my answer in the morning. In the meantime, do you have any homework for tomorrow?"

"Yes. Tons."

"Then I suggest you get busy. I'll fix something for dinner."

Jacob retrieved his backpack and began spreading his books and papers out on the table. Susan left him to his task as she began preparing the spaghetti she'd planned for their meal. As she browned the hamburger, she puzzled through the basketball team request.

"Mom?" Jacob interrupted her thoughts. "Mr. Johnson asked where we moved from. I told him North Dakota. Was that OK?"

Susan chuckled. "Why North Dakota?"

"It's close to Montana, although we ended up not staying there. But I figured it'd be easier to remember."

"Did he ask where in North Dakota?"

"He didn't. That seemed weird to me. Wouldn't most people follow up wanting more specific information?"

"You'd think so. But if he returns to the topic, just tell him Fargo."

"What if he asks where in Fargo? I don't even know where Fargo is."

"Then you'd best study a map. If you're going to make up a backstory, you need to be prepared to sound like you know what you're talking about."

Jacob opened his mouth to protest, but a quick look from his mom caused him to shut it. Instead, he grabbed his phone and started tapping on it. Susan watched him for a minute then returned to her tasks. She knew he was researching Fargo. While she didn't like him doing it on the phone, it was the most efficient way for him to get the information. She'd quiz him later about what he'd learned.

After dinner, while Jacob was still working through the last of his schoolwork, Susan told him he could try out for the basketball team. Jacob looked up from his paper.

"Really? You mean it? Yipee!"

"But there are some conditions."

He immediately stilled. "There always are."

She ignored his sullen response. "If the team is as good as you say, it's going to be featured in local sports telecasts, social media, etc. As much as possible, you need to remain in the background. Do you think you can do that?"

"I may not always be able to control that."

"True. But if you remain aware and work to keep your face out of photos and such, it'll help keep us here. Perhaps long enough for you to finish high school."

Jacob thought about that. In the last three years, they'd stayed in so many places, always on the move. The cabin had been the longest stay in one place he could remember, and that had been in the woods. He wasn't sure he could go back to that lifestyle. Not now. Now that he'd experienced the excitement and feeling of inclusion of a real high school. Granted, it'd only been one day, but he knew he belonged in this new environment.

"I'll do everything I can, but Mom, how can I be aware of every kid with a cell phone recording the game action?"

She sighed. "You can't. And that's what scares me."

"Why do we have to live like this? You've never told me the whole story. I know you haven't. And now the name change on top of everything else. Isn't it time you came clean?"

Susan looked at her son. "It's better if you don't know."

"You say that every time I ask!" Jacob's voice grew louder in his frustration.

"I do. Because it's true." Her response was quiet.

"But why?" Jacob regained control of his volume. "You once said it was because you had something other people wanted. That they would kill for it. Is that the reason?"

"It is."

"Why don't you just give it to them? Maybe then we could live a normal life. Find Cody. Be a family again."

"Unfortunately, it isn't that simple. You must trust me on this. That friend who died in the plane crash that just happened? He was tied to this situation. But only in a peripheral sense. They think there was a bomb on the plane. So you see, the threat is real."

Jacob was silent for a long time as he sorted through what she'd said. When he looked at her, she saw his father in his intense stare. "There's more to all this, isn't there. You told me about the witness protection stuff. But it goes beyond that, doesn't it? You and Dad really were spies, weren't you? You lied about that."

She smiled sadly. "I didn't completely lie. Your father was not a spy. But yes, I worked for the intelligence community at one time. A lifetime ago. Before your father and I even met."

"Did he know?"

"Yes."

"Is that why we were always homeschooled?"

"Partly. But not completely."

"And why we weren't overly encouraged to develop friendships?"

"Yes."

"What did you do?"

"I can't tell you that."

"But—"

"Jacob. I really can't tell you."

"Why are you being hunted? Did you kill someone? Steal something? Both?"

When she didn't answer, Jacob was silent again for several minutes. She wondered what scenarios his brain was formulating. His next question took Susan completely by surprise.

"Do I have grandparents?"

"I—" she stalled. "What prompted that question?"

"Goober lives with his grandparents. It got me thinking. You've never said anything about an extended family. Are yours or Dad's parents still alive? Will I ever meet them? Do I have any aunts or uncles? Cousins?"

"No cousins. No aunts or uncles. Both your father and I were only children."

Jacob nodded, but he wasn't satisfied. "But do I have living grand-parents?"

While Susan was grateful to be off the other subject, this one gave her just as many misgivings. She needed to tread carefully. Tom's parents had passed several years ago. The kids were barely out of their toddler years. But hers were very much alive. And living not that far away. She again questioned the wisdom of coming back to Colorado.

"Perhaps this is a topic for another time. Have you finished your homework?"

Jacob looked about to protest, but instead pushed his papers together and shoved them in his pack.

"Yeah," he murmured.

"When are tryouts for the team?"

"Day after tomorrow."

"Want to watch a movie?"

"Nah. I'm kinda tired. Mind if I go to my room?"

She shook her head and watched him trudge down the hallway. It was several minutes before she noticed his phone still on the table. She stood and walked towards it, staring down at its blank screen. She wanted to check out how he'd been using it and struggled with the need to satisfy her own worries or grant him the privacy he was entitled to. She finally opted to just plug it in and charge it for him.

She quietly finished cleaning up the kitchen, then dimmed the lights and returned to the easy chair she'd claimed as her own. She sat for hours, just staring into space. Thinking. At some point, she dozed off.

23

Cody awoke refreshed and feeling more relaxed than he had in some time. The smell of bacon drifted up the stairs and his stomach rumbled. He tossed the covers back and nearly jumped from the bed. A quick shower and shave later he navigated the stairs, following the delicious scents coming from the kitchen.

Donner was sitting at the table reading a local newspaper. At Cody's greeting, he peeked around a page and indicated the empty chair where Cody had sat the night before.

"Is there a laundromat in town? I really need to catch up on things."

Anna came through the kitchen door at that moment, carrying a large bowl of scrambled eggs and a plate of bacon. Before Donner could respond to Cody, she offered to take care of Cody's laundry.

"Oh, I can't let you do that. Please, the food and place to sleep is more than what I'm paying for already."

"About that," Donner started, but Anna quickly cut him off.

"Nonsense. Just leave it outside your door. I'll take care of it later today."

"Well," Cody hesitated, then capitulated. "At least let me bring it to wherever your washer is."

"Fine. Bring it down the stairs for me. I'll take it from there. Now, eat up."

After everyone satisfied their initial hunger, Anna asked Cody what his plans were for the day.

"I thought I'd visit the town hall. I assume that's where old records are kept? I'd like to try and get a copy of my birth certificate."

He didn't mention that he already had one. It had been in the paperwork from the chest. But his said he'd been born in Montana, not Colorado. He wanted to compare the two documents for other differences.

Anna looked doubtful, mentioning a fire that had occurred many years ago.

"You might have more luck in Denver. Or maybe do an online search. I think most vital statistics are on some new-fangled database."

Cody suppressed a smile at her description of new-fangled. Father Timothy had shown him how to do genealogy searches, but they'd been unsuccessful finding anything relevant connected to the name Winters. Cody now knew why.

"Is there a library here? Do they have computers the public can use?"

"Just use your phone," Donner piped in. "I see the kids, adults too, for that matter, wandering around like zombies, their eyes glued to those tiny screens. I'm surprised more aren't run over. They pay no attention to traffic or anything else going on around them."

"I don't have a phone, either."

"You don't have a—?"

"Leave the boy alone, you old fool. Don't you have places to be, things to do?"

Cody saw a look pass between the two. He couldn't interpret it. But Donner stood and mentioned that he did, indeed, have places to go. He left the room, tossing a casual goodbye over his shoulder.

"We have a computer upstairs. It's several years old, but it should be fine for your purposes. Finish your breakfast. And bring your laundry down. I'll show you the computer after that."

Cody cleaned up the bits of egg left on his plate and asked if he could help with dishes. Anna's refusal sent him up the stairs to sort through his things and gather his dirty clothes.

Two hours later he was still searching a database for birth records when the thought occurred to him to see if he could find marriage records for his parents. He opened a new window and searched under both Winters and Walters. He thought it odd that he could find nothing under either name. *Even if not the correct people, these two names are not all that unique.* He'd barely finished that thought when the computer flashed a warning, lines of text rolled quickly down the screen and large numbers began a countdown to shutting down.

"Anna!" Alarmed, Cody yelled at the top of his voice.

When no answer came, he yelled the name again. Finally, she called up the stairs to him.

"Please come quick! Something weird is happening with the computer!"

By the time Anna made it upstairs and into the room, the computer had gone dark. No matter what buttons he pushed, there was no response. As an afterthought, he reached down and pulled the plug.

"Tell me again what you were doing and what happened," Anna asked in a quiet voice.

Cody did.

"Come. Grab your things. We need to move you to a new place."

When Cody started to protest, she cut him off with a no-nonsense command. Years of obeying his parents had him standing and going to his room without further questions. Her words followed him.

"Make sure there's nothing in the room that shows you were there."

Confused, he did what she said, returning a moment later with his pack slung over one shoulder.

"That's all you have?"

"I travel light. Is my laundry done?"

"Yes. Let's get it. Quickly now."

"Anna, what's going on?"

"Later. It's imperative you or anything that points to you is gone from here."

They'd reached the laundry room and Anna handed him a neatly folded pile of clean clothes. Without comment Cody took them and, unzipping his pack, placed them gently on top of his other possessions. Then he closed the pack and slung it back up over his shoulder, waiting for further directions.

She led him back to the kitchen and hastily threw together several sandwiches, wrapping and putting them in a plastic grocery sack. She dumped the rest of the cookies she'd baked into a zip-lock bag and included that with the sandwiches. Then she grabbed three bottles of water and added them to the bag. She handed everything to Cody, holding up a hand to forestall his questions.

Going to the wall phone, Anna tore a page out of a notebook sitting on the small table under the phone. She began sketching something. Cody came and looked over her shoulder. He could see she was drawing a map. She began explaining the drawing, telling him road names and landmarks to the cabin in the woods she was indicating with a big circle. Turning, she shoved it in his hands and told him to get in his car and go. The longer he stayed, the more danger he might be in.

"What do you mean by that? How can I be in any danger? And wouldn't that also put you in danger? What aren't you telling me, Anna?"

"Please, Cody. Just go. Take this key. Stay in the cabin. Don't leave. We'll come for you when it's safe."

"But—"

"Go, Cody!" Anna practically screamed the words at him as she grabbed his arm and began pulling him towards the front door.

Cody felt her urgency. He didn't understand it, but it was feeding a rising panic within him. He grabbed his car keys from the hook where he'd hung them the previous night. Before he opened the door to leave, he looked at her.

"Will you and Donner be all right?"

"Yes, yes. We'll be fine. Now go, Cody. Don't stop for anything. Just get to the cabin."

He shook his head and turned to leave. Not knowing what prompted it, he turned back and quickly gave Anna a hug, murmuring his thanks and hoping she'd be safe. Stepping through the door, he ran to his parked car, and within seconds was pulling away from the house.

While Anna stood in the open doorway and watched the car drive out of town, Donner came up the walk, a bakery box in his hands.

"Was that Cody? Where's he off to in such a hurry? I bought your favorite pie. Thought we could celebrate something tonight."

"Come inside. Things have changed."

Donner stepped through the door, shut, and locked it. Then he looked closely at Anna.

"What's happened?"

She quickly summarized the events.

"Should we send out the alarm? It's been twenty years or more. Do you think it even still works?"

"I don't know. Maybe I've over-reacted. If it does still work, sending the code could make things worse."

Donner thought about that. "Or it could save lives."

"But Susan always told us—"

Donner reached for Anna's hand. "Susan isn't here. We're not even sure she's still alive. It's been years. Even Cody wasn't sure. I'm sorry we ever agreed to cut ties with her. Our only daughter. And we don't even know if she's still out there somewhere. Hearing of Tom's death was a shock. To think that boy has been on his own for so long, not knowing if his mother or brother are alive. And we couldn't even tell him we're his kin."

Anna barely swallowed a sob. Donner pulled her into his arms and comforted her. "You remember the number?"

"Yes."

"Make the call."

"But what if—"

"I'm tired of living in a world of what ifs. Make the call, Anna."

He led her to the wall phone and took the receiver. Holding it to his ear, he directed her to punch in the digits to the number they both memorized years ago. When a mechanical voice came on asking for identification, he punched in a three-digit code. He heard clicking, then the same voice asked for the appropriate code. Donner gestured to Anna. She punched in the seven-digit code. There was more clicking, then he heard an abrupt thank you and the connection was terminated. He replaced the receiver and looked at his wife with love.

"It's done. Can't take it back now. May God's hand guide the coming events to a positive resolution."

She closed her eyes and nodded. Without opening them she whispered, "You ready?"

"Yes. Let's go. And let's hope we've adequately prepared."

24

The burner phone buzzed in his pocket. He'd almost left it in the drawer today. He'd carried the thing around for two decades. Maybe more. He couldn't really remember. Well, it wasn't the original phone. This was the third or fourth replacement. But it functioned as if it were the original. At least he assumed it did. He'd never had a call or a text on it since acquiring it. He was shocked it had suddenly come alive.

He pulled it out of his pocket and looked at the screen which indicated he'd received a text. A deep feeling of unease began in the pit of his stomach as he swiped the screen to get to the message.

Two lines looked back at him. The first line said 'Colorado'. The second was a series of numbers. A seven-digit code he hoped never to see. He closed his eyes for a second and took a deep breath. Then he carefully deleted the message. He pulled the SIM card out and slipped it in his pocket. He'd destroy it later. He dropped the phone to the floor and crushed it with his foot.

Barely thirty-seconds later he was out the door, his go-bag slung over one shoulder.

SUSAN CHECKED HER BURNER PHONE, as she did every day. Jacob was due home any minute. They'd planned a small celebration dinner to mark his making the basketball team.

Not expecting anything other than its usual silent treatment, she almost dropped the phone when she saw she had a text message. She opened it, noting the time it came in. Sweat formed on her forehead. As she looked at the single word and the seven-digit number, her hand shook. She closed her eyes and mouthed a silent prayer.

She looked around the small apartment. Jacob would be heartbroken. He'd settled in so nicely. She wondered if there was any way she could keep him here instead of them both fleeing. *Maybe he could stay with this Goober kid while I deal with the situation presented by this text.*

She had minimal time to arrange things and she wasn't sure how Jacob would respond. As she heard Jacob's key in the door, she knew she'd have her answer soon enough.

THE MAN LOOKED at the text, then his partner. "Wheels up."

"Where to?"

"Colorado."

25

Cody pulled up to the cabin. It was pretty run down. It looked like no one had been there for years. But the small lean-to attached to the side seemed sturdy. He backed his car into it. While it didn't exactly hide it, the covered space allowed him to not leave the car in the open for anyone to see. He hoped it would be enough.

He got out of the car and reached into his front pocket, feeling for the key Anna gave him. He wasn't sure why he was so reluctant to enter the dwelling, but taking a deep breath he stepped up to the door. The key slid into the lock easily and he entered before he could change his mind. He didn't expect what he saw.

The exterior may have appeared abandoned, but inside looked as if someone was currently living there. One large room comprised the space. Everything was clean and welcoming. An overstuffed chair sat next to a small woodburning stove, with a table tucked next to the chair. Another chair was at an angle to the first. A rug defined the sitting area. A neatly made double bed was pushed up against the wall, a bureau placed at the end of it to create the feeling of a nook. Navigating around a small table with two chairs, he walked into the kitchen area, located in the corner. He pulled open the refrigerator door. The light came on and he could tell the interior maintained a cool temperature. He looked around. He hadn't noticed any wires on his drive in and his mind registered no light switches on any of the walls. No outlets either. *How is this thing powered?* He saw the camp stove on the counter and wondered if anyone actually cooked on it. He knew these types of stoves should only be used outdoors. The fumes would be dangerous inside. He wandered around, touching items here and there, then went back outside and walked the perimeter of the building. He saw a small upright building tucked into the trees and assumed it was an outhouse. He'd explore that later.

Behind a small, fenced enclosure next to the corner of the building, he saw a propane tank and followed the piping, realizing this was the source of the refrigerator's power. He returned to his car, grabbed his pack and the sack of food from Anna.

He put the food in the 'fridge and tossed his pack in the corner of the double bed. That small burst of energy now left him feeling slightly defeated. He slowly turned in a circle surveying the entire interior once more. Small details registered, but although something told him what he was seeing was important, he was too tired to try and decipher anything. He wandered over to the bed and sat. Kicking off his shoes, he swung his legs around and stretched out. As an afterthought, he pulled the folded blanket at the end of the bed over him. He stared at the ceiling for a few moments, then sighed and closed his eyes. He drifted into a deep sleep.

It was dark when he awoke. The cabin looked unfamiliar and intimidating. He tried to remember the footprint of the room as he swung himself into a sitting position. The only light was what came through the side window, the product of a half-moon bravely competing against the clouds in the sky. There was a distinct chill to the air. He wondered if it was safe to start a fire in the stove. He remembered seeing some chopped wood just outside the front door.

He stood and slowly felt his way past the chairs to the door. He opened it slightly and looked around before stepping out onto the wooden porch. He grabbed some small pieces and a few newspapers from a bin he noticed and quickly retreated to the interior. Realizing he needed some light, he made his way back to the bed and rummaged through the pack for his battery powered headlamp. Sliding it onto his head, he flipped it on.

"That's better," he said into the empty room. He wasn't sure if the sound of his voice comforted him or made the utter stillness of the place worse.

As he shredded the newspaper, he noticed the date on one. It was less than a week old. That knowledge sent a chill down his spine. Obviously, someone came here regularly. What if they came while he was here? Would they challenge his presence? Then he relaxed slightly. Why would Anna give him a key and send him here if it put him in danger? She said she was trying to protect him. From what, he didn't know. But he remembered the panic he felt at her urgency to get him away from the house. Then again, what if she didn't know someone else was using the cabin?

His thoughts in turmoil, he realized he was shivering and hurried to get the fire started, using stick matches he found in a container on the table next to the chair. Whatever happened from here forward, at least he'd make sure he wouldn't freeze to death. He smiled grimly at the thought of his death.

The crackling sound of the fire not only made him mentally more comfortable, the warmth overtaking the room's chill relieved his physical distress. He pulled shut the simple window drapes. Then went to the refrigerator and retrieved a sandwich and bottle of water. He sat at the small table while he consumed them. He decided to save the cookies for later.

It occurred to him that continued use of his headlamp risked killing the batteries. He got up to explore the cupboards. He found what he was looking for in the second one. Three camping lamps with bottles of fuel were on the shelves. He quickly set one up and soon had it burning efficiently. He wondered vaguely if it was safe to use the lamp inside even as he turned off his headlamp. Between the fire and glow from the lamp, the place seemed quite homey. He decided to explore.

The cupboards and drawers didn't yield much more than standard kitchen and survival supplies. The small bookcase contained several hardbacks tucked in amongst mostly paperbacks. He recognized many of the titles, having already read them. Those he didn't recognize offered an opportunity for diversion if he was forced to stay for any length of time.

A cardboard gift-type box sat on the lower shelf of the chair table. Perfectly square, his eyes would have gone right over it if he hadn't noticed the word printed lengthwise down one side. Even then he might not have looked at it any closer. But the word had meaning to him. It was one of the names mentioned in the nursery rhyme he knew by heart. He walked over and pulled it off the shelf. He almost dropped it. It was heavier than he expected. He sat in the chair with the box on his lap. Slowly he lifted the lid and looked in.

A small metal safe was inside. He carefully lifted it out, placing the empty box on the floor next to him. Studying the safe, he could see it required a five-digit combination to open. Frustrated, he shook the box and heard the contents inside shift. Without having any way to open the safe, he replaced it in the gift box and put it back on the shelf. He stood and paced the room, stopping to look at the box every time he passed it. He finally convinced himself that it wasn't any of his business and he shouldn't be snooping into it anyway. He glanced around the room one last time. The only place he hadn't looked was under the bed.

He went over to it, got down on his hands and knees, bent his head, and looked. He both laughed at himself and in frustration when he realized it was too dark to see anything. He got up and grabbed his headlamp, then positioned himself to look again. The only thing there was a square metal box. He reached in and pulled it to him. Without bothering to get up, he swung around and leaned against the bed.

The box was old and rusty. It had a key lock. He shook the box and heard what sounded like papers shifting. He shook it again and thought he heard a small ping. He sat and stared at it for a long time, occasionally glancing at the box he'd replaced on the table shelf. He couldn't shake the feeling that both boxes were significant.

"What treasures do you hold?" he whispered to the box, then smiled. "Like you can talk."

He pushed the box back under the bed and stood. He noticed the stove needed some extra wood and quickly took care of that task. Not remotely sleepy, he walked over to the bookcase and surveyed the titles again. He picked an old favorite and went over to the table and sat by the lamp. It gave him just enough light to read. He quickly became immersed in the story.

Two hours later he stood and stretched stiff muscles. Wishing he'd checked out the building earlier as he'd planned, he grabbed his headlamp and made his way to the small outhouse at the edge of the clearing. Although cleaner than he expected, its creepiness encouraged him to finish his business quickly and get back to the cabin.

Deciding to call it a night, he put more wood on the fire, snuffed the lamp, and crawled on top of the bed fully clothed. As he'd done earlier, he pulled the blanket over him and was soon asleep.

He awoke in the early morning hours. He felt both rested and restless. Giving up any attempt to sleep in, he got up and checked the stove. Embers were still glowing. He figured it'd be easier to keep the thing fed and burning rather than start from scratch later. Five minutes later, having stoked the stove, he was looking through the cupboards for coffee. Finding only tea, he sighed but decided it was better than nothing.

He looked at the teapot on the wood stove. Using a towel from the kitchen, he pulled open the top and peered in. All he could determine was that it was empty. He retrieved one of his two bottles of water from the refrigerator and poured it in. A harsh sizzling sound emerged, startling Cody. Recognizing what had occurred, he waited for the water to boil.

He was sipping his tea and half-heartedly munching on another sandwich when he heard a noise outside. He went on full alert as he crept toward a window to look out. His heart thumped as he moved from window to window yet saw nothing outside other than trees and shrubbery. He was about to write off the noise as imagined when he heard it again. He froze. Uncertain whether to hide or confront the source of the noise, he shook his head in frustration when he realized the only hiding place the space offered was under the bed. Without further thought he went to the door and flung it open.

He cried out and stepped back in surprise at the sight before him. His exclamation and sudden appearance frightened the small bear cub that was on its hind feet and exploring the wood pile. As he slammed the door shut, the bear turned towards the porch steps and quickly navigated them. Cody recognized the sound for what it was and opened the door a crack to peek out. He saw the bear running towards the woods. He studied the trees looking for the cub's mother. After a few seconds, his eyes caught movement and a large female bear stepped into the clearing. It stared at him and he began to wonder if it was going to charge when the cub nuzzled it. After sniffing the cub thoroughly, the mother looked in Cody's direction once more before turning and re-entering the woods, the cub following closely.

Cody let out the breath he didn't realize he'd been holding and sagged against the door frame. After a few moments, he stood upright shoving his hands in his pockets as he kicked the door shut with his foot. He laughed out loud at himself as he made his way back to the table. He looked at the sandwich and decided he really wasn't hungry enough to finish it. The act of pulling his hands out of his pockets caused the small key in one to fall on the floor.

As he bent over to retrieve it, he had a sudden thought. Glancing at the bed, he slowly straightened and turned towards it, key in hand.

"What are the odds?" he murmured to the empty room.

He knelt beside the bed and pulled the metal box out. Spinning around he sat with it in his lap and tried the key in the lock.

"Whoa!" he exclaimed as he turned the key and heard a soft click. "Really?"

Hands slightly trembling, he lifted the lid. Inside he saw a bunch of papers and a ring. He picked up the ring, realizing that was the ping he'd heard when he shook the box yesterday. He studied it, noting the crest design and small words that looked to be in Latin. He stood and walked to the table where he could sit more comfortably and go through the rest of the box's contents. He felt no concern at exploring the items. After all, he'd had the key. The key from the treasure chest. Clearly the message was that he should see the contents.

What he didn't understand were the events leading up to this moment. So many coincidences. It seemed as if an invisible hand had guided his journey to this exact time and place. While he laughed at such whimsy, a part of him couldn't shake the thought that every-thing that had happened since he found the chest was part of a bigger plan.

He began pulling the papers out, realizing there were several photographs stuffed in amongst the pages. He stacked those together in one pile. Other papers looked to be official records of some sort. He put those together in another pile. The remaining contents were a mishmash of receipts, written notes, and odd things that didn't fit in the other two piles he'd created. He put all this in a third pile, then placed the metal box on the floor out of the way.

He wasn't sure where to start, but some instinct had him reaching for the photographs. He shuffled through them. Two pictures were of a couple holding a baby. As he compared them, he realized the backgrounds indicated they were taken years apart from each other. He studied the older, black-and-white one first. He dismissed the baby. Babies were babies. They all looked alike to him. But the man and woman looked vaguely familiar. He wasn't sure why.

He looked at the other, color picture and immediately realized he was looking at a younger version of his mother and father. He assumed he was the baby. Before he could distract himself with wondering why this picture was in the box, he sorted through the rest of the photographs. One was a picture of his mother receiving some kind of award or certificate and a small box. He glanced at the ring sitting on the table and wondered if that had been the contents of the box.

Another picture depicted a large ranch-style house. The property around it appeared vast. He didn't recognize it. The fifth picture was the home he'd lived in and seen burn to the ground the night he realized his father had been killed. The sudden pain he felt pierced him to his soul. He realized he'd never gone back as he'd planned. He knew now it no longer mattered.

The sixth picture was a group of people, all looking towards the camera with big smiles. Two sets of adults and two children, both small boys.

He studied it intently. Something inside him shifted. Cody recognized the boys as he and his brother. At least he assumed the toddler was Jacob. He was clearly the young boy standing beside the man he recognized as his father. He looked at the woman. Yes. His mother. But who were the others? When was this taken? And who took it? He had no memory of it. And there was nothing written on the back to clue him in.

It took him far longer than it should have, to realize that the building the group was standing in front of was this very cabin. He sat up.

Heart pounding. He picked up the black-and-white photo and compared it to the group photo. Yes. These had to be the same people. That nagging feeling of familiarity hit him again.

He almost dropped the photos when he realized he was looking at younger versions of Anna and Donner. The significance hit him swift and hard.

"We're family!" he nearly shouted. "These people are my grand-parents!"

26

"**M**om! Are you ready? I'm starving!"

Jacob yelled the words as he kicked his shoes off and headed towards his room to drop his backpack. Not hearing a response, he called out the words again as he headed back to the main living area. He saw his mom texting on a phone. But it wasn't the phone she'd gotten with him. It was something different.

"Mom?"

Susan waved her hand vaguely in his direction, signaling him to wait. Jacob watched her, feelings of unease beginning.

What seemed like hours later, even though it was less than two minutes, she looked up. Before she could say anything, Jacob cut her off.

"I'm not going! I like it here. You said I could attend high school."

Susan looked at him with sad eyes, and in a quiet voice replied, "I also said I hoped we'd be able to stay for your entire term. But that there were no guarantees. What makes you think we're going anywhere?"

"I've seen that look before. And it's always right before you tell me to pack my things and be quick about it."

"Jacob—"

"No! I'm not going! I can stay here alone. I'm old enough."

"You're not," she countered, "but I do have a possible compromise."

Jacob calmed a bit. "What?"

Susan still wasn't sure it was a good idea. Jacob would be in school all day on his own. Goober's grandparents certainly wouldn't be able to protect him. As much as she'd done to prepare Jacob, she knew he wasn't ready. He had skills, but not enough of them. And while he was mature for his age, he was still only fifteen. In her world, there were many who wouldn't care how old he was if he could be used to get to her. And his height and size would encourage them to see him as an adult.

"Do you think it might be possible for you to stay with Goober? Have you been to his place? Is there room? Do you think his grandparents would agree?"

She voiced the questions quickly, before she could change her mind. Once they were out of her mouth, Jacob seized on them. She was committed.

"I can share Goober's room. It's bigger than mine. He won't mind, and I'm sure his grandparents won't mind. Even though they're ancient, they seem with it."

Susan swallowed her smile. She could appreciate that Jacob would think Goober's grandparents were old. He thought she was old. She guessed the grandparents were the same age or younger than her own. But Jacob had never met his grandparents. At least not at a point in life when he could remember them. He never grew up with that generation of the family nearby. He couldn't relate.

"I'll need to meet them. Talk to them."

"I'll call Goober now. We can go right over."

Susan hesitated again.

"Mom, it will work! I know it will!"

"All right. Make the call."

Jacob ran to his room to dig his phone out of his backpack. She heard his voice and assumed he was talking to his friend. She prayed she was doing the right thing.

Three hours later Jacob and Goober were in Goober's room getting him settled. She and Jacob had practiced the cover story again and again on the way over. So much so that Jacob became surly. Susan dropped it at that point and hoped he'd never really need to use it.

While the boys were occupied, she pulled the grandparents aside and insisted they take the generous sum of money she offered.

"He eats like a horse. This will help. Hopefully this situation will only last a couple of weeks. I'll let you know if it's longer."

She handed them a slip of paper with a name and number on it.

"Very unlikely, but in the off chance that you don't hear from me in a month, call this number. This person will know what to do."

"But—"

Susan interrupted. "I really must go. But I appreciate this."

She called out a goodbye to Jacob as she headed for the door. They'd already said their real goodbyes in the car. Still, he came to the bedroom door and responded, adding a caution for her to be careful.

Susan exited the residence and hurried to her car, still hoping she'd made the right decision.

27

"Is she expecting you?" the man asked. He was lounging in the Lear jet's cushy seat, a drink in one hand.

"No. She thinks I'm dead."

The man laughed. "Guess that's gonna be a shock."

"Walt, can you be serious for a moment? That text I got is equivalent to a declaration of a third world war."

"Who sent it, do you know?"

"Her parents."

"And what about them? Are they on our to-do list?"

"No. At least not initially."

"And if they become part of our to-do list?"

"Then we'll do what's necessary."

"Will the others come?"

"Bet on it."

Walt chuckled. "Gonna be a party, then. Looking forward to it. Time to end all this nonsense."

"I agree. Ditch the drink and start getting ready. We touch down in thirty minutes."

28

Anders was on an outbound commercial flight less than an hour after receiving the text he hoped never to get. While he would have preferred a private chartered jet, it turned out that a commercial flight was available, and he grabbed one of the remaining seats. Not only did this save considerable money, it saved time. The private jet would have taken at least two hours, maybe more, to arrange. From that perspective, he felt lucky.

From the perspective of why he was on the plane, he felt anything but lucky. He let his mind drift back to the beginning. He'd been a young lawyer, fresh out of law school and just starting his practice. The young woman who'd approached him had offered several hypotheticals. He was too green to know which might be true, and which completely fabricated. But he diligently researched and answered everything she'd asked about. When she'd provided the burner phone and explained the warning code, he'd felt his first misgivings of what he'd gotten into. But as the years passed and nothing happened, he pushed all those initial concerns to the back of his mind.

His practice had flourished, in large part due to the referrals from the woman. She'd updated her instructions from time to time, but always reminded him of her expectations should he ever receive the warning code. In the beginning, the code would have come by telephone call. But it moved to a text message as technology changed. It was easy to forget about the code's implications when nothing ever happened. But he was acutely reminded of his commitment every time a new burner phone came, accompanied with a new set of instructions.

He checked his watch. He still had more than an hour before he reached Denver. He wondered if renting a car was something he could take care of in-flight. He signaled the attendant and asked. Twenty minutes later he'd completed his arrangements. Nothing left to do but mentally organize his post-arrival activities.

He closed his eyes to shut out unwanted distractions and began planning. Without being consciously aware of his actions, his hand touched the second burner phone tucked in his inside jacket pocket. He wondered when it would come to life. If he was honest with himself, he hoped the answer was never.

29

"Do you think we should have kept the boy with us?" Donner glanced in the rearview mirror as he asked the question. They'd been driving for what seemed like forever. They still had another half-hour or so before reaching their destination.

Anna looked at her husband. She'd been asking herself that question non-stop since she'd sent Cody to the cabin. She'd followed the original plan. One that had been created when Cody was barely five years old. So much time had passed. Things could be drastically different. The problem was, Susan had stopped communicating with her shortly after Tom had died. Anna knew about Tom's death and the events surrounding it. She'd never shared that information with Donner. Maybe she should have. She held her silence. His knowing now wouldn't change the situation they were in.

"He'll be all right. We've got to believe that. I'm just sorry we didn't have more time to get to know him. Perhaps we should have discouraged his research. I'm sure that's what triggered our current situation."

"Tell me again what happened," Donner asked, more to pass the time than because he really needed to hear it again.

Anna repeated what Cody had described to her, wondering again if she'd over-reacted. When Donner remained silent, she looked at him.

"What are you thinking?"

"I'm wondering if the names Walters or Winters had some type of system flag. I'm assuming Cody was researching both. What else would trigger the computer drama? But those names are so common. There must be thousands of people with those names. Maybe hundreds of thousands. Cody didn't even know that we knew his name was also Winters. He wasn't with us long enough for the topic to come up." He released a sad sigh. "If it had ever come up."

"True. But there aren't thousands of people with those names in Colorado. Perhaps that was the trigger? The location?"

"Maybe. We'll likely never know." He hesitated. "I can't help but wonder. If Susan and Jacob are still out there, are they now in even more danger?"

"They're still out there. I'd know if they weren't. I'd feel the emptiness. You have to believe that."

"But it's been years."

"Just over three."

"What?"

"Susan last contacted me after Tom was killed."

"You never told me! How was she? Had she been hurt? And Jacob? What did she say?"

"Focus on your driving dear. I'll tell you all I know. I'm sorry I didn't tell you earlier, but Susan asked me not to. She thought it would be safer for everyone. Things are different now."

"I'll say they are! So you haven't heard from her since Tom's death? You could at least have told me about that. It was such a shock when Cody mentioned it. Now I think about it, you didn't look nearly as surprised as I would have expected you to. That's because you already knew."

Donner's voice had become softer the longer he talked. Anna could tell he was nursing hurt feelings. She hastened to update him and console him at the same time. By the time she'd finished, they were turning the last corner before their destination, a small house in a quiet Denver neighborhood.

"There's a car in the driveway. Should there be?" Anna asked with alarm.

"I don't think so. Maybe we should go around the block and rethink this whole scheme."

Anna took note of the car's license plate as they passed. "It's a Colorado plate."

They stopped three houses down once they'd completed the circuit. They spent the next ten minutes arguing over whether they should approach the house. Then argued whether they should go together or only one go. They finally agreed that one should go, but again disagreed over who could play the best helpless senior in a bid to deflect suspicion. Finally, Anna opened her door and got out.

"I'm going. Stay here you old fool. Don't do anything stupid."

"Mind your mouth, woman. And don't you do anything stupid!"

Anna smiled slightly as she leaned back in to give her husband a kiss. Then she made her way along the sidewalk until she came even with the house. Taking a deep breath to steady her nerves, she walked up to the front door and pressed the doorbell. When the door opened, she just stared in shock.

"Mom! Come in quickly. Where's Dad?"

Susan stepped aside as she motioned for Anna to come into the house. She asked again about her father.

"He's waiting in the car. Three houses down. What are you doing here? Why didn't you call us? Is Jacob here? Is that your car? What's going on?"

"No time for all that now. We need to get Dad in here. Can he see you from where he's at?"

"Yes."

"Then step out and wave him to come."

Anna did as Susan instructed. She watched as Donner got out and started towards the house. He'd covered only half the distance when a small white sedan turned the corner and roared up the street. Susan heard the car and pulled Anna into the house.

"Stay!" she yelled as she ran down the drive towards her father.

Everything seemed to happen in slow motion. The white car slowed. Susan saw the barrel of a gun poke out an open window. She saw her father fall forward and registered the blast a moment later. The car gunned the engine and the tires squealed in protest as the car shot forward down the street. Susan hadn't even had time to draw her own weapon.

"Dad!"

She got to him within seconds, saying his name over and over. He was slow to respond. She was in full panic mode when she heard him cuss.

"Damn knee. Can never depend on it. What was all that ruckus? Susan? Is that you?"

"Dad? Are you all right?" Susan was running her hands over her father searching for blood and an injury.

"Of course I'm all right. Knee just gave out, that's all. Gonna have a bruise. I can tell you that."

Susan released her pent-up adrenalin with a laugh. "C'mon, let's get you up and into the house."

She helped her father to his feet and acted as a crutch until he got his balance and mobility back. Anna came onto the step to greet them as they approached the door.

"Get back inside. He's all right."

Once inside with the door closed, they all just stared at each other. Then as one, they came together in a long, fierce hug, each murmuring their own words of love and comfort.

30

ody worked through the rest of the papers. Most were legal documents that, even after reading twice, he couldn't understand. He set them aside. His objective mind understood they were important. His emotional state, particularly after realizing Anna and Donner were his grandparents, thought them useless to his immediate circumstances.

He glanced at college diplomas for both his parents, noting their majors, but again setting them aside as irrelevant. He wasn't sure what he was looking for, but he knew it wasn't what he was seeing. He continued sorting.

His birth certificate was in the stack. He studied it closely. Place of birth matched what he'd been told, and confirmed in his mind that the baby picture was him. He noted the name of Walters and wondered just when the family changed their name to Winters and why. Since he'd grown up with Winters, he assumed it had to have been shortly after his birth. Perhaps at the same time his parents left this area. *But why?* He rubbed his eyes. He was suddenly tired as well as confused. He didn't have much desire to look through the rest of the papers, but decided that since he'd started, he might as well finish.

There wasn't much. A few hand-written notes describing certain events, a couple greeting cards, a post card from the Grand Canyon, and a copy of the nursery rhyme that he'd memorized. He was pushing that paper aside when he noticed the numbers in the rhyme were written out. Not numerical like the copy from the chest. And this rendering was obviously very old. The paper had darkened, and the edges were curled. His version from the chest was on clean white paper.

"Odd," he murmured aloud. "If this is the original, why use numerical numbers when making the copy? Time saver? Or something more?"

Then it hit him. The first five digits had brought him to this area of Colorado. Although beyond belief, he was obviously meant to be here. But the last five digits. They were the mystery. Another flash of insight hit him. The safe he'd found required a five-digit passcode.

"No! It couldn't be! That would be too much!" His words echoed in the cabin. Even as his mind said no, his body moved to the box, and he retrieved the safe from it. Setting it on the table, he entered the digits in the order they appeared in the rhyme. A light he hadn't noticed before flashed green, virtually begging him to lift the lid. He did.

Inside was an envelope. He lifted it. Lighter than he expected, he quickly opened the unsealed flap and tipped the contents onto the table. A note and computer flash drive fell out. He ignored the flash drive and reached for the note. It was addressed to him.

Cody,

Congratulations on solving the puzzle of the rhyme. I'm sorry you had to work through everything, but it was the safest way I knew to ensure that, other than myself, you and only you found this. The flash drive contains information that has implications for the security of our nation. Some of the information may be outdated, but most is still relevant enough to be desired by those who seek power. It must never fall into their hands.

This information has kept our family safe, yet also put us in danger. It's why your father was killed. Yes, this letter has been updated to reflect recent events. I don't know the circumstances of how you came to be at our cabin and finding this, but you must never let this flash drive fall into any hands but yours or mine. Since it's still here, I've obviously not retrieved it. Therefore, it still poses a danger to you and your brother. Others, also. I ask that you destroy it. And do so before anyone knows or suspects you have it. They'll try to manipulate you. Tell you things to make you trust them. Don't. No matter what anyone says. What they claim I said. DO NOT GIVE THEM THIS DRIVE.

As of this update, please know that Jacob and I are still alive and waiting to reunite with you. Stay safe, son. I love you.

Mom

Cody looked for a date but found nothing to indicate when the letter had been written. Obviously within the last three years. It comforted him to know his mother and brother had been well at the time, but he still didn't know when that was. From his own life, he knew things could change rapidly.

He sat back and thought through the timeline of when he'd fled the farm, his time with Father Timothy, then working for Sal, and finally arriving in Colorado. Some things didn't fit neatly together, and he wondered why that was. But considering the entire set of coincidences and sheer luck that brought him here, he decided the universal forces were simply too mysterious to understand.

He picked up the flash drive, tossed it up and caught it. *Destroy it.* His mother's words echoed in his head. He wondered what was on it. He'd need a computer to find out and there wasn't one in the cabin. He chuckled. There wasn't even electricity. Should he go back into town and see if he could use a computer at the public library? If only because Anna had sent him away, he knew he couldn't go back there.

He started to stand, then sat again, conflicted over his course of action. Natural curiosity made him want to see what was on the drive. An ingrained sense of obedience told him to do as instructed and destroy the drive. But what then? Would that solve anything? Would it remove the danger?

Mom said danger to Jacob and me. But also to others. Who? Anna and Donner? Someone else?

He didn't want to cause his grandparents issues. Even though he hadn't had a chance to get to know them, he knew them to be family and that was enough. He wondered now if they were safe. What did they do after he'd left? Were they still at the house? If so, perhaps he should go back and be there to protect them. The problem was, he didn't know who or what he'd be protecting them from. And seriously, could he even provide any kind of protection?

His head was beginning to hurt from all the thoughts flowing through it. He was so preoccupied he didn't hear the car outside until two doors slammed. Fighting an immediate sense of panic, he shoved the drive into his front pocket, stood and ran to the window. Carefully moving the cloth drapery, he peeked outside. What he saw caused his heart rate to increase.

Two men were staring at the cabin. One motioned to the other who moved to the edge of the building. Cody assumed he was making his way around the back while the other waited. He knew he'd be trapped in a matter of moments. But he didn't know what to do.

"We know you're in there. Why don't you just come out and make this easy on all of us."

The man Cody was watching stayed where he was while calling out the words. He listened closely but couldn't hear the other man. Other than a window on the back side of the cabin, there was no other door. *Poor design,* Cody thought, then grimaced at the fleeting thought.

"Who are you and what do you want?" Cody called the words out. He wasn't sure the man could hear him through the closed door.

"Cody, is that you? Is your mother with you? No, she wouldn't be, otherwise she'd be the one talking. Do you know where she is?"

That the man knew his name startled Cody so badly that he opened the door without thinking.

"Who are you?" he demanded. "How do you know my name?"

"My name is Ray. I'm a friend of your mother."

Cody wasn't sure he believed the friend part. "Who's the other guy and where is he?"

Walt walked around to the front of the cabin and told Cody his name.

"How did you know to find me here? What do you want?"

"I expected to find your mother here, not you. I need to know where she is."

"I don't know where she is. And I don't know that I can trust you enough to tell you even if I did know."

"That's fair. Your mother and I worked together many years ago. There are people looking for her. She has information that's important to them. These people would do anything to get that information. Even kill. I need to know where she is."

The words his mother wrote drifted through Cody's head. *They'll try to manipulate you. Tell you things to make them trust you.*

"I don't know anything about any information. And I don't know where my mother is. I haven't seen her in three years or more. I don't even know if she's alive."

"I believe that you don't know where she is. I saw her only a few months ago. She confirmed you two hadn't communicated for almost three years. But that doesn't change that she's in danger. You, too. You should come with me. I'll keep you safe. I promised your mother I'd keep you safe."

Just then a shot rang out. A loud smack into the wood next to Cody's head sent him to the floor. He scrambled backward on hands and knees into the cabin slamming the door shut. He had no thought for the men outside. Moments later he heard more gun fire. Staying close to the floor, he hurried to the table and grabbed his mother's letter.

He scanned the contents quickly once more before throwing the letter into the stove's flames. He hesitated only a moment before reaching into his pocket and grabbing the flash drive. He tossed it into the fire just as the door burst open and Ray, followed by Walt, stormed into the cabin flinging the door shut behind them.

"Stay down! Not sure there's more than one." Ray ordered.

As if I'm going to stand up, Cody thought as he remained on the floor.

When nothing else happened for ten minutes, Walt suggested he go out and check the perimeter. Ray nodded without speaking, motioning for Cody to rise. Ray walked over to the table and glanced at the papers strewn about. He didn't disturb them but took his time looking at those that faced upward. Cody watched him, thankful he'd removed his mother's note. He didn't think anything left was too incriminating.

"Have you made the connections?" Ray asked.

"What do you mean?"

"I see the photos. You figure out the family tree? Where are your grandparents, by the way?"

Cody just stared at him. He didn't respond.

"C'mon, Cody. Things are moving fast. You need to trust me if any of us are going to get out of this situation alive. Your mother and brother included. Whoever made that shot? They're only the first of many who are coming. They want the information your mother has. If they knew about this cabin, it's likely they know other possible safe houses your mother set up. We need to find her."

"I told you. I don't know where she is. And I don't know anything about any information. It seems you do, though. What is it that's causing all this chaos?"

The two stared at each other. Cody refused to be intimidated by Ray's intensity. Finally, Ray shook his head and half-smiled.

"You're very like your mother, you know. She gives as good as she gets, too. More often, she gives more."

Still Cody didn't speak. Only waited.

"All right. I confess. I don't know what specific information your mother has. I can guess, but she never actually shared it with me. I'm telling the truth about the risk it poses to you and everyone's safety, though. If you have it or know where it is, you need to tell me."

"I don't know anything."

Ray looked at Cody for a long time, then nodded. "OK. I believe you. But we need to get you out of here. Grab your stuff."

Walt came in at that moment.

"No one else out there. No ID on the guy in the woods. Looks like a hired gun."

"What makes you say that?" Ray asked.

"Clothes, tattoos, choice of weapon."

Ray acknowledged the words with a look that Cody saw but couldn't interpret. He jumped slightly when Ray turned to him and repeated his instructions for Cody to grab his things. He turned to the table and pulled all the papers into a big pile.

"Hey!" Cody protested.

"Calm down. Just making it easier for you to bring them. Now get your stuff together. Do it!" Ray raised his voice slightly on the last bit.

It was enough to spur Cody into moving to the bed and grabbing his pack. Since he hadn't really unpacked anything, there wasn't much to do other than take the papers from Ray's hands and stuff them in his pack. He glanced around.

"Ready." Cody said, indicating he was willing to go with the men, even if he hadn't decided whether to fully trust them or not. "What about my car?"

"Anything important in it?"

"No. But the car itself is important to me."

"Leave it. If everything goes well, you'll be able to come back for it. Let's go."

Cody checked the stove, making sure the door was securely closed. The fire would burn down and go out, presenting no risk to the cabin. He went to the fridge and grabbed the remaining sandwich and bottle of water. He was torn between throwing the sandwich into the woods for the wildlife or keeping it to eat later. He decided to keep it. He gave one last glance around the cabin before following the men outside. As he locked the door, he wondered if he'd ever see the place again.

31

"Did you hear?"

"Hear what?"

"Our man was killed."

"How? When?"

"When he didn't check in, his partner went looking for him. Why they split up, I don't know. Anyway, found him dead in the woods by some cabin."

"Cabin, you say?"

"Yes. Why?"

"Did he check the cabin?"

"No. It was locked. Didn't think he should break in."

"Dammit!"

"Boss, what's the big deal? Whoever was there was obviously gone by the time our man showed up. We don't even know for sure it was the woman. I paid the man and told him to disappear. I'll make sure he does, if you know what I mean."

"Sloppy. This whole thing has been sloppy. I should never have listened to you. Just because you knew her years ago doesn't mean you know her now. And we still don't have the information. If we don't get it soon, you and I will be the ones to disappear."

The two men avoided looking at each other. Both were thinking similar thoughts and didn't want to see those thoughts reflected on the other's face.

"We should go to Denver," the first man said.

"Why Denver?"

"Whether it was her at the cabin or not, Denver is her center of operations. Always has been. She's there somewhere. We've just got to find her."

"Denver is a big place."

"Yes, but I have some ideas on where to start looking."

"How long to get there?"

"Too long if we drive. But I've got a buddy who has a plane. I'm sure I can convince him he'd like to fly to Denver."

"Call him. Let's go."

32

Susan pulled back and looked at her parents. She was struck by how old they looked. She had a mental picture of a much younger couple.

"Was it you who sent the code?"

"Yes," Anna answered. "We didn't know what else to do. Were we wrong to do so?"

"Tell me what happened."

Anna did, but not before Susan interrupted her. "Cody? Cody was with you? He's OK?"

"Yes, yes dear. He's fine. Or at least he was when he left for the cabin. But I'm sure he's still OK. He seems a wonderful young man. I'm sorry we didn't get to know him a bit more."

Although Susan wanted to hear more about her son, before Anna could get completely distracted, she redirected her focus.

"Tell me again what the computer screen said?"

"I can only tell you what Cody told me. I didn't see it for myself. He'd already pulled the plug by the time I got there. That was smart, don't you think?" Anna repeated the scenario Cody gave her. But then came back to the gunshot. "Do you think they were shooting at us? Or was it just some random thing. Scary to believe that neighborhoods like this have devolved to random drive-by shootings."

Susan thought for a moment. "It's hard to say which it was. I thought this place was secure. To be honest, I'm surprised the police aren't already here. Is there no one at home who would have called? But either way, we need to leave. If the police show soon, they're going to go from house to house. We don't want to be here to answer questions."

"But where will we go?"

"To the cabin, first. We'll pick up Cody. Then I have another place in mind."

"We've spent hours getting here and now you want to go back? More hours in the car? I'm not liking that." Donner's voice expressed his frustration.

"Hush, old man. We'll do whatever Susan thinks is best." Anna scolded her husband.

"We'll all go in my car. That way you two can snooze if you like. I'll pull your car into the garage here. It will be fine. Stay here while I take care of that."

Susan took the keys from her father and hurried out to move the cars. She was back within ten minutes.

"Anything you need from your car?"

"Yes, we have a suitcase in the trunk. Also a bag with some snacks." Anna responded while patting Donner's hand.

"I'll retrieve that, then we'll get out of here. I'll leave it to you two to figure out who's in front."

Susan quickly took care of transferring the items to her car. Then she went to the refrigerator and collected several juice and water bottles that were there. She turned to her parents.

"Ready?"

"Yes. But, dear, where's Jacob?"

"He's safe. I'll tell you more when we're on our way. We really need to go."

The three of them left the house and piled into Susan's car, Donner in the front. As she was pulling away from the curb, she saw a patrol car turn onto their street. Its lights were not flashing, and it seemed not to be in any hurry. Considering the earlier gunshot, Susan thought that strange but didn't waste time thinking about it. She glanced at it, as anyone would, as she passed it and continued driving. It took another ten minutes for her to realize that the person driving the patrol car was not in uniform. Her foot pressed the accelerator seemingly by its own accord. Susan glanced in the rearview mirror and breathed a sigh of relief when she saw no cars following her. She took several turns within the neighborhood before finally setting a more direct course for the main highway.

Anna and Donner quickly drifted to sleep, and Susan let them enjoy their rest. Or at least, enjoy it as much as the car seats allowed. The quiet gave her time to think. She'd been overjoyed to see her parents. She couldn't believe she'd be seeing Cody in just a few more hours. It had been so long! The drive-by shooting and the non-uniformed officer still concerned her, but she was certain she wasn't being tailed. Therefore, she set those situations aside and focused on the next moves once they'd retrieved Cody.

She glanced at her watch. She needed to check in with Jacob. Make sure all was well with him. She still questioned whether leaving him with his friend's grandparents was wise. Too late to change that now. She hoped Anders was up to his role. She hadn't spoken to the lawyer for at least two years. She'd updated her instructions when she and

Jacob had settled, but that wasn't through a direct communication. She had no idea what his current status was. She'd have to trust that all would work out.

Susan felt the memories flood through her as she absorbed the familiar landscape. She was coming up to the turn-off for the cabin. She slowed to make sure she didn't miss it. The twilight was making things difficult to see. *Yes! There!* She pulled off the highway onto the dirt road. She thought she saw several tire marks on the track, and she felt a light film of perspiration form between her breasts. Once she cleared the first curve, she pulled over and stopped. She knew she couldn't be seen from the highway here. She needed time to think. But first, she'd check in on Jacob. She slid out of the car as quietly as she could, not wanting to wake her parents.

C'mon. Answer! She counted the rings. On the fifth, Jacob answered. He sounded out of breath.

"Mom! Sorry! I didn't have the phone on me."

"Everything okay?"

"Yes. I was just in another room. Didn't immediately hear the phone. Are you good? Nothing wrong?"

"I'm fine. How's it going with Goober and his grandparents?"

"Just great. They're really cool for being old people."

"Jacob!"

She heard him laugh, then he sobered. "Really, Mom. Everything is good. School's going well. The basketball team had a couple of rough games but we're back on track now. I'm so glad you let me stay here. But I'm worried about you. Are you sure everything is good with you?"

"Yes. Listen, Jacob. Please remain very aware of your surroundings. Anything weird happens. Anything that sets your spidey-senses tingling. You contact me. You understand? Immediately. Use the code."

"Okaaay." Jacob stretched the word out. "Mom, what's going on?"

"I just need to know you're staying safe. Don't do anything you know I'd frown on."

"I'll be good."

Jacob said it in a little boy voice, more to antagonize his mother than because he was trying to reassure her. He heard her snort on the other end of the phone. He knew she was aware of his tactics.

"One more thing," she said as she glanced at the car and noted both parents were now awake and looking around. As they saw her, she waived then pointed at the phone.

"What's up?" Jacob heard the change in her voice and reacted to it.

"You may be approached by someone. His name is Anders. If he does come to you, do what he says, OK? Don't argue with him. His instructions are my instructions. Got that?"

"Who is this guy? How will I know him? What's he want?"

"He's a friend. That's all you need to know for now. He'll know you. If he approaches, he will tell you things that he would only know if I had told him. You understand? Personal things about your childhood. No one else would know these things except us. Family."

"Is he family?"

"Not by blood. But I've known him since before your father. He's as much family to me as anyone."

"An old boyfriend?"

"Jacob! This is important! Be serious. You are still in danger, maybe more so because I'm not with you to protect you. If Anders does approach you, it's because he knows it's the only thing to do to keep you safe. Do whatever he tells you to do. Promise me!"

"All right, all right. I get it, Mom." Jacob's voice was sulky.

"I'm waiting."

She heard a sigh. "I promise, Mom."

"See that you keep it. Honey, I've got to go. Stay safe. I love you."

"Love you too. And you stay safe also, you hear me?"

"I will. 'Bye, Jacob."

Susan disconnected before Jacob could respond. She hoped he'd remember and do as she instructed. She hoped Anders would never think it necessary to approach her son. She hoped a lot of things. But she needed to focus on the present. She returned to the car.

"Good to see you two awake. You need to get out and stretch a bit before we go on?"

Both parents agreed that was a good idea and exited the car to walk out any kinks from their naps. Susan watched them, struck again at how they'd aged. Less than two minutes later, they climbed back into their respective seats, Anna suggesting they get on with their journey.

Susan put the car in gear and proceeded slowly up the track. Still concerned about all the tire marks she'd seen, she didn't say anything to her parents, not wanting to worry them. It wasn't long before they arrived at the clearing. Susan saw Cody's car and smiled that he was still driving the same one his dad had helped him purchase. She maneuvered her car so it was facing outward. Even as she hoped the strange vehicle wasn't scaring Cody, her mind questioned whether he was in the cabin. Something seemed off.

"You should stay in the car," she murmured to her parents.

"No way," Donner responded. "We're all going at once."

Rather than waste time arguing, she opened her door and stepped out. As she walked towards the cabin, she glanced around. Things seemed too quiet for her comfort. She reached behind her and pulled her handgun from its holster.

Anna saw it. "Is that necessary?"

"Shhhhh. Stay behind me," Susan whispered, then raised her voice.

"Cody? Cody? You in there?" A hesitation. "Cody? It's Mom. Answer me, please, if you're in there."

Silence greeted her. She hurried up the steps, not caring that her parents couldn't keep up. She turned the knob, realizing it was locked. She turned back to her parents who'd made it to the bottom of the steps.

"Do either of you have a key?"

"I should have one on my keyring." Donner fished in his pocket and pulled out his keys and fumbled with them. Finding what he was looking for, he held it out to his daughter.

Susan took the key and quickly opened the door. One glance told her the place was empty. She stepped in and looked around. Again, memories flooded her, but she pushed them down. She saw the metal box and safe on the table and immediately understood the significance. When she realized they were empty, both hope and fear fought for dominance.

"Stove's still got a bit of warmth to it," Donner's words interrupted her thoughts. She looked in his direction. He had the door open and was peering into it. "Judging by the coals, I'd say the fire hasn't been fed for several hours."

They all looked around the room.

"No sign of any struggle," Donner's words echoed Susan's thoughts.

"If his car is here, why isn't he?" Anna asked, slightly confused.

Susan thought of the tire marks she'd seen.

"He either left with someone, or he's out in the woods."

"But who would he leave with? Nobody knows about this place. And he said he didn't know anyone in Colorado. Why would he go off by himself into the woods?" Anna's voice got more quiet and hesitant.

"I don't know, Mom. But why don't you two get the fire going a bit. I'm going to look around outside before it gets any darker."

She exchanged a look with her father. He nodded and turned to Anna.

"Here, why don't you sit and rest. I'll get some wood." He guided her to the easy chair then followed Susan out onto the porch. Before he reached down for some wood, he said quietly.

"Be careful."

"I will. Stay alert."

Susan noticed the mark on the door by her father's head but didn't comment. She waited until her father returned inside before stepping up and examining the wound to the wood. *Definitely a bullet,* she thought as she rubbed the area and saw the embedded slug. She didn't bother to dig it out. Knowing it was there was enough.

She hurried to her car and rummaged in the glove box for a flashlight. She studied the ground of the clearing, then walked slowly around the house looking for anything that would tell her its story. The ground was leafy and spongy, not allowing for any footprints to show. The one slightly muddy area where prints would show was clear of any disturbance. Either an intruder had seen and avoided the area, or no one had been behind the cabin. Susan didn't know which scenario was more probable.

She widened her circle, looking for tracks going into the woods. She stopped abruptly when she spotted a large boot print pointing away from the cabin. She approached cautiously, scanning the area. She followed the trail of prints into deep foliage until she could no longer see them. Turning in a circle, she realized the cabin's front door was in a direct sightline from where she stood. Likely whoever had put the bullet into the door frame had stood here.

It was getting too dark to make out many details, even with her high-powered flashlight. She sighed and turned to go back to the cabin. Just before she took her first step, she saw a flash in the undergrowth. Stooping down, she ran her hand over the area until she found what had caused it. A shell casing. *Sloppy*, she thought as she picked it up and examined it. *Not from a rifle. Looks like a 9mm. Definitely not what's in the doorframe. Two different guns. Two people?*

She ran her flashlight over the area again. This time she noted the flatness of the undergrowth. Then she saw a dark spot and leaned in to study it. *Blood.* She took a deep breath to calm herself. There was no reason to believe the blood was Cody's. But if not, whose? Susan didn't know if Cody owned a gun. *If he did, would he use it on someone?* Three years was a long time. Who knew what he'd experienced or become.

She shook her head. *Mom said he was a nice boy. That doesn't sound like a killer. But then again, desperate events create desperate actions.*

Realizing the darkness was hiding any more clues, she stepped forward to return to the cabin. Two steps later she stopped, then turned back. She directed her flashlight around the area until she found what she was looking for. She could just make out the path someone had taken from the spot where she'd found the shell casing and blood. While her emotional brain screamed at her to follow, her logical mind knew she would lose the trail in the dark. She turned back to the cabin. The only real question in her mind was whether to stay the night or leave immediately.

She stepped into the cabin and saw her parents sitting comfortably in the chairs by the fire. The picture they created provided Susan all she needed to decide to stay the night. They needed their rest. And she needed to rest also. Besides, she'd be better able to explore things in the daylight.

She told the parents to stay where they were. That she'd bring in their belongings. She hurried to do so, grabbing her own things and the bag of snacks. Once inside, she locked the door and made sure the window coverings were in place.

"I'll check the fridge. Maybe there's some food in it. If not, our dinner will be whatever snacks you put together."

"Whatever, dear." Her mother's voice reflected the fatigue the woman was feeling. Susan had a moment of guilt for dragging them all the way back to where they'd been. But she'd had no choice. Staying in the safe house didn't seem safe at all. Not with the shooting and odd police car thing.

Susan opened the refrigerator and immediately noted the lack of sustenance it offered.

"Snacks it is," she told her parents. "We'll eat then settle for the evening. You two can have the bed. I'll camp on the floor."

"Oh, dear. That won't be at all comfortable," her mom responded at the same time her father said the two women should take the bed.

"I'm younger. I can handle it better. You two take the bed. No arguments." Susan's tone made it clear she would accept no compromise.

"As you wish," her father said as he stood and helped his wife out of her chair. Together they walked to the table. Anna grabbed the snack bag and started pulling items out.

"Not much here, but it should get us through the night. Can you tell us about Jacob, now?"

Susan did. When she'd finished, her parents had several questions which she answered to the best of her ability.

"I can't wait to meet him," Anna said.

"Hopefully, soon." Even as she said the words, Susan wasn't sure how true they were. But she hoped they would comfort her parents.

Donner put an end to the happy conversation.

"Now tell us what's going on. Do you know what caused the computer thing? Is this related to your old intelligence days? Are we really in danger? And if so, what exactly do you think is going to happen?"

Susan looked at her father for a long time, torn between total honesty and some version that would not overly alarm her parents.

"Don't whitewash it, girl. We need to know."

With a sigh, Susan explained.

"You think Cody has the flash drive?" Donner asked when she'd finished.

"I don't know. Either way, I fear he's truly in danger. It's obvious he left with someone. Who, and whether by choice, those are unanswered questions."

"How do we finish this once and for all?"

"I'm afraid there may be only one way."

Donner was silent for a moment, then said quietly, "Kill or be killed."

Silence greeted his words.

33

"Where are we going?" Cody asked Ray. He was in the back seat. Walt was driving and Ray sat in the front passenger seat.

They'd been driving for almost two hours. Cody thought they were headed towards Denver, but he wasn't certain.

"Denver."

"Why there?"

"It's highly probable your mother is there. Just need to figure out where."

"You have any idea where to look? Denver's a big place." Cody doubted Ray would know where to find his mother, but he still felt a small thrill of anticipation that he might see her soon. "Tell me again how you know her?"

Although Ray had given him a brief explanation of his relationship with Susan, Cody still had doubts whether he could trust these two men. The words his mother had written kept repeating in his head like the lyrics to a bad song. He wanted more. And he wanted to know if his father's death tied into any of this. When Ray didn't respond, Cody pushed him again. Finally, Ray told Cody more of the history.

"So Mom was some sort of spy. I think I already figured that out. But these people who are after her are spies, too? Our spies? Why would they come after Mom? Aren't they all supposed to be on the same side?"

"The world is a bit more complex than that."

"But you worked with Mom? You're also a spy?"

Ray laughed. "I was. Once. I'm retired now."

"I didn't think spies could retire."

"Your mom did."

Cody was silent while he absorbed that simple truth. "What about Dad? Was he a spy?"

"No. But he knew what your mother was involved in before they married. He still married her, believing they could make a peaceful life together. And they had."

"Until it all fell apart." Cody again experienced the grief of seeing his father's dead and burned body. He glanced at Walt. "What about you? Are you a spy? Or were you one?"

"No and No." Walt answered, not volunteering anything further.

Cody debated asking more but decided not to. He wasn't sure he wanted to know the answers he might get. Walt was a bit younger than Ray and seemed like he regularly worked out. Cody drew his own conclusions.

"Cody. This is important. All our lives might depend on this. I need to know if your mother gave you anything. Maybe you're not even aware that you have the information she has kept for so many years. But somewhere, somehow, she's managed to control the situation through this information. You need to give it to me if you have it."

"I don't know what you're talking about. Really. I don't. She never said anything to me. The only papers I have are what you saw on the table."

While that wasn't strictly true, Cody believed it was close enough. He made his statements with authority. In any event, he no longer had the flash drive. He'd tossed it into the stove's fire. He only hoped it had completely burned. He would never divulge that he had it at one time. What difference would that make? It was gone now, and he didn't even know what was on it. He shifted his position. When he did, he felt a small poke from something in his pocket. He moved so he could slide his hand in.

When he felt the Allen Wrench memories flooded into his mind. The Lincoln log, the decoder ring, the wrench, and the belt buckle. He'd never figured out the meaning of any of the items. Yet he still had them. Could they somehow be tied to the flash drive he'd tossed into the fire? He doubted he'd ever know. Maybe they were just random objects from his childhood. But he rejected that thought. He was sure they had meaning. But what? Should he tell Ray? He shook his head as he also rejected that thought.

"What?" Ray asked.

"What, what?" Cody responded, confused.

"You shook your head, like maybe you'd thought of something."

Cody's heartbeat increased. He took a quiet breath to calm himself.

"I did? Wasn't aware of it. No. Nothing's come to me. I still don't know anything about any information."

Ray was quiet. He shifted back around and didn't look at Cody. But after a few moments he said quietly, "have it your way, kid."

No one spoke for another half hour, until Ray told Walt to stop at the next service station. They could all do with a stretch, and they should gas up the car. Twenty minutes later, Walt took an exit and they pulled into a gas station. Ray turned to look at Cody.

"Take care of whatever you need to take care of. But don't do anything stupid. You really are safer with us than on your own."

Cody gave a brief nod as he opened his door to exit the car.

34

Anders watched the game with interest. Jacob was a talented basketball player. His team was ahead by several points and the game clock showed two minutes remaining. Anders had no concerns over which school would take the trophy. He did have concerns over how he would keep an eye on Jacob throughout the celebrations that would follow. *I can only do my best,* he thought as he studied the crowd in the gymnasium one more time.

So far, he'd seen nothing that indicated evil was lurking. That's how he'd categorized it. Evil. Susan had been blunt. Jacob's life was in danger. And from people who should be working to secure the nation, not tear it apart. He wondered again how he'd gotten drawn into the intrigue. But he knew, deep down, he'd wanted something more than the boring law practice he'd dedicated his life to. His youthful yearning made Susan's offer too good to turn down. He just hoped that now reality had set in, he wouldn't completely mess up. He had no training for this lifestyle. His talent was looking at pages of facts and arcane law and finding the one kernel of hope to hang a case on. He was very successful at that. Secret spy stuff? Not so much.

And even less so now that the years had caught up with him. He wasn't sure he could dodge a car coasting towards him at slow speed, let alone a fist or something worse.

He shook his head. *It probably won't come to that. Susan said no one knew Jacob was here. That increased his safety, right? I'll only need to maintain surveillance and report back that all is well. Easy-peasy.*

The game buzzer sounded, startling Anders out of his thoughts. He checked the scoreboard. Jacob's team had won by fifteen points. Everyone was pouring off the bleachers and onto the court. Anders couldn't see Jacob in the chaos. His heartbeat and breathing increased. He stood and scanned the crowd.

There! Anders watched as Jacob skillfully avoided the local news cameras pointed his way by keeping his head down and pretending to deal with uniform and shoe issues. *Clever.* The coach quickly rounded everyone up and herded them to the locker room. Just as Anders thought that would provide a reprieve, he noticed two men hovering in a corner by an exit door. They looked completely out of place. Anders wasn't sure why they did. It was just some vibe they put out. He was convinced they didn't belong, and he watched them closely, careful to not actually stare at them.

When they moved to mingle with the crowd and follow the team towards the locker rooms, Anders climbed over the bleachers to the court without being consciously aware he was doing it. He was so focused on the two men he didn't see how the crowd shifted as two rambunctious students pushed through. One rammed into his shoulder spinning him around into the other student who lost his balance and fell. Anders fell also. Others were tripping over them and with the constant push and pull of the crowd, soon the number of bodies on the floor increased. Anders struggled to regain his footing. By the time he did, the team was gone. And so were the two men he'd spotted.

Feeling desperate, Anders pushed his way against the streaming kids. When he reached the locker room door, he was turned away by uniformed security. They ignored his questions about the two men, simply telling him to move along.

Not wanting to draw further attention to himself, Anders decided to wait for the team to exit the gym. He'd approach Jacob then. Introduce himself. Prove that he was sent by the boy's mother. All would work out.

He positioned himself at what he thought was the most likely exit point and waited. Twenty minutes later, members of the team began to leave the building, their hair still wet from their showers. Anders barely held his patience as the boys met up with various friends or parents. But still Jacob didn't emerge.

Finally, when Anders realized that almost the entire team had left the building, he hurried up to one of the boys.

"Excuse me. I was waiting for Jake." Susan had warned him not to use Jacob. "Is he still in the locker room?"

The kid looked at him with some suspicion. "No. He left with a couple of guys. Never seen them before and Jake didn't introduce us."

"A couple of guys? Kids or men?"

"Men. Why? Who are you? What's Jake to you? Haven't seen you around before."

"I'm a friend. Please, can you describe the men Jake went with?"

The boy did, and Anders felt nauseated. "Thank you," he said as he turned away.

"Hey! Who were those guys? Jake didn't look happy to see them. In fact, he looked kinda scared. Is he okay?"

"I'm sure he is," Anders said hastily. "Thanks for your help."

He hurried away before the boy could ask or say anything further that would delay him even more. As it was, he was convinced he'd lost Jacob. In addition to his concern for Jacob, was his utter fear of telling Susan what had happened.

35

The small Lear jet touched down and taxied to the non-commercial side of the Denver airport. The man looked at his partner and spoke.

"OK, genius. How we gonna find the woman?"

"She'll come to us."

"And why would she do that?"

"Because we have her son."

"What? How?"

"Picked him up after the school basketball championship game. Got him safely tucked away."

"But how did you know where the kid was?"

"I've been keeping an eye on all the local happenings. Saw a brief news story about a high school's multi-year basketball playoff success. It was only for a second, and he was slightly turned away from the camera, but I saw a kid who looked so much like Susan, had to be related. Did some research. Found a familiar name. Put two and two together."

"And got five. Seriously? That's it? A second's view of some kid?"

"I've got the son. Positive. Trust me. I can't tell you the details, but I've got the son. She'll come to us."

"And what if you screwed up? What if it isn't her kid? Player on a successful high school team missing? The cops will be all over this!"

"No they won't. I'll take care of that. The only one who will be all over this is Susan. And she'll do anything to protect her son. Mother's instinct and all. We'll get the information. Everything will work out as planned."

"It better. I don't fancy a long prison term."

The first man didn't say anything. If this didn't work out, he wouldn't have to worry about prison. He'd be dead long before a prison sentence came into the picture.

36

The vibration in Susan's pocket woke her. She sat up more fully in the easy chair glancing at the bed as she did so. Her parents were sound asleep. She pulled the phone from her pocket and read the text message several times, her brain trying to process what she saw.

J gone. 2 men. ?? Sorry. 74932.

The number at the end told her the text was from Anders. But even without the code, she knew it. Anders was supposed to be watching Jacob. Keeping him safe. But obviously he'd failed. She barely kept herself from leaping out of the chair and rushing to her car. She glanced at her watch, then quickly typed a reply.

Call. 5m.

She didn't bother with her own numerical code. She knew Anders would do as instructed. She got up and quietly stepped outside the cabin and walked some distance away. The cell service wasn't the best, but she had enough signal to complete the call.

Her burner phone rang.

"Tell me."

Anders did, all the while profusely apologizing.

"Stop with the apologies. They serve no purpose. When did you last see him? And describe the kid who told you about the men."

Anders complied.

Goober. Anders talked to Goober. What are the odds? But when Jacob doesn't come home after a reasonable time, will they sound an alarm? Of course they will. They might already have done so. Why didn't Anders call me sooner? Susan's mind was spinning. She felt completely out of control. She needed to act, and act now. But do what? She still didn't know the story with Cody. And now Jacob was also missing. Both taken. But by whom?

One thing was for sure. She couldn't stay at the cabin. But she also didn't want to involve her parents any more than they already were. Having them with her would only complicate things further. After everything that had happened, she decided they would be safer at the cabin than anywhere else. Doubtful anyone would circle back this way. But they needed supplies.

She gave Anders new instructions then disconnected. She decided that since she was outside and it was light enough to see, she would finish her investigation from last night. She headed to where she'd found the shell casing and seen the blood. Regardless of what she might find, she'd return to the cabin and update her parents on the situation. Twenty minutes later, with no additional insight, she was back at the cabin. Her parents were up and both expressed relief when she came through the door. Susan described the recent events.

"We'll go with you!" her father declared.

"No. It's better I go alone. Anders is on his way here. He's bringing supplies. You'll be safer here than with me. And I won't have to worry as much."

"And this Anders fellow? He's from your past?"

"Yes, but not in the way you think. He's a lawyer. He's handled my affairs since my days in the intelligence field. Since before Tom. If anything happens to me, he has instructions. You'll be taken care of. And so will the boys."

"We should be taking care of you, not the other way around. And right now, the future of Cody and Jacob appear to be well and truly in question."

"Donner! Don't say such things!" Anna protested.

"Well, it's true! There's no denying it. And I'm not sure our daughter can fix that. Talented as she is."

Before her parents could devolve into a full-blown argument, Susan intervened and tried to calm the situation. It took a bit of effort, but soon the three of them were collaborating on a plan of action.

A half-hour later, she was in her car driving towards Denver.

37

Cody sat up and looked around with interest as they entered the outskirts of Denver. It wasn't how he'd pictured it in his mind. He expected to be on the top of a mountain. After all, it was called the mile-high city. But he now realized the city sat in a basin surrounded by mountains. He couldn't decide if he liked that better or was disappointed the city he imagined didn't exist. Nevertheless, it was exciting to be here and the thought that he might soon see his mother filled him with a mixture of need and hope.

He listened as Ray gave Walt directions, wondering at the destination. He was confused when they turned down a residential street and pulled into the driveway of a small house.

"What's this?"

"A possible stopping place for your mother."

"Mom's here?" Cody's voice squeaked and he quickly coughed and cleared his throat to mask the sound. He was relieved when Ray didn't comment.

Walt got out and went to the door. After a bit of fumbling, he opened it and stepped into the house. Watching him from the back seat, Cody wondered if Walt had picked the lock somehow. He doubted either Ray or Walt had a key.

Walt was gone only a couple of minutes. He slid into the driver's seat and reported the house empty but a car in the garage. Ray cursed softly.

"We can't leave our car here. I was hoping to put it in the garage. Any papers in the car?"

"Yes. Registration says Donner and Anna Winters."

"Susan's parents." Ray said the words at the same time Cody blurted out, "My grandparents!"

As if Cody hadn't spoken, Ray continued, "That means she was here. They must have all left in her car."

"Unless the grandparents were taken by someone else," Walt responded.

"Doubtful. But not totally improbable."

Ray turned to Cody. "Any idea where they might have gone?"

"Why would I know that?"

"Think, Cody. If your grandparents' car is here, that means they were here. Which means they came after they sent you to the cabin. Either your mom was already here or someone else was and they now have your grandparents."

"But why would someone take them?"

"To use as leverage. But I think your mom was here or came shortly after they arrived, and all left together. Where would they go?"

"Maybe back to the cabin?" Cody asked hesitantly. When Ray didn't respond, he felt foolish for mentioning it and sank back into his seat.

Ray looked at Walt. "Let's get out of here before some nosey neighbor comes asking questions."

"Right."

Walt backed out into the street and accelerated towards the corner. As he slowed for the stop sign, a patrol car pulled up across the intersection. Ray glanced at it, then did a quick doubletake before he bent his head and looked to the floor.

"Turn right here. Take it easy. No drama. Don't get the attention of patrol car's occupant."

Walt did as instructed. When they were half-way down the street, with Walt glancing in his side and rearview mirror multiple times, he asked Ray what that was all about.

"I recognized the driver of the patrol car. He wasn't in uniform and that caught my eye. I looked closer. It's not a local officer. I only hope he didn't see me. But it confirms the house is being watched. Which means the wrong people know about it. If Susan was here, she won't be coming back. If she wasn't here, but does come, things are going to get ugly. Count on it."

"What's going on?" Cody asked from the back seat.

"Never mind," Ray responded. "Just stay low in your seat and keep your seatbelt fastened. We may need to do a little race car driving."

Cody snorted. "Don't talk to me as if I were five."

"Noted. But do as I say."

Cody checked that his seatbelt was fastened, then slid down in his seat a bit. "Are we going to the cabin?"

"No. Whatever is going to happen, it's going to happen here in Denver."

"What do you mean by that?"

"Cody. I'm going to ask you one more time. Did your mother give you anything to keep for her? Or did you find something in the cabin besides the papers I saw on the table?"

"No. I already told you. I don't know what you're talking about."

Cody was careful to keep his voice neutral. Non-defensive. He was beginning to fully realize that while he had followed his mother's instructions and destroyed the flash drive, that act may or may not have put him in deeper danger. And he was again questioning whether being with Ray and Walt was in his best interest. The fact Ray kept going on and on about the information made him wonder if Ray really wanted it for his own benefit, and not to keep Cody or his mother safe.

He didn't react when Ray told Walt to find a motel, but his mind started working at the possibility of getting away from these two men. His thoughts kept him quiet as the car traversed the streets of Denver's suburbs.

38

Jacob didn't bother to struggle against the two men. They were obviously larger and stronger than him. He figured a confrontation would only lead to him being injured. Worse, students around him might be injured. He tried to catch Goober's eye as he left with the men, hoping to send a message that his leaving wasn't voluntary. He wasn't sure Goober got the message.

His biggest concern was whether he'd have an opportunity to send his mom a coded text. He knew he had to do that soon. Before they realized he had a phone and took it away. In fact, he was amazed they hadn't already checked him for one, but he counted that a blessing.

They hadn't wasted any time in pushing him into the backseat of a car. One slid in next to him, the other quickly got into the driver's seat and pulled out of the space they'd stashed the car. One part of Jacob's mind wondered how they'd managed to get the car so close to the gym's back door without someone stopping them. Another observed the car's acceleration once on the main street. No possibility of escaping the vehicle now. They were going too fast. He focused on trying to get as much information as he could.

"Who are you guys? What do you want with me?"

"Shut up." The man next to him spoke roughly. He was the bigger of the two and if Jacob was honest with himself, the one he feared the most. But he persisted.

"Are you sure you have the right kid? Maybe you wanted someone else. I'm new to the area. Haven't had time to make a lot of enemies."

"Don't be a wiseass. I said shut up. Don't make this harder."

"Harder than what? Where are you taking me?"

"Some place you'll never be found, if you don't do as my buddy says and shut up," the driver said.

Jacob contemplated that. He was scared, but he knew from watching TV shows that whatever they wanted him for, he was more valuable alive. He decided to push for information. Any small thing might be helpful. How, he didn't know. But he knew he had to try.

"Yeah? Well, you won't kill me. I'm useless to you dead. So why not tell me what you want. Maybe I can help."

"We want your mom, and the information she has. Can you help with that?"

"Shut up, Butch!"

The man beside Jacob reached out and cuffed the driver on the side of the head. It caused the man to swerve, but he quickly regained control of the car, cursing as he did so.

Jacob thought Butch was probably not the guy's real name, but he filed it away in his memory anyway, along with a detailed description of the man. He was glad now that his mother had made him play the various memory games that required a quick look at items followed by distractions, followed by asking for detailed descriptions of the objects. He'd thought the games stupid and participated only to keep his mother from getting more annoyed with him. He realized now that she'd been training his brain for just such a moment as this without really telling him she was doing so.

He wondered if his mom was okay. He'd just talked to her the night before. She'd sounded funny but wouldn't share anything with him. There'd always been a small part of him that didn't believe they were in any danger. That his mother used the tactic to keep him in line. After today's event, he now understood the truth. But understanding and doing something about it were two very different things. He had to figure out how to warn his mom and how to get away. And he knew he had to do both soon, or all hope of completing either task would disappear.

He glanced out the window. He wasn't familiar enough with the Denver area to know where they were. Even if he did, he wasn't sure how much help that would be to him. Particularly since he didn't know their ultimate destination. But he made a half-hearted attempt to observe landmarks that might later help him.

They left the city and traveled deep into the suburbs. Jacob stopped trying to remember things about their route. He could never see the street signs fast enough or long enough to read them, and all the houses looked the same to him. He felt all hope receding.

The driver suddenly braked and turned into the driveway of a home. Jacob looked around the neighborhood with interest.

"Get out and don't be stupid," his seat mate told him.

Jacob opened the door and stepped out of the car. Before he could contemplate doing anything, the man was out and had a strong hold of his arm. Jacob was hustled up the walk and to the front door. Using a key, the man opened the door and shoved Jacob in before calling over his shoulder.

"Ditch the car then get back here as soon as you can."

He didn't bother to verify his instructions were being followed. He stepped into the house and closed the door. Jacob stood in the center of the small living room.

"Why are we here? And just where are we?"

"Your mother knows this place. She'll know where to come for you."

The man's words gave Jacob hope, but his next words crushed that hope as quickly as it blossomed.

"Once we get what we want from her, neither of you will have any value to us."

Jacob didn't need an explanation. He knew what the man meant. His first fear was for his mom, followed quickly by fear for his own life and a regret that he wouldn't see Cody again. He turned slightly from the man and stared at the window which was covered by dark drapery.

"You have a phone? Of course you do. All teenagers have phones. Pull it out."

Jacob was surprised but did what the man asked.

"What's your usual way of communicating with your mother? Text or phone call?"

When Jacob didn't answer, the man repeated his question more aggressively and took a step closer to him.

"Usually text."

"Then send her one telling her you need her. No funny business. Tell her you're at the safe house. She'll understand."

"Safe house?"

"Just do it! And let me see it before you send it."

Jacob composed his text.

N3ed Help. At saf3ho7se. Pleas4 come.

The man stepped up and looked over Jacob's shoulder. "What's with the numbers? Some kind of code?"

"No. Just nervous. My fingers are fumbling." Jacob hoped the man would believe him. "I can fix it, if you want."

"Just send it."

Jacob breathed a quiet sigh of relief and hit send before the man changed his mind. As soon as the man heard the swoosh sound that the text had been sent, he grabbed the phone from Jacob's hand and turned it off.

"You won't need this anymore."

The man slipped the phone into his back pocket and told Jacob to sit on the couch, stay there, and be quiet. Jacob did as he was told, seeing no viable alternative. He hoped he sent the correct code. He hoped his mom understood. He knew all he could do was wait. But nothing prevented him from planning his actions in response to various imagined scenarios.

"What's your name?" Jacob tried once more.

"What'd I tell you? Shut up."

"I'll call you George. You know, like that character Curious George? Because I'm curious what your name is, George."

The man took three quick steps to the couch, reached out, and cuffed Jacob before Jacob could even raise a hand in defense.

"I told you to shut up."

Jacob rubbed the side of his head, fighting the reactive tears that came to his eyes. Before he could say anything, the door opened and Butch stepped into the house.

"Parked the car a couple streets over. Should be okay there. Lots of other vehicles. And did you know there's a car in the garage here? No keys in it and none readily noticeable nearby."

Butch looked between his buddy and Jacob. "What's going on?"

"Nothing. The boy just can't follow directions, that's all. Thinks he's clever or something." He looked at Jacob. "Do as you're told and that won't happen again."

Jacob nodded without speaking.

"You contact the mother? Is she coming?"

"Sent a text on the boy's phone. She'll come. Have no concerns about that."

"Think she'll be alone or have backup?"

Jacob looked up at that question but quickly looked away again, hoping neither man had noticed his interest in the conversation. He was torn between hoping his mom would come and hoping she'd stay away.

"I think she'll be alone. She was always arrogant about her skills. We should plan for backup just in case."

Butch nodded, but added, "It's been twenty years. Doubtful she's as skilled as she thinks she is. And there's two of us."

Jacob didn't know what skills the man referred to, but he assumed they must be significant if they were considering their own actions based on them. He felt a tiny bud of hope begin to form again. *Maybe everything will be OK after all.*

<h1 style="text-align:center">39</h1>

Susan's phone buzzed on the seat next to her. She glanced at it, seeing she'd received a text. Not taking her eyes from the road, she reached over and felt for her phone. Once in hand, she used her thumb to tap in her access code. Her wheel hand jerked as she read the text, causing her to refocus on the road and control her vehicle.

She glanced at the text again to verify she'd read it correctly the first time. The six words offered more information than the average person would ever understand. Jacob was at the safehouse. She'd been correct to question the non-uniformed officer. The house was compromised and under surveillance. She'd instinctively known that. The proof was more unsettling than she wanted to admit. However, the real question still hadn't been answered. Who had Jacob? His code only told her he was held by hostiles. She already knew he wasn't at the safehouse voluntarily. He didn't know it existed. But he also wouldn't know the players, so giving her a clue as to their identity was a false hope. And, she didn't know how many were involved.

Her sense of urgency increased. As she focused on the road, her mind began playing through different scenarios. Ray's death left a huge hole in potential resources. Worry about Cody also intruded into her plans, as well as whether he had the flash drive with him. She shook her head, as if she could shake the unwanted thoughts away.

She read the highway sign approaching. *Just a few more miles and this situation will be resolved. One way or another, good or bad, this will end. I just hope my family is not who's ended.*

She took the exit that would put her close to the safehouse neighborhood. She needed to rest. If she didn't, she'd be useless to herself and her son. She saw the sign of a chain motel that was generally clean and inexpensive, and pulled into the parking lot. Ten minutes later she stepped into her room, her go-bag over her shoulder. She showered and changed into her only other set of clothing. It was enough to refresh her.

She was performing a routine check on her handgun when a soft knock sounded on the door. Holding her weapon in both hands in a ready position, she moved to the side of the door and waited. The knock came again.

"Susan, let me in."

Her mind went blank at the familiar voice. *No! He's dead!*

"Susan, please."

She quickly glanced through the peephole as she undid the chain and opened the door. Ray stepped through, closed and locked the door behind him. They both looked at each other for a long minute, Ray noticing the weapon in Susan's hand.

"You don't really need that, do you?" He nodded towards the gun.

Susan holstered it. "I thought you were dead. I saw it on the news."

"That was the point. Everyone was supposed to think I was dead. But as you can see, I'm very much alive."

"What are you doing here?"

"The alarm."

She nodded. She'd forgotten Ray's number was one tagged to receive the coded messages. She mentally kicked herself for that, with his supposed death, she'd never thought to change the process. And now she realized others would have been notified. She'd gotten stale.

"I can read your thoughts. Yes. Others also got the message and are either already here or on their way. This is going to be a shit-storm."

"How'd you know I was here?"

"Pure coincidence. I'm also staying here. With Walt. The safehouse is compromised. Saw you walk into the office."

"Walt's here? I thought he'd retired."

"He's as retired as I am."

Both smiled at that. Then Ray got serious.

"Susan, do you have the information?"

At her head shake, he groaned. "Then we need to get it."

"Can't."

"Why not?"

"It's missing from where it was hidden. Have no idea where it is now or if it even still exists. But that's the least of my concerns. They have Jacob. He's at the safehouse. That's all I know about the situation, but he's my number one priority right now. I'll do anything to protect him. You understand? Anything."

"I understand. But the information is my priority. I need to have it."

Susan was silent while she processed Ray's words. *He said he needed to have it. Not we need it.* Ray appeared agitated at her extended silence.

"Susan, if you're lying and you do have the information, it—"

"I'm not lying. I don't have it. It was at the cabin. So was Cody. Neither are there now."

"Cody? You think he has it? He said he didn't, that he doesn't know anything about any information."

Susan stilled and looked fully at Ray.

"You spoke to Cody?"

She didn't go on to ask if her son was okay or any of the other questions that immediately came to her. She was studying Ray's expression, not sure exactly what she was looking for.

"Where is he?" Her voice was deadly quiet. When no response came, she reached behind her and placed her hand on her holstered handgun. She put a slight distance between them and asked again. "Ray, where is my son?"

"He's safe. He's with Walt."

Ray didn't look directly at her. He'd heard the change in her voice and felt a twinge of unease form in his stomach.

"He's here? Take me to him!"

"Soon. The information, Susan. It's important."

"Not as important as me seeing my son." Susan removed her handgun and held it at her side, barrel pointing down. Ray saw it and forced himself to remain calm.

"That's not necessary. Cody is under no threat from me. Or Walt. We've kept him safe. If not for us, he might already have a bullet in his head."

Susan thought of the scarred doorframe at the cabin. She took a deep breath and changed her tone.

"Take me to Cody, Ray. We'll talk about the information after that. Please. It's been over three years."

Ray nodded, then glanced at the gun in her hand. Susan took the hint and replaced it in her holster.

"Now, Ray."

He turned and opened the door enough to put his head out and look in both directions.

"C'mon," he tossed over his shoulder as he stepped out and walked down the hallway, not looking to see if Susan followed.

~

"Mom!"

Cody flew off the bed and grabbed his mother in a bear hug. She returned it just as fiercely. The next minute was filled with an excited gibberish as their two voices talked over each other.

"Heartwarming as this reunion is, we have business to discuss."

Ray's voice cut harshly through the moment. He stood in a casual pose, his back against the door. Walt sat in a corner chair, his demeanor calm. Susan wasn't fooled. She knew he was able to move with deadly intent in an instant. Or at least he could. Just like her, the past twenty years showed.

"The information."

"Told you. Don't have it."

"Then your son must, even though he denies it."

Cody started to protest, but Susan gestured for him to stay silent.

"We need to get Jacob. We need a plan."

"Not before you hand over the information."

"I told—" Susan began, but Cody interrupted.

"I burned it! Threw it in the stove's fire at the cabin. Whatever was on that flash drive is gone!" He turned to Susan, agitated. "Mom, what did you mean about getting Jacob? Where is he?"

Susan turned to Cody and tried to calm him. Ray's voice had her diverting her attention back to him.

"Burning the flash drive is an unfortunate turn of events. Unfortunate indeed."

Ray had straightened. He was also pointing a gun at Susan and Cody. He used it to gesture towards the bed. "Have a seat."

He looked at Walt. Without words, Walt stood and walked over to mother and son. Susan took Cody's arm and pulled him onto the bed next to her. She looked up at Walt.

"What? You going to kill us?"

"Don't be melodramatic. I'm just here to ensure you do as Ray suggests." Walt reached around Susan and removed her handgun from its holster. "You don't really need this right now."

Susan gave Cody's leg a soft squeeze and felt him relax slightly as he interpreted her signal to stay put.

"Gotta admit, feel a little naked without it."

Ray interrupted. "I'll ask one more time. Where's the information? That couldn't have been the only copy."

Susan stared at Ray without speaking for several seconds. "Why do you want it, Ray? Is this a personal power play, or have they gotten to you?"

"It's complicated."

"Everything is. Why don't you start with why you needed the world to think you'd died in a plane explosion."

She looked at Walt. "Do you mind? I prefer you not standing over me like some giant in a children's story."

Walt glanced at Ray who nodded. He went back to his chair in the corner. She looked back to Ray.

"Well?"

"They have my daughter."

"Daughter?!" Susan was stunned. She also noted Walt's reaction. She figured this was news to him, too. She knew Ray had never married. Then a memory surfaced. "Cairo?"

He nodded, dropping his hand so his gun pointed at the floor.

"If they think you're dead, why would they bother with your daughter? And how would they even know about her?"

Susan was still uncertain if Ray was being completely truthful. Her trust in him was fractured. She told herself to remain on guard. Not get sucked into a sob story.

"Mistakes I've made. First, I surfaced too soon. Was seen. They know I'm not dead. How they found my daughter, I don't know. But they did. Obviously my fault, since she doesn't even know about me. And now they have her."

"She doesn't know you exist? How?" A pause, then, "Never mind. That's for another time. Do you know where she is?"

"No."

"That complicates things considerably. At least I know Jacob is being held at the safehouse. One location to focus on. Might they have her there also?"

"I don't think so. The message I got was from overseas. Not local. I think they're holding her somewhere close to where they grabbed her. She was living in Paris."

Susan was quiet while she thought through things. After several moments, she looked at Ray.

"OK. We now have two rescue missions to pull off, on near opposite sides of the planet. A challenge, to be sure. You have any contacts in France? I may still have one."

"Even if I did, which I don't, coordinating the action is near impossible. While we focus on one, the other is put in further danger. Time differences only adds to the problem."

"Then I guess we tell them we'll give them the information."

"I knew you made a copy! Where is it?"

"There was only the one flash drive. The information was too dangerous to copy. If Cody says he burned it, it's gone."

Everyone looked at Cody. He vigorously nodded his head. "I did throw it in the fire." He looked at his mother. "It's what your note said to do!"

Susan patted his leg again and murmured some comforting words.

"Then we have nothing to bargain with!" Ray's voice showed his desperation.

"They don't know that."

Everyone in the room was quiet while they thought about the implications of her statement. Susan broke the stillness.

"We need a plan. But first, we need to know if whoever has our children is working for the same entity. If not, things become trickier. Any idea how we can determine that basic fact? It will drive the rest of our actions."

Ray looked at the floor, then at Susan. "Has anyone contacted you?"

"No. Just Jacob with a coded message. Any idea who sent you your message?"

"No."

"Then we're going to have to figure a way to draw everyone out."

40

Anders arrived at the cabin as dusk was setting in. He sat in his car for a few minutes, wondering if he should just go up to the door and knock, or wait for them to notice him. He still hadn't decided when the cabin door opened, and an older man stepped out holding a shotgun pointed at the car.

"You that fellow Anders?" Donner called out.

Anders quickly opened his door and stepped out with his hands high over his head.

"Yes. Yes. Please don't shoot! Susan sent me. She said you were expecting me."

Donner lowered the gun causing Anders to breathe a sigh of relief.

"You have food?"

"Yes. Backseat is full of groceries. Can I bring them in?"

"Of course you can, you young fool." Donner turned and said something Anders couldn't hear. Anna stepped out onto the porch next to him.

"Don't mind him. He gets grumpy when he hasn't eaten for a while." Anna stepped down and walked towards the car, holding her hand out. "I'm Anna. You've met my husband Donner. Is Susan okay?"

Anders shook her hand lightly, repeating his own name. "I don't know. I haven't spoken to her since she gave me instructions to come here. Do you think your husband can help bring in the supplies?"

Anna moved to the back door, opened it, reached in, and grabbed a sack off the back seat. As she turned to walk back to the cabin with it, she called for Donner to put the gun away and help. Anders didn't wait to see Donner's reaction. He simply grabbed two more sacks and followed Anna. It took only a few minutes for the three of them to empty the car of its bounty.

As Anna found places to stash things, Donner rummaged through the sacks looking for something to snack on. Finding a package of cookies, he greedily tore into it.

"Donner!" Anna scolded.

"What? I'm hungry!"

"Go sit down. I'll fix something for us as soon as I clear this mess away."

"Can I help at all?" Anders asked.

"No, no. Please, it's easier if you both just stay out from under foot."

Donner and Anders retreated to the chairs in front of the wood stove. Donner looked at Anders.

"Susan says you're a lawyer. Her lawyer. Why would she need a lawyer?"

"Everyone needs a lawyer at some point in their lives. A few understand that fact sooner than others. Susan came to me over twenty years ago."

"What do you do for her?"

"Donner!" Anna admonished. "That's none of your business."

"She's our daughter. That should give us some entitlement."

"I'm afraid it doesn't," Anders interrupted before the two could argue. "Attorney-client privilege is real. I can't discuss Susan's affairs with anyone but her. Unless she instructs me to do so."

"And what has she instructed regarding us?"

"To bring you supplies and stay with you."

"Can you shoot a gun?"

"No."

"Fight?"

"No."

"Then what good are you to us if we get attacked?"

"What makes you think you'll be attacked?"

"It's already happened. I was shot at! And both Cody and Jacob are missing."

"Susan will sort it out. In the meantime, she instructed me to stay here with you. So here I am."

Donner was about to express his thoughts on that when Anna called the men to the table. She'd prepared a simple meal and wanted them to eat it while it was hot. She closed the window she'd opened to air the cabin from use of the camp stove and joined them at the table. As they were eating Anna asked Anders her biggest concern.

"Do you think Susan will be okay?"

Anders swallowed before answering. "I have complete faith that she will resolve the situation at hand. We simply need to be patient and wait."

Donner snorted his contempt at Ander's reply but didn't comment.

Anna wasn't ready to let it go. "Do you think there's anything we can do to help? Staying here seems so useless."

"If Susan wants you here, she believes you're safe here. That's the best thing you can do for her. She's already got her boys to worry about. You won't be helping her if you put yourself in a situation that adds to her worries."

It wasn't what she wanted to hear but she admitted to herself Anders was probably right.

41

Their plane landed without incident and the two men quickly secured their rental car.

"Where's the kid?"

"He's being held at the safehouse."

"Are you insane? We're not the only ones who know of that place!"

"Doesn't matter. Susan knows. That's all I care about."

"Who's holding the kid?"

"Just a couple guys. Nobodies. We won't need them once we get to the house."

"You sure about that?"

"Absolutely."

"You gonna do it in front of the kid?"

"No. You're going to do it. And not in front of the kid."

"Me?"

"Yes. You. And you'll be efficient about it if you want to remain part of this game."

Both men were silent as they traveled toward their destination. For one, the silence was welcome. For the other, it was uneasy. He glanced at his partner. Things were not going as anticipated. And now he was being tasked with eliminating the two who'd been hired to grab the boy. He had no issue with the task itself. It wasn't as if he hadn't done that type of work before. What concerned him was the not-so-veiled threat he'd just heard. He suddenly wondered if he and his partner had the same end goal in mind. He began contemplating his own plan. One he could implement if his partner's plan revealed an unexpected twist. A twist that didn't include him.

Traffic was relatively light, and it didn't take long to arrive at the house.

"You think we should leave the car in the driveway? Maybe we should just park it on the street? Draw less attention that way."

"Good point."

The pounding on the door startled the three inside. Butch stood and went to the door without waiting to be told to do so. As he opened it, the two outside stepped in and one put a knife in Butch's chest. The act was violent, but efficient. Butch dropped almost where he stood. The second man jumped from his chair, but a bullet stopped him before he'd taken two steps. Jacob rolled off the couch and hit the floor, his hands covering his head.

"I thought you said not in front of the boy."

"Changed my mind. Close the door." The man looked at Jacob on the floor. "Boy. Get up. Jacob, isn't it? Don't worry. We're not here to hurt you."

Jacob slowly raised his head and looked at the two men.

"Who are you? Did Mom send you? Are you here to rescue me?"

"I'm Sam. This is Bill."

Jacob noticed the man referred to as Bill looked at the one speaking.

"Are those your real names?"

"Real enough. You okay? They didn't hurt you?"

"I'm fine. What's going on? Who were those guys? Why did they bring me here? Why'd you kill them? You think someone heard the gunshot? Will the police come?"

"You ask a lot of questions. Your health would benefit from not asking so many questions."

Sam's voice was harsh. He looked at the second man. "Gag him. And while you're at it, tie his hands."

Jacob slid back onto the couch, alarmed. He realized these men weren't here to save him. In fact, considering the fate of the two that had brought him here, he wondered if his situation had just worsened.

"Please. Don't gag me. I won't ask any more questions. I promise. I'll stay quiet."

Sam indicated for Bill to complete his instructions and Jacob's hands were soon secured behind his back along with a makeshift gag in his mouth. Neither added to his physical comfort. Both increased his fear.

"Now what?" the man Jacob knew as Bill asked.

"Now we wait. But we need to contact Susan."

"How?"

Sam looked at Jacob. "Through him."

Both men looked at Jacob who made noises through his gag. Sam gestured with his head and Bill removed the gag. Jacob coughed a bit then looked at the men expectantly.

"You got a phone?"

Jacob nodded towards one of the dead men. "He took it. Put it in his back pocket."

Without a word, Bill walked over to the body and patted down the man. Finding the phone, he pulled it out and handed it to Sam. Sam turned it on and noted the low battery.

"You're running out of juice on this thing." He opened the message application and saw the last text Jacob had sent. "What's with the numbers?"

"I was nervous. I offered to fix it, but the guy said to just send it."

Sam looked at Jacob with speculation but didn't comment. Instead, he began typing rapidly. In the quiet of the room, everyone heard the swoosh that indicated a sent message.

"What'd you send her?" Jacob asked.

"Not your concern. She'll understand. That's all that matters."

Sam looked at Bill again and made a gesture towards Jacob. Bill quickly stuffed the gag back in Jacob's mouth, and walked back towards Sam. The two had a whispered exchange that Jacob couldn't hear. Then Bill grabbed one of the dead men and pulled him down the hall to one of the bedrooms. He did the same with the second. Both men looked at the floor.

"Gonna be a mess to clean up all this blood," Bill said.

"Not our concern. Others will deal with it." Sam hesitated, then added, "Or not. Take the kid to the bathroom. Let him use it if he needs to. Lock him in. Make sure he's secured and has no means of escaping. Then check around the house. Susan will be coming, and she likely won't come via the front door. We need to make sure we're not surprised."

42

Susan read the text that came through on her phone. Her anger momentarily surpassed all other emotions.

"What?" Ray asked.

"Message from Sam. He's at the safehouse. Wants the info."

"Sam? He's behind this? I would have never guessed."

"Why not? It's who I suspected. Now I have confirmation."

"You think it's just him?"

"No. I think someone's pulling his strings. And I don't think he's alone at the safehouse."

"What makes you say that?"

"He was never a loner. Always needed an audience. He'll have someone there with him. Maybe more than one person, but I doubt it. The question is, how loyal is he to that person? Or that person to him?"

"You think we can stir up some conflict between them?"

"Possibly. But we need to confirm how many are there. If Sam is texting me, did he originally snatch Jacob? Or was that someone else. Are they still part of this or did Sam eliminate them?"

"That's a lot of unknowns."

"Maybe I can clear the air a bit."

Susan tapped on her phone screen. A quiet whoosh indicated she'd sent a text.

"What'd you say?"

"Just playing along with him for the time being. Trying to buy us some time. You think of anything regarding your daughter?"

"No." Ray's voice indicated his frustration and worry.

"You're sure they have her?"

"Yes. The message was very specific."

Walt cleared his throat. "Something doesn't add up. Even I didn't know about your daughter, and I probably know more about you than anyone else in this world." He looked at Susan, "with the possible exception of you." He looked back at Ray. "How could anyone else? Especially if she doesn't know about you. With no communication between you, who could possibly put the pieces together and figure out you have a daughter living in Paris?"

Susan picked up Walt's thoughts. "Have you been over there? Have you observed her? Do you have others observing her? Have you in any way tied yourself to her in real time?"

"No! I've purposely avoided all of that!"

Susan stared at Ray for a long time. She knew her next question would anger him, but she asked it anyway.

"Are you sure you even have a daughter? How did you find out about her?"

Everyone in the room watched Ray take several deep breaths. Each had their own thoughts of how Ray would respond. None expected the answer he gave.

"Her mother told me. Sent me a picture. The resemblance is clear to me. She's my daughter. I have no reservations about that fact."

"Maybe you just want to see a resemblance? When's the last time you had contact with the mother? I mean before you got the picture?" Cody's voice was hesitant. Susan glanced at him but did nothing to silence him. She was curious where this would go. She also wondered if Ray was grasping at straws. She was amazed at Cody's insight. He'd matured a lot these past three years. She couldn't wait to hear about his life. But they had to get through this current situation before she could indulge in thoughts of a true family reunion.

Ray was silent so long Susan didn't think he was going to respond to Cody. Just as Walt opened his mouth to say something, Ray spoke. He admitted to having had no contact with his former love interest since leaving Cairo many years ago. But he was convinced the communication he'd received had been legitimate.

"Did you research to see if the woman is still alive?"

No response prompted Susan to nudge him. "Ray? Is she even still alive? That was so long ago."

"Stop referring to her as if she doesn't have a name! You know her name. It's Heba! Use it."

Susan let Ray's momentary anger wash over her. It didn't distract her. "Did you check?"

"How could it be anyone else? Who knew about us other than you?"

"Ray! Did you check?" Susan's voice was firm. "You know as well as I do that some secrets don't remain secrets. That some were never secrets in the first place. Did you check?"

"No!" Ray's anguish was clear.

Walt pulled his phone out of his pocket and asked for Heba's last name and any other pertinent information. Both Susan and Ray gave him different responses, Ray's more personal. Susan's more observational. Walt tapped on his phone without actively acknowledging either of them. No one spoke.

"Heba Badawi doesn't exist. Never did, as far as I can tell."

Walt's voice was flat. He continued staring at his phone, scrolling through screens, and tapping on things he saw.

"Impossible! I didn't have a relationship with a ghost!" Ray exploded.

"I'm sure you didn't. You have any kind of picture of her? It'll be tricky to do remotely and on my phone, but I can try to run it through facial recognition. How about the daughter's picture? You said you were sent a picture. You got it?"

Susan and Cody exchanged looks. Neither spoke. Both looked back to Ray and waited.

Ray fumbled with his phone. After a few moments, he sent Walt the picture of the woman he was convinced was his daughter. Walt studied it but didn't comment on any likeness.

"And the mother?"

"All I have is a picture of a picture. She never let me photograph her. I had one of those instamatic cameras—you remember those? One time when she left the room, I snapped one of her family photos. She didn't know I'd done it. Later, as technology changed, I scanned it into my phone." A whoosh sound was followed by his muttered, "Here. She's on the left."

Walt opened the picture and stared in silence at it for a long moment. Then his fingers got busy again.

Ray began pacing the small space. Susan's phone buzzed with another text. She quickly read it and responded. Ray stopped and looked at her. "What?"

"Nothing. Let's focus on this right now. I have a bad feeling about your entire history with Heba."

Ray walked over to the other chair in the room and slumped into it. He looked totally defeated. Cody looked at him and internally sympathized. If anyone understood the shock of discovering that everything you thought you knew was not what it really was, he did. But his sympathy didn't detract from his resentment and frustration with this entire situation. No one was talking about his brother Jacob. And Ray's situation paled in comparison to the fact that Jacob was being held prisoner by someone who wanted the information he had destroyed. Cody knew that if anything happened to Jacob, it would be his fault. He turned to his mother.

"What about Jacob? How are we going to rescue him?"

"I'm still formulating a plan. Some of it will depend on what Walt finds."

"I can help, Mom."

"While I'm sure you think you can, it isn't necessary. I'll take care of it."

"I'm not a child anymore. And you don't need to shield me. I want to, no I need to help. If anything happens to him, it'll be my fault. I destroyed the flash drive."

Susan looked at her son and realized what she should have realized right away. She hurried to comfort, as well as disabuse, him of his guilty thoughts. But she also understood that she needed to include Cody in her plans. Just how, she wasn't yet sure. Walt's voice interrupted her thoughts.

"I'm sorry Ray, but there's no record of Heba. However, facial recognition offers a high probability of a match with a woman named Zhara Samaar."

"Why only a high probability?" Susan asked.

"The picture is old, the woman young. I had to run it through an aging program first. No telling if the results are anywhere close to accurate."

"So, your results could be totally off base." Ray commented.

"Possibly. But you might be interested in this bit of info. I ran that name through the agency database. I still have access, you know. That name is tied to an intelligence agent that operates throughout the Middle East. Still operates, I might add."

The room was silent while everyone digested that information.

"You slept with a spy?" Cody broke the silence.

Susan gave him a quick elbow in the side and shook her head.

Ray stood and walked to Walt. "Show me."

Walt flipped through the various screens. Ray read everything without comment, but his expression got darker with each new piece of information he absorbed. His next words shocked Susan.

"If it is her, and it appears she's still alive, then it's very possible I do, in fact, have a daughter."

"That's it? That's your takeaway on this?" Susan looked at Ray, her disbelief evident. "You're not concerned that you may have been compromised all those years ago? That this woman is now using a daughter, who may or may not exist, as leverage to further compromise you, and our country?"

When Ray didn't respond, Susan stood and pulled Cody up with her. "C'mon, Cody. Let's get out of here."

She wasted no time pulling Cody to the door.

"Wait! Where are you going?" Ray's physical reaction reflected his panicked response.

"I'm going to get Jacob."

"But what about my daughter?"

"I don't think she exists. And if she does, I don't think she's in any real harm. My son is. I'm going to remedy that."

Susan opened the door and pushed Cody ahead of her. She let the door close behind her with a finality as she hustled her son down the corridor.

43

Cody stared at his mother, noting her singular focus as she drove through the city streets. She looked older than he remembered. Three years didn't seem long enough for that big of a change. He knew his life had been full of unexpected challenges. He guessed his mother's had contained more. He wondered if he'd even recognize Jacob. Kids change a lot between the ages of twelve and fifteen. He couldn't wait to see his brother.

Thinking of Jacob reminded him of the direness of the situation.

"Mom, do you think Jacob is all right?"

"If you mean still alive, then yes. If you mean injured, I can't answer that. I hope not. But I think he's okay. They can't afford to hurt him too much. They'd lose all leverage."

"How are we going to save him? We don't have what they want."

Susan glanced at Cody, then refocused on the road in front of her. She'd been thinking a lot about the situation and had formulated a rough plan. She shared it with her son. The question-and-answer session that followed further refined the details. If Susan was impressed with Cody's ability to analyze and find both the strengths and weaknesses of the plan, she didn't show it. Instead, she acknowledged to herself how like his father he was. She pushed away the immediate stab of pain that acknowledgement caused. Time enough for all of that later.

"We're about five minutes out. Are you ready? Can you do this?" Susan tried to keep the doubt from her voice.

"Yes. I can do this," Cody's statement was full of confidence. "Don't worry, Mom. I won't mess this up."

"This isn't a game. There will be real guns. Real bullets. A real possibility of death."

"I know." Cody took a deep breath. "You can count on me."

At that moment Susan's phone buzzed. She handed it to Cody.

"See what that is."

Cody took the phone and looked at the text that had come through. "It's from Grandma. From Anna."

Susan glanced at him. "You figured that out?"

"Yes. The papers in the cabin. She sent me there. Do you know? Are they safe?"

"They should be. They're at the cabin themselves. With a trusted friend of mine. Call the number. Put it on speaker."

They listened to the phone ring twice before it was picked up.

"Susan? Susan is that you? Are you okay? Where are you?" Anna's voice came through the speaker.

"Mom. I'm fine. I have Cody with me. Are you two good? Is Anders there with you?"

"You have Cor—"

There was rustling, then Ander's voice came on.

"I'm here Susan. All is fine here. They wanted to come find you, but I convinced them you'd rather they stayed here."

"Indeed. Thank you."

"What about Jacob? I'm so sorry about that."

"I told you, stop apologizing. Cody and I are on our way to get Jacob. If all goes well, we should be able to finally indulge in a true family reunion."

"Do you need any assistance? Is there anything I can do?"

"No. We're good." She hesitated. "On the other hand, perhaps you can help."

Susan explained what she had in mind. Cody looked at her in disbelief. He opened his mouth to object, but Susan gestured with her hand for him to stay silent.

"Do you think you can do that, Anders?"

"Yes. You'll send a signal when you're ready?"

"Yes. Absolutely. Mom, Dad. I love you. This will all be over soon. Then you and your grandkids can finally get to know each other."

They heard Donner's voice in the background but couldn't make out his words. Anna's voice came through strong and clear.

"Godspeed, dear. We'll see you soon."

The line disconnected. Cody looked at his mother. "Will this really be over soon?"

"Yes. One way or another. This will end."

Cody wasn't sure he liked the way she phrased that.

44

Jacob sat on the toilet. Other than the floor, there was nowhere else. The bathroom didn't have a tub. His arms ached from being tied behind him for so long. He was tired, hungry, and thirsty. He was also worried and afraid. He knew Sam and Bill were waiting for his mother to come rescue him. In fact, they had done nothing but manipulate the situation to get her to come. He hoped she had whatever it was they wanted.

He thought of the two dead men in the other room. Was that to be his fate? Or his mother's? He knew his mom had not done intelligence work for many years. At least he thought he knew that. Seemed like every time he thought he had something figured out, he learned differently. Was this a similar situation? Had his mother continued her intelligence work even when they were on the farm? Is that why his father had been killed? Not because of something that happened years ago, but because of something happening now. He wondered if he'd even be in this situation if he hadn't insisted on staying in Denver and going to a public high school. Maybe he should have continued his home schooling and moved when his mom thought it necessary to do so. He felt pangs of guilt that he might be the cause of her demise.

He sighed. All this thinking just made his head hurt and caused him to feel even more hungry and discouraged. It certainly wasn't helping his current situation. As he took another deep breath to let it out in a sigh, he had a sudden thought that he should be trying to escape. Not just passively sitting here and following instructions. He began looking around his small prison for anything that could help him.

He stood and faced the sink. Leaning forward, he pressed his cheek against the edge of the mirrored medicine cabinet and pulled backward attempting to open it. His third try was successful, and the door swung outward on its hinge. The narrow shelves revealed several personal hygiene items, including two toothbrushes in their original packaging, a fresh tube of toothpaste, a can of shaving cream, a razor with a package of extra blades, mouthwash, shampoo, and soap.

His eyes focused on the blades. He turned around and stretched his arms outward, trying to reach the item. His attempts left him with aching shoulders and no closer to his goal. He turned back and stared at the items in the cabinet. Frustrated was a mild description of his current state. He tried again, but no matter how much he leaned or twisted his body, he couldn't reach the blades.

He returned to his perch on the toilet. As he sat there, he wondered if he could manipulate his body through his hands so that they were in front of him. He'd seen action movies where the hero had done it. *Don't be stupid. Those were movies.*

Still. Worth a try. He sat on the floor and squirmed and strained. He tried everything he could think of. He finally admitted to himself he wasn't flexible enough, or his arms weren't long enough, or his legs and hips were too big to fit through the opening. Even if it were possible to pull off the technique, his body refused to cooperate. He struggled to his feet and sat on the toilet. He was almost ready to admit defeat when he saw the toilet brush in its corner stand. He stared at it, tossing about various ideas. He realized he only had two options. Hold it in his hands and wave it around behind his back to knock the cabinet contents into the sink or hold the brush in his mouth so he could see what he was doing.

He gagged at the thought of using his mouth. But he also realized that blindly flailing the brush behind him would likely make too much noise when the items fell. Even if they only fell into the sink and not on the floor. It took him only another second to realize the same outcome would occur if he used his mouth to hold the brush. He'd still have to knock things into the sink or onto the floor to be able to pick them up.

He stared at the towel hanging on the shower door as he tried to decide what to do.

The towel!

He realized he could use it to cushion the fall of the items. He stood and stepped to the shower. Grabbing the towel with his mouth, he pulled it down and took the two steps to the sink. After several moments, he was able to position it to cover the sink and counter. Shutting down his disgust, he went back to the toilet and leaned over, and grabbed the handle of the brush in his mouth. He had to shake it a little to free it from its stand. Straightening, he went back to the sink.

It was hard to control the brush, but he was finally able to sweep the items off the shelves. Releasing the brush, he waited to see if his actions had alerted the men. After several moments where nothing happened, he assumed all was well. He looked over the items and thought through his next moves.

Turning around, he felt through the items finding the package of blades. Once he had them in his hand, he realized he was no closer to his goal. Even if able to open the package and remove the blades, he'd only end up slicing his fingers and hands versus his restraints. Without being able to see what he was doing he'd never manipulate the blade correctly. Recognizing the truth, he knew even if he could observe his actions, the likelihood of severing his bonds was minimal to non-existent.

He dropped the package and returned to the toilet. A small tear escaped from the corner of his eye as he stared into the shower.

45

Susan pulled up behind an old pickup truck four houses down from the safe house. She looked at Cody.

"You ready?"

"Yes."

"Any questions? Concerns?"

"Questions, no. Concerns, yes. What if this doesn't work? What if they kill Jacob?"

"It'll work. You must believe that with all your heart. C'mon. Let's do this."

They got out of the car and walked towards the house. When they were two houses away, Cody split off and made his way to the back yard of the neighboring house. He would approach the house from the rear. His job was to create a distraction to allow his mother to breach the front door. As he snuck up to his position, he appreciated his mother's knowledge of the house and it's surrounding yard. Everything was exactly how she'd described it. He began counting towards the number they'd agreed upon.

Susan approached the front door, sliding along the corner of the garage to stay as much out of sight of the narrow window that framed the door as she could. A part of her hoped no neighbor was looking out their window. Her movements would definitely be suspicious.

She pulled her phone out of her pocket and sent Anders a text. *Do it now.*

She waited.

A few seconds later she heard glass splinter and assumed Cody had found his target. The first broken window was followed by two more. She smiled as she moved quickly to the front door, gun in one hand, door key in the other. Since Walt had taken her holstered gun in the motel room, she was glad she'd had a backup in the trunk of the car. All of this would be impossible without a weapon.

She'd thought of kicking the door in, but remembered how reinforced it was. Not only was it unlikely she'd be able to kick through the door, but having the key made the action unnecessary. She remembered once asking that additional locks be put on the door. Her request had been denied and now she was grateful for that as she quietly slipped her key into the slot. As she slowly turned the knob, she heard voices.

"What the hell was that?"

"Check it out," Sam said as he grabbed his gun off the coffee table. He started towards the hallway that led to the bathroom door.

"Window's broken," Bill yelled from the kitchen. He opened the back door and stepped out just as Cody threw his second and third rocks, aimed at two other windows.

"Hey!" Bill yelled as he ran down the steps of the small porch. By this time, Cody was pushing his way through the shrubbery on the far side of the yard. Bill raised his gun, but realized he couldn't fire it as he watched Cody disappear.

He returned to the kitchen, closing the door behind him. "Just some kid making mischief," he called into the room. Hearing no response, he added, "Sam?"

He entered the living room and took in the scene before him. Sam was sitting on the couch with a woman holding a gun to his head. She looked at him, and even the brief glance was enough to send chills down Bill's back.

"Drop your gun where you stand and come sit over here. Don't do anything stupid or your friend Wade will lose his brain matter." Susan's voice was low and intense. As Bill hesitated, she said harshly, "Do it! Do it now. I'm not kidding."

Bill put his gun on the floor and sat on the end of the couch. He looked at her with curiosity.

"Wade?"

"Yes. You probably know him as Sam. He likes to use that name. But his real name is Wade Bronson. Introduce yourself."

"You can call me Bill."

"OK, Bill," she emphasized the name, making it clear she didn't believe it was his real one. "Where's my son? Where's Jacob?"

"Locked in the bathroom."

Susan's expression caused him to add that her son was fine. Maybe a little hungry, but otherwise unhurt. As he said the words, Bill observed that Susan's finger was on the trigger, not along the side of the weapon. That told him she was ready to follow through on her threat. He calculated the distance between them and realized she could shoot Sam, or Wade, or whoever the man was and still have time to shoot him before he could get to her.

"You have the information?" he asked, as he wondered how he didn't know Sam's real name. They'd worked together for over two years. Then again, he was pretty sure Sam didn't know his own real name.

On the other hand, was Wade Bronson the man's real name, or only the one she knew him by. He half smiled as he again realized the smoke-and-mirror world he lived in.

"What's so funny?" Susan asked. Bill hadn't realized she'd been watching him.

"Nothing. Just appreciating the life we live is never what we think it is."

"My life is. At least it was." As she said the last words, she pushed her gun against Wade's head. "You couldn't let it go, though, could you?"

Wade spoke. "It wasn't me. You should know that. There are others above me. If you kill me, someone else will come. They want the information. They'll do anything to get it."

"Then they'll be disappointed. There is no information. It was destroyed."

"Even if that's true, they won't believe you. Or, they'll figure you can personally provide what they want. They'll still come."

"Who else knows about the information? Who wants it? And why?"

When Wade didn't respond, she pushed the barrel of the gun harder into his temple.

"Tell me!"

"You kill him, you'll never know," Bill stated in a calm voice.

Without any warning, Susan turned the gun on him and pulled the trigger. The suppressed gunfire was still quite loud in the small space. Even as Bill slumped forward, Susan returned the gun to Wade's temple.

"Who else knows about the information?"

"You'll never get to him."

"Why do you say that? Who is it?"

When Wade didn't answer, Susan thought through the situation. Her gun hand trembled a moment before she controlled it.

"Why would he want it? It's been over twenty years. Most of the information is now irrelevant."

"Not to him."

"Anyone else?"

"Not to my knowledge. You going to kill me, too?"

"Haven't decided."

"You might as well. If you don't, he will. I won't survive the week if you let me go. Better I get it from an old colleague than some new idiot that has no idea why he's been tasked to take me out."

"Interesting perspective." Susan smiled as she said it.

"You ever miss the old life? We were a good team back in the day."

"I don't. You should have gotten out when I did. Why'd you stay?"

"Thought I could save the world."

They both laughed at that. A siren sounded in the distance. It seemed to be coming closer. Susan knew Anders had completed his task and that her time frame was quickly closing.

"I'm sorry, Wade."

"For what?"

Even as he asked the question, Wade felt the butt of the gun smash into his head. His awareness darkened into unconsciousness as he slumped over, his head falling against the body of Bill.

Susan ran down the hallway calling Jacob's name.

"Mom! In here!"

Jacob's voice revealed both fear and relief at the same time. Even though he'd failed at his escape attempt, he'd managed to get the gag off earlier. Although still a prisoner, he was slightly more comfortable.

He'd heard the gunshot, recognizing immediately what it was. Not knowing what was happening, he'd been mentally preparing himself for death. His mother's voice caused him to shake uncontrollably.

She slammed into the door. It shook but didn't budge.

Jacob! Can you unlock the door?"

"No. There's nothing on this side."

She looked at the doorknob, remembering the one-way lock mechanism so that the room could be used exactly as it was currently being used. As a small prison.

"OK. Keep away from the door."

She stepped back and gave two strong front kicks. The door caved slightly but still held. She could hear the sirens. The authorities would be here any minute. She didn't want to be caught here. In desperation she ran at the door throwing all her weight into it. The pain in her shoulder was nothing compared to the relief she felt when the door gave way.

"Mom! I knew you'd come! What was that gunshot? Are you OK?"

"No time for that. Are you OK? Can you run?"

"Yes, but I'd be faster if you undid my hands."

"Later. We must go now. Follow me."

Susan led the way into the kitchen and out the back door. She ignored his gasp as he saw the men on the couch. She hurried Jacob across the yard and into the shrubbery.

"Watch your step. Keep going straight."

She guided him as best she could. At one point he over-balanced and she yanked on his arm to get him upright. She heard his grunt and understood he'd experienced pain at her action, but he didn't complain. Just kept moving his feet forward.

Once through the natural barrier, she told him to turn right and follow the hedge to the end. He did as instructed, and she led him to the street just as the first police car turned into the safehouse's driveway. She pulled back on her son, waiting for the officer to decide whether to wait for reinforcement or enter the house.

She breathed a sigh of relief when he exited his car and approached the front door. While he was occupied with that, she pushed Jacob down the street towards her waiting car. They reached the car as three more vehicles turned onto the road, their lights flashing.

Susan reached out and opened the back door, pushing Jacob in with little ceremony. She climbed in beside him and pulled him down so he couldn't be seen by anyone casually looking at the car.

"Pull out and drive like you own the street," she instructed Cody. "Glance at the officers like anyone would but keep going. Don't speed."

"Got it."

A few tense minutes later, they were two blocks away from all the action. Susan undid Jacob's bonds and he rubbed his arms as he brought them to his front. He shrugged and rolled his shoulders. Susan watched him in silence, thankful to have both sons with her. Alive.

"Where we going?" Cody interrupted her thoughts.

"Get on the highway. Head away from Denver. Just drive. We'll figure out the rest later."

Cody didn't comment as he navigated the roads, looking for signs to the interstate. When he saw a junction sign, he followed the arrows and was soon taking the onramp to the highway. He glanced several times in the rearview mirror, looking in amazement at the tall young man that was his younger brother.

"Eyes on the road," his mother said softly. "You can pull over at the first rest stop. We'll take a few minutes there to celebrate our reunion."

Cody nodded and focused on his driving.

"Mom?"

"Later, Jacob. Just a few more miles. Then we'll catch up."

46

Ray watched the news with dismay. The safehouse sat clearly in the background of the news camera's shot. The reporter was going on and on about a gun fight, one dead, one unconscious, no witnesses, no theories.

She did it. I should have known she would. I wonder why she left Wade alive? An inconvenience, if ever there was one.

Walt looked at him. "Looks like she was successful. What now? What are you going to do next?"

"This."

Before Walt knew what Ray's intentions were, he felt the sudden pain in his chest. His eyes registered the gun in Ray's hand as everything slowed and faded.

"Why?"

"Sorry, old pal. Had to be done. You knew too much."

"It was you all along. You wanted the information. But the joke's on you. It's gone. The kid burned it."

"Maybe," was all Ray said as he watched his long-time friend die before his eyes.

Without another look at Walt, he holstered his gun, grabbed his duffle off the bed and walked to the door. Opening it slowly, he looked both ways down the hallway then stepped out and quietly closed the door behind him.

Five minutes later, he was in his car. He had one thought in his mind. Get to the cabin before Susan did. Because he knew that's where she would go.

Cody pulled into the highway rest stop and found a parking space at the farthest end of the lot, away from the main foot and auto traffic. All exited the car and gave each other long hugs, softly murmuring words of love.

Susan was the first to step back and as she stood there gazing at her two sons, she was both grateful and concerned. The first time in over three years she and her sons were together. But she knew they were still in danger and couldn't spend much more time where they were.

"Do either of you need to use the facilities? Are you hungry?"

Both looked at her then shook their heads, understanding instantly she was prompting them towards leaving.

"OK, then. Let's head out. I'll drive. You two can catch up in the back seat."

She slid into the driver's seat, adjusting it to her liking and glanced at the fuel gauge, as Cody and Jacob climbed into the backseat and fastened their seatbelts.

"Where are we going?" Jacob asked.

"To the cabin. Then you and your grandparents will leave for their house."

"Grandparents?" Jacob asked at the same time Cody asked why she wasn't coming with them.

She didn't answer either one of them for several minutes. When the silence stretched beyond what Cody could absorb, he asked again, "Mom, why aren't you coming with us?"

"There's more to be done to finish this situation. I want all the rest of you safe. You'll be safe at your grandparent's house."

"Are you sure?"

"Positive. Now let me focus on the road while you and Jacob compare lives over the past three years."

Cody was about to object, but she caught his eye in the rearview mirror and slightly shook her head. He sighed, then settled back and asked Jacob about school. Their conversation turned into background noise for Susan as she let her thoughts sort through what she knew and what she thought she knew.

Two hours later she pulled into another rest stop to refuel the car. She gave the boys money to purchase food and other snacks. While they were inside, she pulled out her phone and called Anders. He answered on the first ring.

"Are you all right?"

"Yes. I'm coming to you. And I've got both boys with me. Tell my parents to be ready to leave as soon as we get there. I don't care who drives, but I would encourage you to do so. Take your car. Everyone should fit, although it will be tight."

"Where are we going?"

"To their house. You should all be safe there."

"And you?"

"I'll be staying at the cabin. I expect to have company."

"But—"

"It will work out. Trust me. I'll join you as soon as I can. And when I do, this should all be over."

"And if you don't join us?"

"Then you know what to do. You have all the instructions and paperwork."

"I don't like this, Susan."

"You don't have to like it. You just have to do what I tell you to do." After a short pause she added, "The boys are coming back. We'll see you in a couple hours. Maybe less. Be ready."

She disconnected and shoved the phone back in her pocket before Cody and Jacob reached the car. She saw their soft drinks and bags of fast food and smiled.

"That should hold you for a bit."

"We got some for you, too," Jacob said. "Bacon cheeseburger. I know you like them."

She laughed. "I do, indeed. Thank you. I'll just run in and pay for the gas. Cody, could you start the process?"

"Sure."

Ten minutes later they were back on the road, all munching on their food. Less than two hours later, Susan was pulling onto the dirt road that led to the cabin. As she navigated the bumpy road, she explained what she expected of everyone and would tolerate no objections.

Once at the cabin, she was happy to see that Anders had positioned his car such that she could back up in front of Cody's vehicle that was still in the lean-to shed.

"Why can't I drive my car with Jacob, and Anders can take Anna and Donner?"

"I want you all together. It's more efficient. And there's no chance you'll be separated."

"But—"

"Cody. Please. Don't argue. You'll be able to come back for your car later. It will be fine where it is."

Cody's expression made clear his thoughts on the subject, but Susan ignored him. She had too many things to prepare and she needed to get everyone out of here. Fast.

As she turned off the car, Anna and Donner came out of the cabin. Both were talking over each other as they strove to get their own questions answered. Susan gave each a brief hug, introduced Jacob, who stared at them with wide eyes, then hustled everyone towards the car Anders had readied.

Over all the protests, she bullied everyone into their seats. Pulling Anders aside she questioned him on his role. Satisfied with his assurances, she squeezed his shoulder.

"God Speed. Take care of my family."

He reached out and put his hand on her shoulder. "I promise. But you will be able to do that yourself. We'll see you soon."

With that, he slid into the driver's seat. Without another glance at Susan, he started the car and accelerated out of the front yard. She stood and watched the car carrying everyone she loved drive away. Before the dust had settled, she turned and hurried into the cabin.

48

R ay left his car a half-mile from the cabin. He didn't want to alert Susan of his presence. But it was getting dark fast, so he started with a quicker pace than originally planned. After tripping twice, he realized he couldn't sustain his speed and arrive in one piece. He slowed. It wasn't long before he saw a light through the trees.

Brave or stupid. Can't decide which. I wonder if everyone is there, or just her.

When he reached the edge of the clearing, he saw her car, as well as Cody's, but that didn't tell him how many were in the cabin. He approached cautiously. Her voice made him nearly jump out of his skin.

"I've been waiting for you. Come on up. Don't do anything stupid."

He strained his eyes to find her. He wasn't sure but he thought she was sitting on the porch.

"Susan?"

"Were you expecting someone else? Where's Walt?"

"I'm alone. You?"

"Same."

He walked across the clearing, his hands loose by his side. When he was about ten feet from the bottom step he stopped. His eyes widened slightly at the sight of the rifle across her knees. He was glad the darkness disguised his reaction.

"You expecting trouble?"

"I'm expecting you. Come up and have a seat. Slowly. Keep your hands where I can see them."

He climbed the steps and looked around. The only other place to sit was a wooden crate across from her. She motioned towards it with the barrel of the rifle.

"Sit."

"Not very comfortable."

"I don't care if you're comfortable. Sit down."

As Ray lowered himself onto the crate, he noticed a handgun on the small table beside Susan. He wondered if she knew he was carrying. Then realized that of course she would just assume he was.

He nodded toward the handgun. "All this fire power necessary?"

"You tell me. In fact, why don't you tell me everything Ray. It should make for an interesting conversation. You played your role well. You had everyone fooled. Everyone thinking you were as much a victim as the rest of us."

"It wasn't difficult. You saw and heard what you wanted to. But tell me why you left Wade alive."

"Wasn't necessary to kill him. And despite his recent actions, I always liked him. Besides, he wasn't the real threat."

Ray glanced at his watch. "Well, I'm sorry to say he didn't survive his injuries."

"I figured. And Walt? The reason he's not with you?"

"An unfortunate case of getting in the way of a bullet."

Susan took a few seconds to make sure her voice was under control. "You've become quite ruthless in your old age."

"I always was. You just never wanted to see it."

She stared at him, knowing he was right. After another few seconds she simply asked him why. She knew he'd know what she was asking.

He smiled sadly. "You never figured it out?"

She remained silent.

"The information. It's really destroyed?"

"Yes."

"And there's no copies anywhere? No one, other than you, knows what was on the drive?"

"You know the truth of that. Ray, what am I missing? Why is that information so important to you? Almost everyone referenced is dead or beyond understanding what it means. How could it possibly be worth all the lies and recent deaths?"

When he didn't respond after several moments, she asked, "Do you really have a daughter? Or was that also a lie? You certainly had us all convinced in the motel room."

"No. Not a lie. I do have one. She's not being held hostage. As far as I know, she's happy and healthy, living a productive life. But the information ties me to her, and my legacy is not a burden she needs. She thinks I died a war hero. I wanted her to never know the truth."

"What do you mean?"

"What does it matter? Without the information, those with suspicions can't confirm them, and if I tell you, you'll likely kill me." His laugh came out on a harsh cough. "Maybe that's for the best. Saves others the trouble of doing it just to put their suspicions to rest. And relieves me of having to do it myself."

"I don't understand."

"Susan. Think. All those years ago. Egypt."

He stared at the wooden floor of the porch, refusing to meet her gaze. After several minutes, she softly gasped.

"You were compromised."

"Yes."

"You became a double agent."

"Yes."

"And now?"

"Still am. If I'm found dead, both sides will assume the other caused it. Neither will mention it. Case closed."

"Then why all the effort to get the information?"

"I thought I might be able to use it to bargain."

She laughed. "Always looking for an angle. You should have known that would never have worked. For either side."

"I thought it worth a shot."

"If it came down to it, would you really have harmed me or my family?"

Ray didn't answer. And his silence was the only answer she needed. Her hands involuntarily tightened around the rifle on her lap.

"Answer me this. And tell the truth. Are you the only threat to my family? There's no one else?"

"No one else. Those who posed a risk to you were under my direction. They're either dead or paid off with no understanding of why they were asked to do what they did."

"You're sure? What about Zhara?"

"Yes. I swear. Zhara is not a problem. She knows nothing of the situation. We severed ties years ago. My handler perished recently in an unfortunate accident." The way he said that convinced Susan Ray had caused the unfortunate accident. "His agency only knows my code name. I made sure of that. I wanted the information to negotiate with our side."

"And is there anyone on our side I need worry about?"

"No. The only one who suspects is firmly in your court. No matter what, you'll be protected, even if you aren't aware it's happening."

"Then I guess we're done here."

Susan stood and picked up the handgun from the table and slid it into the holster tucked into her jeans at the small of her back. It didn't fit well, but it was secured enough for her purposes. She walked past Ray towards the steps. When she was on the second one, he spoke.

"Wait. That's it?"

"Yes. It's your mess. You take care of it."

She cleared the steps and walked to her car. Without looking at him, she placed the rifle on the floor of the back seat then opened the driver's door. As she slid behind the wheel, a single shot rang out. Her glance at the porch told her everything she needed to know. She was about to drive away when she had a sudden thought.

Maneuvering her car forward and to the side of the drive, she got out of the car and transferred everything from her car to Cody's. Then she entered the cabin and quickly gathered a few items of personal importance. Snatching Cody's keys from where they hung next to the door, she shoved everything into the back seat, then drove his car out of the shed and to the end of the drive. Leaving it there, she walked back to the cabin and stood staring at Ray. So many unanswered questions. She thought about burning the cabin and her car but realized that sooner or later, property records would likely bring the officials back to her doorstep anyway. It would take time to unravel the ownership trail, but if they were persistent, they'd figure it out. Unless an unseen hand derailed the effort. She shrugged. Whatever.

She stared into the woods for a moment. No need for the destruction. Better to formulate a feasible story, if needed. She still had a few local contacts who could help if things got messy. Besides, she had a good lawyer.

She gave one last look at the man who had been her colleague, mentor, friend, then betrayer. Possibly the murderer of her husband.

"I hope you find peace in death," she said softly.

She walked to Cody's car, slid behind the wheel and began the drive to her parents' house.

49

SIX MONTHS LATER

"**C**an I have seconds?" Jacob's question caused everyone to laugh.

"Boy, I swear. You're a bottomless pit." Donner's response brought more laughter.

The family was gathered around the table in the house Anna and Donner owned. Dinner had been an extended celebration of Donner's birthday. Jacob's question referenced the remaining cake.

Susan wasn't sure, at first, if they should stay there. But Anna convinced her they were as safe there as anywhere, and more comfortable due to its familiarity. And the house was big enough to cater to everyone's needs. After some thought, and an unexpected message, Susan had to admit her mother was probably right.

A month after Ray's suicide, Susan had received an encrypted message saying all loose ends had been resolved. She no longer need worry about further threats. She should enjoy her retirement to its fullest. There was both an apology and appreciation for her role in the cleanup process.

While she didn't like to think of all the deaths as simply a cleanup process, she was grateful for the reassurance about her family's safety. Apparently, Ray was truthful on that part. And the following months had been quiet, giving her hope. The horror of the last three years was over.

The only real question was where they would plant their roots. Jacob still needed to complete high school, and she hoped Cody might consider college. They could stay in the small town, but unless Cody took remote classes, he'd need to leave it to further his education.

Dinner finished, everyone moved into the sitting room. The boys sprawled on the floor while Susan and her parents commandeered the available chairs.

"We need to talk about the future," Susan started the conversation. Everyone groaned although they all recognized the truth of her words. She looked at Cody. "What are your thoughts on college?"

"I always wanted to go, but never thought it would happen. I should get a job and start supporting myself."

"It could happen."

"But the cost!"

"Don't worry about that. If you want to pursue college, there are ways to do so. Just takes a little planning."

"If you went, where would you go?" Jacob asked.

"I don't know. What about you, kid? You still need to finish high school. Although at this point, you'll probably have to start all over again. You want to go back to Denver?"

"I'd like to see Goober again, but I can't say I really want to go back to that school. There'd be too many questions on where I've been. It might be better to start fresh somewhere."

Susan breathed a quiet sigh of relief. She worried that if Jacob went back to the same school, she'd have to deal with the Turner Johnson issue. It would resolve itself if they didn't go back. She'd already thanked Goober's grandparents and assured them all was well, while at the same time making sure they had no financial needs in the immediate future. She waited to hear the outcome of the discussion.

"You could all stay here," Anna joined in. "Our high school is quite good. Jacob could finish out here."

"But there's no college in this town," Cody commented.

"There's a community college a few miles away in the next town. You could start there, then transfer your credits to the university when you figure out what you want to do. Be cheaper, too. And you could all stay here. We've a lot of time to make up."

Susan wasn't convinced that was the best plan, but she waited to see her sons' reactions. She was surprised to see that neither one of them looked excited at the prospect. She wondered why. Cody was the first to express his thoughts.

"I'd kind of like to be in a big city. Or at least in a bigger one than here. It would be nice to explore a life of new opportunities. I haven't really had a chance to." He smiled sheepishly as he said the words.

Susan recognized the truth of them. Living on the farm, with only summer camp counseling as a diversion, he'd been sheltered. Coming home to find his father dead and home burned, then thrust into a world of stress and hiding, Cody hadn't experience much of a normal life. Even Jacob's short stint in high school had given him a more normal existence than what Cody had lived through. She would forever be thankful of those who had guided and protected him, but she knew she needed to offer a solution that would allow his true transition into adulthood.

"Are you game for changing states?" she asked him. "We have property in Montana."

"But you said it was in the middle of nowhere!" Jacob protested.

Susan smiled. "I might not have been completely truthful about that. Yes, the property is rather large, but it's not that far outside of Missoula. Cody could attend university there, and still be able to commute from the ranch. Once he got his bearings, he could possibly find a place in the city. Then he'd have his independence, yet still be accessible to us. Would also give us an excuse to come into the city more often."

"But what about me? High school? Remember?"

"There's a perfectly good high school nearby."

"But you'll be so far away. We were just getting to know the boys, and you, again," Donner protested.

"We could visit often. Or, better still, you remember there's a second home on the property. Might need a little fixing up, but that's easily accomplished. You and Mom could come with us. We'll take the main house, you two can live in the smaller home. We'll be close, yet separate."

The room was silent as everyone contemplated Susan's words.

"I like it!" Everyone spoke the same words at the same time. Laughter followed.

"Then it sounds like we've plans to make." Susan looked to her parents. "Will you sell this place or rent it?"

"Sell," Anna said with finality. "It's too big to rent or manage from Montana. And we could use the funds to pay for whatever renovations are needed on the ranch homes."

Donner hesitated for a moment, then agreed with her. "I'll call a real estate agent in the morning."

"Yeah! We're going to Montana!" Jacob said the words with excitement. Then sobered. "Do you mind if I head up to my room? I want to read a bit before I go to bed."

Susan had a feeling he was going to research Missoula as opposed to reading any book, but she didn't mind. She was glad he seemed willing to embrace his new life. She wished him a good night's sleep.

"We're off to bed, also," Anna said and gave Donner a look that allowed for no objection. Susan wished them both a good night and waited to see if Cody was also going to make his escape. She was surprised when he stood and settled into Donner's chair.

"Mom, can I ask some questions? There are still things I don't understand."

Susan looked at him, wondering where this conversation would go. "I'll do my best to answer."

"Can we start with a little more background on your previous life? Before you met Dad? Why you changed your name?"

Susan knew she couldn't tell him everything, but she summarized most of her earlier years. She watched his reactions closely and was relieved when he didn't show anything other than curiosity.

"Is that the reason for the whole quest thing? Wouldn't it have been easier to just tell me what I needed to know? Why the treasure chest, rhyme, clues, and so on?"

"Most of that was your father's idea. He was always into the fantasy genre. Did you never notice the books he read? He thought it would take some of the fear away if you approached everything as if it were a game. I didn't fully agree with him but didn't see any harm. I wish I'd thought through that more. It might have saved years of our being separated. And possibly reduced your risk. On the other hand, it did allow you to meet people that offered you guidance and protection."

"Yes. I'm forever grateful to have had Father Timothy and Sal in my life, even if only temporarily."

"You could always reconnect with them. Let them know how you're doing. You'd pose no risk to them doing so."

"That's a great idea. I think I will."

The room was quiet for a few moments. Then Cody spoke again.

"I've still got the decoder ring, Allen wrench, Lincoln log and belt buckle. I never understood their significance. They didn't seem to connect to the overall quest Dad sent me on. Care to enlighten me?"

Susan chuckled.

"I told him you'd never figure it out, but he insisted on including the items in the chest. The decoder ring and Lincoln log were meant to remind you of your childhood. Hopefully happy memories. The Allen wrench was used to put the swing set together. Why your father would think you'd figure that out, I haven't a clue. I think he put it in there for his own benefit. It took him hours to put that thing together, all the while you and Jacob were pestering him to hurry up. The belt buckle? You'd never have figured that out, either. Well, possibly. But the research you'd have needed to do, and with no point of reference from where to begin, it's unlikely you would have solved the riddle."

"What, then?"

"Your dad won that buckle in a small-town rodeo event. He managed to stay on a bucking bronco longer than anyone else. His back was never the same, but he staunchly refused to admit he wasn't the rodeo king he made himself out to be. He and I met at that event. He was so intent on impressing me, he strutted around like he owned the town and was the undefeated crown-holder in all events. It was years before I found out he'd never ridden a horse in his life before that."

Cody laughed. He couldn't quite picture his dad acting like that, but he was sure his mom was telling the truth.

"Thank you for telling me all that. I'll cherish the items more for this knowledge."

He was quiet a moment, then switched topics.

"Can I really go to college? We can afford it?"

"Yes. There's enough to cover the cost. And if not, there are student loans available. But your father inherited a large sum from his parents when they passed. We put the money aside thinking we could use it for yours and Jacob's college expenses. I haven't checked the account, but I'm sure it's grown substantially over the years. Things will work out."

"I love you, Mom. I'm sorry I haven't said that enough. And I'll forever regret not telling Dad more often."

"I love you, too. And your father knew you loved him even if you didn't often outwardly express it."

"But the last words I spoke to him were words of anger. I never got the chance to apologize."

"The words were from an angry seventeen-year-old, frustrated to have not gotten your way on something. Your father would have forgotten them almost as soon as you spoke them, knowing the source of your anger. Don't carry that burden, son. He wouldn't want you to. He loved you more than life itself. And was so proud of you. Remember that. Be kind to yourself. The world is cruel enough."

"But—"

"No buts. Your father loved you dearly. He's probably laughing at you from heaven right now. Thinking how silly you are, wondering if you're ever going to grow up."

Cody smiled even as he wiped a tear from his cheek. After a moment, he looked at his mom.

"Thank you."

Susan nodded, swallowing away her own tears. "Go on, off to bed with you. We've got a lot to get done before this family can start over in Montana."

"I wish Dad were part of this new life."

"I do too. But the past is the past. Just know he's happy we're all together again."

Cody stood and walked to his mother, dropping a quick kiss on her cheek.

"G'night."

"Good night, son."

Susan sat for several minutes after Cody left. She let her mind wander through memories she'd suppressed for far too long. She knew, deep in her heart, that having the family together pleased Tom. She often felt him with her. She wasn't sure she fully believed in this whole life-after-death, heaven thing. But she knew without a doubt that there was much in this world that couldn't be explained with logic. So perhaps there was a spiritual realm, and those in it could offer support in ways mere humans weren't meant to understand.

With that thought, she stood, switched off the lights, and climbed the stairs to her room.

OTHER BOOKS BY THE AUTHOR

<u>**The Unexpected Series**</u>
Unexpected Benefits
Unexpected Rewards
Unexpected Results
Unexpected Beginnings
Unexpected Revelations
Unexpected Endings

<u>**The Twin Assassins Trilogy**</u>
Assassin School
Mission Status: Active
Next Generation

ABOUT THE AUTHOR

Naiditch has had a varied professional career that includes hospital administration, practicing attorney, director of a multi-million dollar nonprofit organization, adjunct college professor, and Human Resources professional.

She also holds a 6th Degree Black Belt in Shaolin martial arts, as well as a Black Sash in traditional Shaolin Kungfu animal forms. Retired from her various day jobs, she fills her days in New Hampshire with teaching the martial arts, yard work, bicycling in her annoyingly hilly neighborhood, and of course—writing.